Asking Questions

By the same author

H. R. F. Keating

Asking Questions

An Inspector Ghote Mystery

St. Martin's Press ✿ New York

Library of Congress Cataloging-in-Publication Data

Keating, H. R. F. (Henry Reymond Fitzwalter).
    Asking questions : an Inspector Ghote mystery /
H. R. F. Keating.
        p.   cm.
    ISBN 0-312-15057-1
    1. Ghote, Ganesh (Fictitious character)—Fiction.
2. Police—India—Bombay—Fiction. 3. Bombay
(India)—Fiction. I. Title.
PR6061.E26A93   1997
823'.914—dc21   96-48771
                                              CIP

First published in Great Britain by Macmillan

First U.S. Edition: March 1997

10   9   8   7   6   5   4   3   2   1

Asking Questions

By the same author

Death and the Visiting Firemen
Zen there was Murder
A Rush on the Ultimate
The Dog it was that Died
Death of a Fat God
The Perfect Murder
Is Skin-Deep, Is Fatal
Inspector Ghote's Good Crusade
Inspector Ghote Caught in
Meshes
Inspector Ghote Hunts the
Peacock
Inspector Ghote Plays a Joker
Inspector Ghote Breaks an Egg
Inspector Ghote Goes by Train
Inspector Ghote Trusts the
Heart
Bats Fly Up for Inspector Ghote
A Remarkable Case of Burglary
Filmi, Filmi, Inspector Ghote
Inspector Ghote Draws a Line
The Murder of the Maharajah
Go West, Inspector Ghote
The Sheriff of Bombay
Under a Monsoon Cloud

The Body in the Billiard Room
Dead on Time
Inspector Ghote, His Life and
Crimes
The Iciest Sin
Cheating Death
The Rich Detective
Doing Wrong
The Good Detective
The Bad Detective

The Strong Man
The Underside
A Long Walk to Wimbledon
The Lucky Alphonse

Murder Must Appetize
Sherlock Holmes: The Man and
his World
Great Crimes
Writing Crime Fiction
Crime and Mystery: The 100
Best Books
The Bedside Companion to
Crime

Questions

I

'Asking questions. Too many questions. Nobody asks Abdul Khan questions.'

The tall Pathan, eyes concealed as always behind black-lensed glare glasses, held Chandra Chagoo by his neck at arm's length against the rows of glass-fronted snake cages.

'So, now you will find out answer. Answer to what happens to whoever is so stupid as to try to get evidences for the policewallas to put Abdul Khan behind the bars.'

Chandra Chagoo made a feeble effort to kick out. The blows that hit the Pathan ganglord's iron-hard, widespread legs might have been taps from a chicken's beak they were so ineffectual.

Behind, a Russell's viper, ten feet in length, black, spot-marked, threshed to and fro, excited to fury by the repeated slamming against its cage.

'Soon you will find out what happens to questions-asking. Soon-soon.'

II

Chandra Chagoo, Dr Gauri Subbiah thought, tugging out of her mouth the end of her long thick plait of hair she had, in her absorption, allowed herself to suck at like a schoolgirl.

3

Those seemingly idle questions the sly devil had asked. How much did they show he knew?

Or was it that he had merely guessed? Nothing in what he had asked, apparently so innocently, which could be replied to with an outright denial. And certainly nothing to make it possible to get him necked out. As he ought to be. However good his handling of the snakes.

She wanted to go down that instant to the Reptile Room, to stand in front of the fellow and ask and ask him what he had meant. To treat those half-hints of his as if they were a problem in research. To ask about them every question needed until the truth had been cut clean away from whatever obscurities surrounded it. Until she knew. One way or the other.

But what if those questions brought to light the whole truth about what she had done? What if she would have to face the fact that she was truly in the power of that devil?

III

Ram Mahipal faced the upward-rising benches filled with the smooth, unmarked faces of first-year students.

'Asking questions,' he pronounced. 'Let me say, at this the very start of your careers in medicine, that here is the one and only key to your futures. You must ask and ask. Whether you are going in for research or whether you are hoping to practise general medicine, you must ask questions always. Ask until you have found out what is the truth. Ask in the months and years, just now before you, what are the truths already discovered about the human body and its workings. Ask, when at last you will be able to put before your name the word *Doctor*, what is the truth about whatever illness is affecting the patient you are examining. That is what you must do. Ask questions. Ask questions.'

And is it, he thought, what most of you will do? No, you will want now simply to fill your notebooks with enough facts to jump or scramble you over the hurdles of the exams that face you. And then, when you are Dr Mehta or Dr Miss Mehta or Dr Mrs Mehta, you will be content to give the wretched patient seeking your help whatever is recommended in some textbook or even some pharmaceutical advertisement and hold out your hand for the fee.

He compressed his lips in a line of bitterness.

Already, he saw, some of the students had actually brought out pencils and ballpoints, wanting nothing more than to be crammed with information like so many baskets in the vegetable market. Resenting every word I am saying as idle talk of questions-pestions.

Or am I being too cynical? No, I have the right to be cynical. If anyone has. The man who lost all he most cherished by asking the wrong question. Or the right question at the wrong time. Forced to come down to this. A life of dull grindingness. And even that in jeopardy. If anyone, even some badmash like that fellow Chandra Chagoo, asks a certain question about myself . . .

But what I have done, I have done.

'No,' he snapped out, almost shouted to the sweep

5

of greedy faces in front of him – But were there some
who would take heed? Was there just one? – 'Kindly pay
attention. This is the one and only time you will hear
this said. So take it to your hearts. Questions. Questions.
That is what you must ask and ask. That is the path to
take, whatsoever thorns lie upon it.'

IV

Professor Phaterpaker, Director, Mira Behn Institute for
Medical Research, sat in his office glaring, unseeingly,
at the cover of the file in front of him.

R. K. Mahipal MB, Ph.D.

Damn the fellow. Why had he, too, asked questions?
Is it not enough I have had to deal with that wretched
snake-handler? Why did this fellow have to have ideas
about me also? And why, if he had more questions to
ask, did he not ask? Why suddenly fall silent? And why,
after that, resign? Give up his research and go off and
lecture first-year medical students only? Giving no good
reasons. Causing others to begin asking questions they
would not at all have thought of before. Why didn't he
ask and ask himself, go on asking?

Even if in the end he was getting to the truth.

And perhaps that would have been best. For the
truth to come out at last. No more parrying and parrying
the questions then. No more finding answers that satisfied to some extent. And then having to wait for the
next question. To wonder and wonder when some nasty

busybody would hit on the one that could not be answered. Except by the truth.

But to have the burden lifted. All the heaped lies and half-truths and inventions and evasions of the years suddenly cascading down into ruin like some termite tower in the desert with a charge of gunpowder put under it. All the ant work of years crumbling to nothing in an instant.

And it would need only one question. If it was the right one. And then it all, everything that over my lifetime I have built up and built up, would come crashing down.

It would have needed only one more question from Mahipal. Only one more perhaps.

And he had not asked it.

It had been plain from the look on the man's face that he had glimpsed the truth there in front of him. He had gone grey. Grey as ashes. But he had not dared to face the outcome. He had drawn back from that last question.

So it will have to go on. For all the years to come. Till my body has been consumed by the fires of the burning ghats. Or, more likely, by the controlled heat of the Electric Crematorium.

Then the world can know. And it will not hurt me.

As, now, it would hurt. Would have hurt as much as if I was under torture itself. To have all revealed.

Answer

Chapter One

Inspector Ghote, idly glancing outside as he came to eat the crisp fried poories his wife had made for him, the jangling morning arguments of the crows pleasant in his ears, saw standing in the road nothing other than the car of the Commissioner of Police, Greater Bombay. The pennant at its front fluttered for a moment in a little puff of breeze.

Now why is Commissioner sahib here just now? he asked himself. What for can he have been coming so early as this down the road here? And why is the car stopped? Why is the Commissioner's driver no longer at the wheel? What can the fellow be doing?

The questions that had flooded into his mind received their answer almost at once. A fierce tattoo of knocking.

He hurried to the door.

And there the Commissioner's driver was, throwing him a cracking salute.

'Inspector sahib, Commissioner is wanting to see.'

'Now? He is wanting me now?'

What could this be? If, for some unimaginable reason, the Commissioner wanted to give him, and no other officer, some particular task, the order should come through the proper channels. He should receive it from the Assistant Commissioner, Crime Branch, when he arrives at Headquarters in one hour's time. So why . . .?

'Ji haan, Inspector. You are to come out to car now only.'

But his hair was not combed. It was sticking up all over his head after his bath. He could feel it. Dealing with it was something he always left till just before departing.

Should he dart back in? Run across to the little mirror by the doorway of the kitchen? Pull out his comb? Flick, flick, flick at his hair?

But these, he knew at once, were questions not worth asking. When the Commissioner said *Now* it meant now.

'Very well, I am coming itself.'

Just a minute later he was sitting beside the Commissioner on the well-polished leather of the wide seat at the back of the car. With more questions springing up in his head, like bats flying from a cave.

'You will be wondering, Inspector, why I have called you so early.'

'Oh, no, sir, no.'

'No? I would have thought that a summons of this sort would have had any detective officer worth his salt asking like hell what it was all about.'

'Oh, yes, sir, I—'

'But no matter. This is what I want you to do, Inspec-

12

tor. I will mention it to Assistant Commissioner Dhasal
as soon as he is in his seat.'

'Yes, sir.'

So what was he going to be asked to do? What could
be so urgent that the Commissioner himself had inter-
cepted him in this way? Was it some anti-corruption
inquiry that Vigilance Branch could not, for some
reason, handle? Or something somehow one hundred
per cent secret? Even something *national importance*?

'Inspector, a very good friend of mine – the film star
Asha Rani, as a matter of fact – has brought to my notice
a certain matter.'

'Yes, sir?'

Asha Rani, the star of stars. Of course, she would be
a friend of the Commissioner. They would meet at social
functions. Asha was famed for her charity work. The
Commissioner also took great interest in such matters.
It was well known. So some dirty works going on behind
the scenes at a very very respectable charity? Fraud
investigation? Lakhs and lakhs of rupees involved?
Utmost discretion required? Not a word to be breathed?

'It is not perhaps very serious, something you should
be able to handle without trouble, Inspector. But Asha,
that is Miss Rani, is extremely anxious about it. So I
have undertaken to have it looked into by an officer
from Headquarters rather than anyone from the local
station.'

The Commissioner gave a little cough and hurried
on.

'And there is a side to it also that is not – what shall
I say? – perhaps not strictly as it should be.'

So what was this? What something not very serious? He felt himself bumping down to earth.

No great kudos to be gained after all then. No vitally important anti-corruption inquiry. Not even something gone badly wrong in the higher reaches of Bombay society. Just a matter *you should be able to handle without trouble*. But what?

What?

The Commissioner leant forward and slid open the glass panel between himself and his driver.

'Jadhav, take a walk along the road.'

'Sir.'

Hastily Jadhav got out, closing the car door with more force than necessary.

'Never needs oil to clean his ears, that one,' the Commissioner murmured, watching him march stiffly away.

Then he turned and faced Ghote directly.

'Yes. Well, Inspector, it is like this. One of the charities Miss Rani is most concerned with is the Mira Behn Institute for Medical Research. I dare say you've never even heard of it. It's comparatively small – run by a man called Phaterpaker, first-class fellow – but they do some very interesting work.'

'It is that place out in Sewri, sir?' Ghote put in, phrasing his chance piece of knowledge as a question since it seemed the Commissioner had expected him not to know of it.

'Yes, yes. Well, you see, one of the things they're experimenting with there is some sort of drug – I believe it comes in the first place from the venom of a certain kind of snake – that keeps people who are prone to heart attack safe and well. Pretty useful, of course.'

Useful for business burra sahibs having stress and eating–drinking too much, Ghote thought. But not anything much for the common man.

But he contented himself with simply putting a bland question. After all, the Commissioner was, in his way, the same sort of burra sahib.

'And there are some troubles, sir?'

'Yes. Well, the long and short of it is that there are some people, in the *filmi duniya* you understand – different values and all that – who have been getting hold of experimental samples of the stuff for their private use. Apparently we're well in advance in this field on America and Europe, and in any case their stuff is damned expensive, even smuggled.'

A film world affair? Something of troubles here. But say nothing. Just prod it along.

'Yes, sir?'

'Well, getting samples like that was all right. In its way. Only, it seems one in the last batch to come out of the place, by whatever route, was not up to par. Well, to be frank, a certain film director who's very close to Asha, that is to Miss Rani, damn nearly died because of it. Bengali fellow called Mihir Ganguly. Can't say I'd ever heard of him. Now, we can't, of course, have that sort of thing going on, even in that incorrigible set-up. So, at Miss Rani's particular request, I'm seconding you, Inspector – think you're the man for the job – to find out who's selling those samples and to see he's dealt

with. Discreetly, of course. Some other charge. Anything. You know the ropes.'

There were dozens of questions he wanted to ask.
Such as, why exactly did the Commissioner believe he
was the man for this job? And why did he assume
he would be willing to put someone behind the bars on
a charge altogether different from the crime they had
committed? And what precisely was this miracle drug?
What snake venom was it made from? And how was it
that samples were there to be secretly sold?

Let alone, how could a Commissioner of Police wink
at such goings-on?

But there were questions you did not even ask. So,
instead, he put forward a practical objection in the tenu-
ous hope it might get him out of a business that had
begun to seem altogether trickier than it had looked.

'Sir, there is one thing only. Sir, at this moment itself
I have another case on hand. Sir, a case I am thinking
may bring very much of congratulations and praises to
entire Bombay Police. It is a matter of Abdul Khan
himself, sir.'

'Khan, eh? And what have you got to do with a
Number One public enemy like him, Inspector?'

'Sir, it is matter of chance only. You see, sir, I was
out at Sahar Airport some time ago, obtaining some
informations, when I was spotting this girl, one Miss
Nicky D'Costa, sir, Goan lady, an air stewardess. She
was just only coming out from airport staff security
check, and I was straight away noticing her change of
manner. From walking in a very very idle way, sir, she
was in one moment only starting almost to run. So

I was deciding to follow and observe what she was next doing. Sir, to my surprise she was hurrying back into airport building. Into public section, sir. And, inside there, what was she doing but, once more walking idly, going into Ladies itself, sir.'

'Inspector, what is all this nonsense?'

He would have liked to answer that irritated question with *Not at all nonsense, sir.* But there were some questions that had to be answered in a very indirect manner, if at all.

'Sir, it was then coming to my mind that this Miss D'Costa must be smuggling something. You are knowing, sir, that in some cases smugglers are swallowing drugs wrapped up in – well – in condoms, sir. And that these may in some circumstances cause one such smuggler in question to need to – to evacuate bowels, sir, with great urgency.'

'Inspector, I have not spent twenty-five years in the Police Service without being aware of facts such as that.'

'No, sir, no. Of course not, sir. But, sir, this is what I was telling. When Miss Nicky D'Costa was emerging from Ladies, in view of suspicions aroused, I was at once taking aside and questioning. Damn hard questioning, sir. And soon she was breaking down and confessing all. That she was bringing in cocaine from America, at the request of Abdul Khan himself, sir. Khan had made her his mistress, sir. Short-time only, I am thinking.'

'Yes, yes, Inspector. I do not really wish to hear every sordid detail.'

'No, sir, no. So, sir, this lady was bringing in, for Khan to distribute, sir, just only a small quantity of crack cocaine. What they are calling the champagne drug, sir. She was saying other airlines' staff were doing it also.'

'Yes, yes, Inspector, I know all about crack cocaine, and that Abdul Khan is the main supplier of the stuff to the élite. Someone like myself has his contacts in that sort of world, filmi people and whatever. I'm ready to make use of them when the time is ripe.'

'Yes, sir. Definitely, sir. So, sir, what I was doing, when I was seeing I had got Miss D'Costa one hundred per cent under my thumbs, sir, was to tell her I would overlook this one illegal act if, and on condition, sir, that she would tell me when the police could nab Abdul Khan two hundred per cent red-handed, sir.'

He looked at the Commissioner with a gleam of hope.

'Yes, well, all very fine, Inspector. But I don't think our friend Khan is going to be caught as easily as that. You know what sort of a ruthless swine he is? That story of how he began his move to the top? The three nine-year-old boys who had played some prank on his mother, beaten her with shoes for refusing them a sweetmeat or whatever? And of how Khan then forced some members of his gang to strangle the little devils, one after the other? No, frankly, Inspector, it'll take a better man than you to put paid to Abdul Khan.'

For a moment after telling his story the Commissioner sat there frowning. Was he asking himself, Ghote wondered, if there was anybody at all under his command capable of dealing with such a super-best badmash.

Then the Commissioner looked up.

'However, I'll mention the matter of your air stewardess to Mr Dhasal, and I dare say he'll put some other officer on to it. Nicky D'Costa the girl's name, you said?'

'Yes, sir.'

'Right then. Just call Jadhav back, Inspector, and then you'd better cut along up to the Mira Behn Institute.'

'Yes, sir. But then can you be giving me any more informations at all, sir? Sir, such as what exactly is this drug that is being taken out? How is that happening itself?'

'No, no, Inspector. I've given you quite enough to be going on with. Just get up to the Institute and start asking questions. That's the way to go about it, man. Ask questions. Ask questions.'

'Yes, sir.'

As if asking questions was not what he had been doing from the very first day he had become a detective.

Chapter Two

Ghote did not, however, 'cut along' at once to the Mira Behn Institute as the Commissioner had suggested. As soon as he had begun to ask himself a few questions about the whole business of drug samples being stolen he realized no inquiries there would get him anywhere unless he knew more to begin with.

Why on earth had the Commissioner given him so ridiculously few facts? But, he realized at once why that must be. There would be questions the Commissioner could not, as friend to friend, have asked Asha Rani. The answers he might have got could have been altogether too embarrassing for a senior police officer to hear.

So that was what he would have to do himself. Go and question Asha Rani, star of stars.

It was not something he at all liked the idea of. The stars of the Bombay film world were creatures apart, gods and goddesses, and they knew it. For a simple inspector of police to go asking questions of such a person as Asha Rani would be like summoning Goddess Laxmi from swarga above and treating her like a brothel madam under interrogation. But it had to be done. With the minimal information he had he could not even begin to make proper inquiries.

He looked at his watch. It was still good and early. Asha Rani would not have left for her morning shift at whatever studio she might be bestowing her presence upon, before moving on to some other one, some other film of the ten or twelve she might be making at this moment. So he would find her at home. And he knew where that was. The location of the home of a star of such magnitude was a piece of common knowledge, there to be read in every Bombay guidebook.

But presenting himself at the gates of Asha Rani's garden-surrounded house on Pali Hill was one thing. Getting to see the star herself, it proved, was quite another.

Behind the tall curly iron gates there were no fewer than three uniformed Gurkha security guards. Already, as he came up, he had heard one of them say to a cameras-laden photographer, 'Madam not seeing. Today Madam is working-working.'

He stopped and thought. How to overcome this infuriatingly ridiculous obstacle? At once a possible answer came to him.

He took from his pocket one of his cards and underneath his own name and rank scribbled three words: *From the Commissioner*.

Would they do the trick?

'Inspector Ghote, Crime Branch,' he snapped out as soon as one of the Gurhas stepped up to the gates and gave him a glaring look. He thrust the card at him.

'Give same to Miss Rani ek dum,' he barked.

'Ji, Inspector sahib.'

The Gurkha hurried away into the great white pillared and porticoed house.

And, in less than three minutes emerged, a wide welcoming grin on his face.

'Please to come, Inspector.'

Asha Rani, when he had been conducted into her presence, blotted out everything in the whole huge room where she was half-lying, half-sitting, on a deep-buttoned, cushions-spread sofa, rich in purple silk. She looked exactly as she did on the giant painted hoardings advertising her films which, one after another over the years, had towered over the Bombay streets. Except that her face, instead of being many square inches in extent, was of normal dimensions. Or only a little more than normal. Her figure, too, was nothing like as enormous as when she was shown spread across the hoardings. But it was nevertheless wonderfully full, straining her deep-green, silver-edged sari to the utmost at every vulnerable point.

On an ivory-inlaid table beside her there was a large glass dish filled with darkly luscious grapes with next to it a smaller dish of plump white almonds. Ghote, who after leaving the Commissioner had felt obliged to do no more than dip back indoors and, calling out that he had to go, snatch up just a single one of the crisp poories he had expected to consume, experienced a fierce stomach rumble of thwarted hunger. But he had a task in front of him. Questions to put.

'Madam,' he said to the great star, dry-mouthed, 'it is most good of you to see me at a so-early hour.'

'But, Inspector, I would see any officer of Bombay Police at whatever hour they wished. I am so much admiring the work you are doing under that nice, nice Commissioner. What it is he is named?'

Ghote felt this was a question that should be passed over as if it had never been asked.

'Madam,' he said, 'I would not keep you long. I know you must be going to the studios in just only some minutes.'

'Studios, studios, Inspector. They must wait for me. Asha Rani does not go when studio is calling. Ask each and every question you are wanting. Duty before pleasure. That has been my motto always. Yes, pleasure before duty. Always.'

Ghote cleared his throat.

'Very good, madam, there are some questions I would like to ask concerning the matter Commissioner sahib was ordering me to investigate.'

'Yes, yes. I will answer. What is it that nice, nice man has sent you to investigate?'

Could it be that she had not, after all, asked to have the business of the stolen experimental samples looked into? Or had she actually now forgotten all about it? Or, worse, could the Commissioner, somehow, have misunderstood? No, that was something not even to be asked in the privacy of his own head.

Before he had thought of a way to answer the star's air-floating enquiry she leant forward spreading her hands wide in invitation.

'But you should not keep standing, Inspector. Like a make-up man itself, or my dialogues coach. Sit, sit.'

Ghote looked round. The big room, he saw now, was full of chairs. But they were all immovably large and at no small distance from Asha Rani's purple sofa. If he went over even to the nearest of them, he would be much too far away in the shuttered light of the big room to see the effect of any question he might ask. All right, Asha Rani was hardly a suspect under interrogation. But he had his methods.

What to do?

Nothing else for it but to go to one of the chairs that looked a little more easy to manoeuvre than the others – it too was covered in rich purple silk – and begin to drag it forwards.

'Oh, Inspector, Inspector, no, no. Just sit, please. Sit where you are.'

He abandoned his tugging and perched himself on the edge of the chair, leaning forward as much as he could. It would have to do.

He gave a little cough.

'In so far as I am understanding, madam,' he said, 'your friend Mr Mihir Ganguly, who was keeping his health by using some drug supplied from Mira Behn Institute experiments, one day received a sample that was somehow wrong. And he was nearly dying from effects of same? Is that correct?'

'Yes, yes, Inspector. How clever you are. Just that was what was happening. Poor Ganguly-mooly. He was taking his daily medicine of that wonderful A-C-E. It is called A-C-E like that, Inspector, because it is an altogether ace medicine. What he was having before from

24

the States, smuggled-smuggled, was causing definite symptoms of impotence.'

Her full, overwhelmingly healthy face took on a look of simpering coyness. A look that would have radiated from a thousand silver screens to the furthest dark reaches of the cinema.

Ghote, inwardly suffused with embarrassment, could not at this moment think of any other question to put.

But he need not have worried. Asha Rani was in full flow.

'Oh, yes, as soon as my Ganguly-mooly had begun to take wonderful, wonderful A-C-E all those problems were over and done with. Until that terrible day. A day I will never forget so long as God is giving me life.'

'What day was it, exactly, madam? It may be important to know.'

'Oh. Oh, I cannot say, Inspector. You policewallas, always wanting to know this and that. Times and dates, dates and times. Inspector, we artists are not like that. We respond. We feel. We do not go here and there counting and numbering. Inspector, I am betting if I ask you when you last were making love to your wife, you would be able to tell me down to the last five minutes. Yes? Or no?'

Ghote thought like a whirring firework.

A question. He must find some question, demanding enough of an immediate answer to put this demoness on to another track.

'Madam— Madam—' Inspiration came. 'Madam,

kindly explain what for exactly this A-C-E medicine is needed?'

'Questions, questions. Have you nothing better to do, Inspector, than ask all these questions?'

'Madam, it is in that way that police investigations are carried out. By asking questions. Yes, madam, the very last words Commissioner sahib was saying before I was setting out to come here were just those. *Ask questions. Ask questions.* So, madam, it is my bounden duty to put.'

He felt the smallest twinge of shame at this re-directing of the Commissioner's orders. But since they should not have been necessary in the first place . . .

'Then ask, ask, ask, Inspector. I will answer, answer, answer, answer. But what was it you asked? I have some-how forgotten.'

There followed Asha Rani's famous giggling laugh. Which Ghote had heard described more than once, though he had never cared to expose himself to it from the screen.

'Madam,' he said, 'I was asking what for exactly is this A-C-E medicine given?'

'Oh, yes. That is easy-easy to answer. It is for— Now, what is it my little Ganguly-mooly is always telling me? It is for— High— High— High something.'

'High blood pressure, madam?'

'No, no, not at all. Something else, quite different. Some long, long medical word. Yes, hypertension. That is what this ace medicine is preventing, Inspector. Hypertension. And not at all interfering in impotence matters. That is why she is so brilliant.'

'She, madam?'

He felt as if he was some thin-planked little boat swirled back and forwards, this way and that, on rushing, cross-currented flood waters.

'Yes, yes. Who did you think we were talking, Inspector?'

She looked at him now, all intensity, all demandingness. And it was a question he could think of no possible way of answering in any sensible manner.

He surrendered.

'Madam, I regret. I am not following to one hundred per cent.'

'Oh, what a nuisance you are. How could my nice little Commissioner send me such a – such a dish of curds?'

Ghote gritted his teeth. And returned to the fray.

'Madam, please to inform. You were mentioning a *she*. Who, please, is this lady?'

'But I was telling you. Gauri Subbiah, that marvellous scientist from somewhere beside Pondicherry. A girl from nowhere, Inspector. And yet she has learnt all the things a scientist has to know. In school, in college. Then she was getting Ph.D. She is Dr Subbiah, Inspector. Dr Subbiah. I myself have gathered funds to buy for her some special thing she was needing for her work. From France. Lakhs and lakhs of rupees needed, as much as the cost of four–five big cars from foreign. And it will make her a world champion. She is already, you know, best scientist in all India, my Dr Miss Gauri Subbiah.'

'Oh yes, madam?'

He wanted to keep the note of doubt out of his voice.

No girl from nowhere could be as good as that. But he found he had not succeeded. Hastily he covered up with another question, feeble though it was.

'And Miss Subbiah is working at the Mira Behn Institute?

'Yes, yes. Where else? It is there she is taking all that venom from snakes, cobras, kraits, all, all, and making her ace hypertension cure. How could my Ganguly-mooly be getting it, if it was not coming from there?'

And, miraculously it seemed, he found he had been brought at last to the key question he needed to get answered. How was it that this drug was being removed from the Mira Behn Institute and getting into the hands of the director Mihir Ganguly? And whoever else in the world of Bombay films who was using it.

But that was a question it was not altogether easy to put to Mihir Ganguly's mistress, if that was what he had understood Asha Rani to be.

'Yes, madam,' he said, groping for the right words, 'but can you also kindly inform: how does this A-C-E medicine – you were calling it that, yes? – come from the Mira Behn Institute to— To those who are needing it in filmi community?'

Yes, that had not sounded too impolite.

'Oh, Inspector, such questions. Do you really need to be knowing such things?'

'Yes, madam, I do.'

And he looked the screen goddess straight in the face.

For several seconds she remained blankly silent.

'Inspector,' she said at last, 'you must go now. I must

be getting ready for my shooting. Studio cannot wait. You know we artists have our duty.'

She rose.

It was like some television goddess in the epic Mahabharata emerging, complete and bone-dry, from a wide river.

Ghote simultaneously shot to his feet from his perch on the deep-cushioned purple chair.

'Madam,' he said, 'just only one moment if you please. One moment only. Madam, I must have answer to the question I have asked. Otherwise I would not at all be able to carry out any investigation. Madam, how does A-C-E medicine get out from the Mira Behn Institute to you or to Mr Ganguly himself? This I have to know.'

For an instant it looked as if Asha Rani was going to call her security men and have this impudent questioner thrown out. But it was an instant only. Then she sank back on to the sofa behind her.

'Oh, if you have to be knowing,' she said. 'Then it is quite simple. It is coming, of course, from the same smuggler who was getting us the American stuff.'

'He was obtaining from Mira Behn Institute, madam? But how? Kindly explain.'

'Oh, Inspector, Inspector. One does not at all ask questions of people who are supplying things like that. It is enough that they can bring what one needs at a good price.'

'Madam, I am not wanting to hear about smuggling practices, however much against law they may be. Those I am leaving to Customswallas. But about the taking of drug samples from such a place of medical research as the Mira Behn Institute, that I am needing to know in full particulars.'

'Particulars this and particulars that. So many questions you are asking, Inspector.'

'Madam, it is just only one question. But I must have answer.'

'But I tell you I don't know, Inspector. It is not something to ask.'

'Nevertheless, madam, have you at any time heard a whisper only about what exactly is happening at Mira Behn Institute?'

'Inspector,' Asha Rani asked, exuding coyness as if it was some rich attar wafting on every breeze, 'if I tell, will you once and for all leave myself alone?'

'Madam, I would.'

So long as I get an anyway decent answer.

'Well then, there is a man at the Institute. He is giving it to our supplier. A man. But that is all I know, Inspector. That only. A man.'

'I see, madam. And you are not at all having any idea of the name of this individual?'

'Inspector, I have told. I know nothing-nothing. It is just that I was hearing once from Ganguly sahib that there was this man. Do you think I concern myself with such matters? Do you think I was asking what was the man's name? What his wife was called? His children also?'

Ghote ignored that last stream of questions.

'Then, madam, I must ask Mr Ganguly,' he said. 'Kindly say where I may find him just now.'

'In London, Inspector,' Asha Rani said.

She gave a great gusty sigh.

'Our audiences in these days are insisting and insisting on having many, many foreign locations,' she went on, a look of piteous suffering spreading across her hugely vibrant face. 'Yes, and we are their slaves. So someone has to go to wherever they are demanding. London, New York, Paris, all those places. Someone has to go to shoot backgrounds. My Ganguly-mooly has gone. So you will not at all be able to find out from him itself. Not today. Not tomorrow. Not for many days to come.'

'Very well, madam. Then I must do my level best with what you have been so kind as to tell.'

Chapter Three

It was still early when at last Ghote arrived at the Mira
Behn Institute in its slightly cooler, somewhat higher
than sea-level area of Bombay, dotted with hospitals and
research establishments. The place itself, he realized as
he stood outside it, must be in fact a distant annex of
the big Peerbhoy Hospital, one of the city's most
respected. The same high wire-topped wall appeared to
surround them both, broken here by the gate for the
Institute, as tall and formidable – if not as ornate – as
the gates at Asha Rani's home.

Must be as hard to get in here as to Asha's house, he
thought to himself. But here high gate is more needful.
Cannot have dangerous drugs and all at mercy of whosoever passes by.

Surrounded by its own garden – an aged, bare-
chested mali was feebly thwacking at a scrawny bullock
tugging along a big metal water-tub on wheels – the
Institute was simply an old house built in the same dark
knobbly English-looking stone as Police Headquarters
at Crawford Market or one of the churches the British
had put up in the days of their raj.

There was, however, in one of the stone gate-pillars

a very modern-looking electric bell with a grille to speak into. He put his finger on the button and was rewarded after a few seconds by a voice emerging.

'Yes, please? Kindly state business.'

'Inspector Ghote, Bombay Crime Branch. I am wanting to see Director sahib as soon as he is coming in.'

'Ek, moment only.'

The door of the house opened and the chowkidar, in neat khaki uniform, boat-shaped cap on head, came hurrying towards him along the Public Works-style black tarred path.

But before he had got halfway he stopped in his tracks.

'Mali, mali,' he shouted.

And at a knees-pumping run he set off towards the ancient gardener and his equally ancient bullock.

And I am left to wait outside this gate itself, Ghote thought, his patience still scratchy from his meeting with Asha Rani. But there was nothing he could do now but listen, fingers irritatedly tapping at his side, while the chowkidar berated the old mali.

'Once more you are doing it. You were entering house to take water straight away after I was letting you inside compound. Yes? Yes? Yes?'

The old man's reply was inaudible.

'Then I am telling you. Do it one time again, and I will report-report to Directorji himself. You have broken lock on that window for your nefarious in-comings. You should pay. You should be necked out itself. And pay. Yes, pay, pay, pay.'

But, when the chowkidar turned away and came

across the well-greened grass towards the gate, Ghote saw his shoulders were heaving with uncontrolled laughter.

'Oh, sorry-sorry, Inspector sahib,' he spluttered out. 'But that fellow is always and always stealing water from inside house. How many times have I told him this is last time, and how many times he has done same thing again. Oh, he will never stop. Never.'

He wiped away the tears of laughter that had begun to run down his cheeks.

'I am wanting to see Director, urgent police business,' Ghote said, coldly as he could make himself. The chowkidar's maniacal mirth tended to be infectious.

The fellow calmed down a little.

'Yes, yes, Professorji has just come to his seat,' he said, carefully unlocking the tall gate and swinging it open. 'He is here always very, very early. And here late in night also. No one is working so hard, they are saying. Come inside, come inside. There I will state per telephone to Professorji you are here.'

'Very good.'

I was losing no time then, Ghote thought as he watched the chowkidar carefully relocking the gate, by going to see Asha Rani before coming here. And some information gained from her also, however much of difficulties she was making. The name of this drug that is being illegally taken away, A-C-E. The fact that there is someone here, a *man*, who is selling the samples.

Should be enough to start asking questions with, questions that should obtain some answers worth

34

having. Get to the bottom of the whole business with some luck today itself. No need to go asking Mr Mihir Ganguly whenever he is getting back from UK. Be able to report to Commissioner sahib all dealt with. Some kudos perhaps to come my way after all.

He followed the happily bouncing chowkidar up the path to the house, its tarred surface already hot to the feet. Inside, in the pleasant cool of the old stone building, the chowkidar carefully closed the big door and then dipped into a small glass-walled sentry-box beside it and took up his phone.

Ghote looked around.

The tall, narrow hallway, gloomy and ill-lit, reminded him a little of his college days in the city. A flight of wide stairs leading upwards and a narrower one going down; bare wood shining with years of polishing. A wooden bench where visitors lowly enough to have to wait could sit. In a dark corner a green baize noticeboard scattered with pinned-on sheets. The standard pair of red-painted, sand-filled fire buckets, dusty and littered with cigarette butts. Just inside, opposite the chowkidar's box, another reminder of college days, an In/Out board with a list of a dozen names, most of them preceded by *Dr.* All the little wooden sliders bar two were clicked across to *Out.* Only two primly registered *In,* the one marked *Director* and one other.

Dr G. Subbiah, Ghote read.

The young scientist from Pondicherry Asha Rani had said was so brilliant. Perhaps some of her success was due to starting first thing in the morning.

Well, good for her.

The chowkidar at his phone seemed to be having an unaccountably long conversation with the Director. Already two or three bursts of noisy laughter had penetrated the glass of his box. Professor Phaterpaker must be more jovial than most senior academics.

But when would he get to see him?

In a burst of impatience he marched across to examine the noticeboard in its gloomy corner. Along its top, he saw as he reached it, there had once been painted in bold, white letters, now so time-dimmed it was difficult to make them out, the motto *Truth Is God*.

Well, let me hope to find such words still acted upon here. After film star Asha it will be very much of a change to ask questions to people believing in strict truth. To scientists.

But he had hardly glanced at any of the notices pinned on the board's faded baize, a few new and white, most yellowed with age, all either incomprehensible or solidly dull, when the chowkidar poked his head out of his box.

'Inspector, kindly go upstairs. Directorji is waiting.'

He abandoned the noticeboard and set off up the wide polished stairway. A turn. Another flight. Another turn. And there stood the man who must be Professor Phaterpaker. *First-class fellow*. The Commissioner's words. Great joker with the chowkidar. Dressed in a white atchkan and tight-to-the-thighs churidar trousers. Slightly stooped. Grey-haired. Little jut of grey-white beard sprouting from his chin. Heavy spectacles perched on a long nose.

But somehow, for all the slightness of his frame, for

all the laughter he had indulged in with the chowkidar, giving the impression of implacably barring the way.

'Inspector Ghote? Was that what Laloo was saying? Crime Branch, was it? Now, do you have any scientific training?'

The oddity of this last question stopped him in his tracks.

What for could this professor be wanting to know if he himself had scientific qualifications?

Then he guessed. Or thought he might have.

'No, sir, no,' he answered. 'It is not at all a scientific matter I have come for. It is just only a question of administration.'

'Come up, come up then, Inspector. If— If there is any way I can be of help, you may count upon me.'

'Thank you, sir.'

He still felt a tiny trickle of unease, of something not quite accounted for, as Professor Phaterpaker ushered him through an empty outer office and into his own room. Large, airy, its walls surrounded by wooden filing cabinets with rows of heavy books above them. Stored knowledge.

At once the Director took his place behind a wide desk. A desk, Ghote noted, singularly free of papers. Its large blotter was an unmarked white. In front of it three glass inkwells glinted with fresh blue, red and green ink. And all over its surface were scattered little metal paperweights, more than he had ever seen on one desk before. But under them there were no documents, no working papers weighed down against the draught from the big fan whirring lazily overhead.

Odd.

Leaning forward a little, he observed that each paperweight, so far as he could see, bore the initials PPP, presumably the professor's own. He saw then, too, that the shallow drawer directly in front of the Director was not quite closed. Papers seemed to have been hastily stuffed into it. Perhaps, after all, this had been the reason for the question about his own scientific training. No prying eyes wanted?

'Sit, sit, Inspector.' Genially Professor Phaterpaker indicated the three chairs ranged up in front of his desk. 'Now, what is it exactly that I can do for you?'

This was better than Asha Rani's empty gushing. Perhaps some good progress lay ahead.

'It is just only a simple matter, sir. It has come to police notice that samples of a certain drug being produced at this Institute have come into the possession of certain individuals in the city.'

Professor Phaterpaker's geniality faded away like the sun dipping under the horizon at day's end. A sudden darkening everywhere.

His spectacles began to slide down his long nose, flushed suddenly with sweat. With a jabbing middle finger he pushed them back up.

'What do you mean, Inspector?' he snapped out. 'Are you stating that my Institute is being conducted in an irresponsible manner? That I am failing in my duties?'

'No, sir, no. What I—'

'Inspector, let me make this altogether clear. This Institute, over which I have had the honour to preside for the past fourteen years, has a reputation second to none in India. I will not tolerate the least breath of suspicion touching upon it.'

Then he must have seen the look of surprise Ghote had been unable entirely to suppress.

What for is the fellow so much hot under his collar, he asked himself. Why is he thinking I am attacking this Institute itself? When all I am wanting to do is ask some simple questions?

'Inspector, you will think I am unnecessarily defensive. But what perhaps you will not understand is that an establishment such as the Mira Behn Institute depends very largely upon its day-to-day reputation. We are not one of the great research faculties of America or Europe. Indeed, all our work is conducted from this by no means large house, built in British days simply as accommodation for the Resident Medical Officer at the Peerbhoy Hospital. So, if anything is done to damage that reputation, even by inference, it is a very serious matter indeed. If our standing in the world of science should go up in smoke, as they say, every paper produced by our researchers could all too easily come under fire from what I may call rival bodies. Inspector, let me tell you I would go to any lengths to protect the Mira Behn Institute's good name. To any lengths.'

His spectacles had, once again, slipped down his nose. And, once again, he thrust them ferociously back up with a poking middle finger.

Then, abruptly, he smiled.

'In my own case, of course,' he went on, 'such considerations scarcely apply. My personal reputation, I am happy to say, is utterly secure. Some hundreds of papers, published in journals all over the world, attest to it. But with more junior members of this Institute the case is rather different. Take, for instance, the work our Dr Gauri Subbiah is doing. She is a young person, Inspector, and from a background that is in itself no guarantee of probity. A person of altogether humble origins, not to put too fine a point upon it. Coming from somewhere near Pondicherry. Daughter of a domestic servant. Learning English and French by listening to the little girl of the house. But possessed of remarkable intellectual qualities. She may yet go far, if she does not encounter unnecessary opposition. A researcher of great promise. Yes, of great—'

'But, sir, sir,' Ghote could not help interrupting, coming up from under the battering of self-justification. 'It is what Dr Subbiah herself is producing that is subject of my inquiries. A substance going by the letters A-C-E, a name, I am told, for the ace cure for hypertension.'

Professor Phaterpaker smiled once more, all tolerance for a scientific ignoramus.

'Well, no, Inspector,' he said. 'You are not altogether correct in your nomenclature. I fear you have been somewhat misinformed. Or perhaps, if my friend the Commissioner was giving you your orders directly, you may have misunderstood him. The substance you are referring to is an inhibitor, an Angiotensin Converting Enzyme inhibitor, more familiarly an ACE-i. Dr Subbiah is deriving it from the venom of one of our Indian snakes. A chemical process, I may say, of truly dazzling originality.'

He produced a sudden sharp look from behind the spectacles still up on the bridge of his nose.

'But you were telling me you had no scientific training, Inspector,' he said. 'It was because, you know, misunderstandings of this sort were likely to crop up that I thought it right to enquire what qualifications you might possess.'

'Yes, sir. Thank you, sir.'

But was that really why he had asked that question on the stairs? The very first words he spoke? Before he knew in any way what for I was coming here?

'Yes, Inspector,' Professor Phaterpaker went on, smiling still. 'For one moment I thought, when you first asked me about this, that you must be referring to some irregularity concerned with my own researches. But I am not working on ACE-i. No, no, my field is the malaria vaccines. Their study has occupied me for many, many years. In fact, I think I can say without undue boasting I am considered the leading authority in the world on the subject.'

'Yes, sir.'

He put on an expression of deep respect. It was clearly expected of him. But he could not help asking himself why the professor was feeling it necessary to tell him all this. Even for a second time.

Not something, however, that could easily be put to a person as influential as the Director of the Mira Behn Institute.

Back to the matter in hand.

'But this ACE-i, sir. Can you, please, suggest any way in which it could be taken out from here? Is there some

individual in the employ of this Institute, some altogether Class Four person no doubt, who would have
access to these samples?'

At this question Professor Phaterpaker sat in silence.

Ghote had just reached the point of wondering
whether he could break into such deep cogitation – but
what was it about? What could have set off such a long
train of thought? – when abruptly the Director came to
life again.

'Ah, as to our humbler employees, Inspector, I fear
I cannot be of much assistance. The minutiae of administration is not something I find I have time to pay
attention to. My strictly scientific work . . .'

He left the overriding importance of that speak for
itself.

'Then, sir,' Ghote said, allowing himself a touch of
sharpness, 'who must I go to?'

'Ah. Well, yes, Dr Mahipal is your man. He is in
charge of day-to-day administration.'

He broke off.

'That is, Inspector, Dr Mahipal was until recently in
charge. Unfortunately, however – Mahipal is a harijan
by birth, and you know how there is always an element
of instability among the Untouchables – unfortunately
he chose just the other day suddenly to offer his resig-
nation. I hardly know why, although naturally I did my
best to dissuade him. A researcher of some ability, you
know. One must give him credit. But, alas, no longer
with us.'

Ghote sighed with half-concealed impatience.

'I see, sir. But then who am I to go to?'

Professor Phaterpaker's hands rose in a judicious steeple.

'Yes. That is a question of some difficulty. You do well to ask it, Inspector. Let me see. Ah, yes. I think the person you had better see is Dr Subbiah herself. She makes most use of the refrigeration facilities we have in the basement here. She, doubtless, will know who we have working there. I am afraid I cannot claim even to know by name every employee.'

Ghote felt a small lowering of optimism. If the Institute had so many employees . . .

'So, sir,' he said, 'there are a great number of Class Four workers here?'

Professor Phaterpaker looked, for an instant, put out.

'Well, no. No, Inspector. Not so many.'

He brushed the inquiry aside with a gesture of mild vagueness.

So, Ghote thought, if you are knowing so little of your juniormost employees, what about your joking-this and joking-that with Laloo, the chowkidar?

But that, again, was hardly a question he could ask.

He contented himself with another. An altogether simpler one.

'Then, sir, please, where can I find Dr Subbiah?'

Chapter Four

Following Professor Phaterpaker's directions – he had apologized for having no peon at this early hour to show him the way – Ghote climbed further up the broad polished stairway to the very top of the old house. There he found a door bearing the single word *Laboratory* with, stacked beside it, four or five tall gas cylinders their red or blue paint scarred and battered with much handling.

He paused for a moment before knocking.

A laboratory. The place where the mysteries of nature yielded to the questioning of scientists. The place where little by little the truth would be wrested from the impenetrable. *Truth Is God*. A truly holy, shoes-off place.

Or is it altogether such, he asked. I am not having, as Professor Phaterpaker was so often mentioning, any scientific education. Am I giving too much of respect to what is happening on the other side of this door?

Time to find out.

He knocked.

'Yes? Who's there?'

The voice that answered was female and terse.

He opened the awesome door.

The sight that met his eyes was not at all what he had expected. Once, in the course of his duties, he had had to arrest on a charge of receiving stolen property the owner of a shop selling second-hand chemistry apparatus. Standing here in front of the door marked *Laboratory*, that place had come vividly back to him. The narrow galli leading to it, almost night-dark in full day, the crumbling old building at its end. Then the shop itself, dusty and dim, in one corner of the dirty, hemmed-in courtyard. Retorts, flasks, coils of glass piping, Bunsen burners, racks of test-tubes, cotton-tied bundles of pipettes, old brass balances, iron stands spider-legged with sprouting clamps, microscopes focusing endlessly on their little dust-smeared glass plates, all in mass confusion on the shelves.

Here things could not have been more different.

The room, light and airy at the top of the house, seemed to be filled with nothing other than big, grey metal boxes of varying shapes and sizes. On them, here and there, tiny red lights glinted and gleamed. There was not a single test-tube or retort to be seen. Not a whiff of alien metallic odours in the air. Not a sound of bubbling or mysterious hissing. Only in one corner, one of the bigger grey-painted pieces of apparatus was, apparently, pursuing an interminable programme of its own. A wide, grey arm moved backwards and forwards, backwards and forwards, along its length, giving out at each end of its tireless journeys a subdued click followed by a tiny wheeze.

But in a moment his attention was drawn to the figure in a white coat over a plain, pale-green sari with a long, girlish plait of lustrous dark hair dangling down her back. She was sitting on a tall stool in front of the furthest of the square grey boxes. From time to time her outstretched hand clicked one of a pair of bright red plastic knobs protruding from a small device on the bench beside her.

Without turning away from from her task – in a flash of understanding Ghote realized she must be operating a counting machine, recording a series of events occurring on the VDU screen she was intently regarding – she called out.

'What do you want?'

'Madam, it is Dr Subbiah? Dr Gauri Subbiah?'

She pressed a button on the VDU's control panel and with a sigh of mild exasperation turned round on her high stool to face him.

She was, he saw, as young as Asha Rani and Professor Phaterpaker had indicated, in her late twenties or early thirties. No great beauty, but pleasant-looking enough. But what held him were her eyes. There was about them an unyielding earnestness, a quiet gravity, that transformed her face into one, for all its ordinariness, not easily to be forgotten.

And there was, he saw as he walked over towards her, a tiny white scar running horizontally across the broadish tip of her nose.

'Yes, I am Dr Subbiah. What is it you want?'

The directness of it chimed in with that look of searching earnestness.

'Madam, Professor Phaterpaker sent me to you,' he answered, finding himself equally to the point. 'He was saying you could give me certain information. I am from Bombay Police Crime Branch, Inspector Ghote.'

For a second or two she was silent, her large unblinking eyes regarding him almost cautiously it seemed. Then, making up her mind, she spoke.

'Well, what information does our Director think I might have?'

'Madam, I am here to investigate the disappearance, as I understand it, of some samples of the ACE-i you yourself are producing in this laboratory.'

With a thump she jumped down from her stool.

'Disappearance?' she snapped out. 'What is it you are saying? That specimens of my ACE-i have been stolen?'

'Madam, there is evidence.'

She looked swiftly round.

'But, good God, Inspector, this is a serious matter. Where exactly are these specimens meant to be disappearing from? Not from this laboratory itself?'

She strode over to one of the cupboards under the benches on which her apparatus stood, flicked open its steel doors, took a long look inside. Over her shoulder Ghote saw, at last, test-tubes. Neat racks of them each filled with pale almost colourless liquid.

'Those are your specimens?' he asked.

'Yes, yes. But none is missing, I promise you. I will double check against my records. But I am not mistaken.'

'But you are keeping other specimens elsewhere in the building?' he asked. 'Professor Phaterpaker was mentioning refrigerated storage. In, was it, the basement here?'

For the second time she hesitated before answering. But, when she did so, what she said was as straightforward and direct as she had been in her other answers.

'Yes, true, I send specimens down there to be kept under refrigeration. Specimens I may need if there is some question of my results being challenged. And, as controls also, any that were deficient in some way.'

'Those are ones, is it, that would not cure the hypertension they are designed to?'

'Not all of them, Inspector, no. Or not as effectively as they should. There would be some that would be useless certainly.'

'Then, madam, it looks as if the stolen specimens must be coming from there. We are having a report of a person nearly expiring from using one of them.'

'A person? What person, Inspector?'

Ghote stopped to think before replying. No, this was a question he ought not to answer, if only because the person mentioned was a friend of the Commissioner's friend, Asha Rani.

'I regret,' he said, 'I am not at liberty to give you any answer.'

'But if I don't know who has got hold of one of these failed specimens, I cannot help you. Or, what is more important, I cannot arrange for help for this person, whoever he or she may be.'

'Madam, I am told danger there is past. What is more important now is that I should find who is responsible for these thefts and bring to an end such antisocial activities.'

By – the thought suddenly came back to him with a chill of internal dislike – in the end, putting the thief behind bars for some other, invented offence.

'Yes, I see that you should do that, Inspector. And as quickly as possible. To have drugs stolen from an institute such as this is something that has to be stopped. At once.'

He felt that direct approach as a distinct rebuke. How had he got into the way of mouthing things like *antisocial activities*?

He would end it, as from today.

'And I think I know,' Gauri Subbiah added cautiously, 'who it is you should be questioning.'

With a quick decisive movement she glanced at the watch on her wrist. No delicate feminine affair, Ghote noted, but a working timepiece, broad in face, steel-rimmed.

'Yes,' she said. 'Yes, Chandra Chagoo should be down in the Reptile Room by now, and I very much suspect he is the man you are wanting.'

'Very good, madam,' Ghote said following her out, delighted at this swift advance. 'But can you kindly explain who is this Chandra Chagoo?'

'Yes. Of course. He is our snake-handler. Many of us here are working with snake venom in various ways. I use a great deal of it, as does Professor Phaterpaker. So it is an asset to have a technician, if you can call him such, who is particularly adept at extracting the venom.'

'Oh, yes. I suppose he has to hold a sponge or some

rag for the snake to dart in the forks of its fangs? Must be dangerous work.'

Gauri Subbiah gave a little laugh and came to a halt at the first turn of the stairs.

'Oh, Inspector,' she said, 'It seems you know very little about snakes. What you are calling the fangs are no more than the tongue, which is bifurcated at the tip. No, the true fangs are the teeth behind the tongue. One of them has a canal running through it. By it, the snake injects into its prey venom stored in a sac in the jaw. Venom, let me tell you also, that is not in all cases very injurious to human beings.'

Questions sprang up in Ghote's mind. He had hesitated to ask them as the young scientist had begun to go on down the stairs. But she seemed, abruptly, to have changed her mind and had turned to him. So he launched into the first of his queries.

'But cobras? And kraits? Surely kraits are very dangerous snakes. So I was always told as a child in our village.'

'Oh, yes, you are right. The krait's venom is highly dangerous to a human being. Often fatal. And the cobra's is only somewhat less so. But do you know which is the most dangerous of all? Did anyone warn you of that when you lived in your village?'

'Madam, I did not think there was any snake more terrible than the krait.'

'Then let me show you, Inspector, in one minute's time, the Russell's viper. It is from that species the venom I am using comes.'

'And Chandra Chagoo,' Ghote asked, 'who is obtaining this venom for you, how does he do it, if not by holding a sponge for the snake to strike? It is a very, very skilled task?'

'Oh, the milking, as it is called, is not enormously skilled, though it is best done by someone used to handling the creatures. You hold the snake with its mouth at the edge of a beaker and by squeezing the venom gland from above you cause it to eject the fluid. It is something that has to be done about once a month, when enough of it has collected in the sac. The snake-charmers you see here and there in Bombay, at places like the Gateway of India where there are plenty of tourists, they do that. So, you know, their cobras are never really dangerous. But it is more important to us to have someone for the day-to-day handling of the snakes. That requires skill and confidence born of much practice. Chagoo, actually, comes from Village Sitala about two hundred miles south from here. Do you know of it?'

'No. No, I do not think so.'

'Well, the people there have for hundreds of years worshipped cobras. It is said they once prayed to Shiva to free them from a plague of snakes, and he promised that if they worshipped them they would be safe. Of course, speaking as a scientist, I am bound to state that there are deaths each year in the area from snake bites. But that does not stop their great annual celebration.'

'No, madam, I am supposing not.'

'Yes, about two weeks before the Naag Panchami festival the men of the village go out into the fields and catch as many cobras as they can. They keep them in their huts, in large metal vessels, until the day itself.

Then there is a big mela. People come to it from miles around. They take out a great procession. Bands are hired for lakhs of rupees, all hooting-tooting brass instruments. Everybody in their best clothes. Each group of cobra hunters with its decorated bullock cart vies with the others. Red powder is blown everywhere, just as if it was Holi itself. And at the end all the cobras are put through their paces, made to dance by waving vessels in front of them. There can be as many as three hundred snakes on display. And at last they are taken back to the fields and released.'

'I did not at all know this. We are not doing so much for Naag Panchami in Bombay itself,' Ghote said, wondering a little why Dr Subbiah was taking so much time to explain all she had.

Down in the basement the man who, very likely, had stolen specimens to sell to people such as Asha Rani's Ganguly-mooly, was there to be questioned.

'Why should you know about Sitala?' Dr Subbiah replied, still making no effort to go on down the stairs. 'I know the place only because Chagoo goes back there for the mela every year, and when I was a newcomer here I once went with him. I had asked him where he learnt his skill with snakes.'

Then, as abruptly as she had stopped on her way down, she seemed to make up her mind.

'But, come,' she said decisively. 'It is time to see the fellow himself.'

They arrived at the basement. To the left of the stairs, guarded by a notice in red, *Danger – Reptiles –*

Authorized Personnel Only, there was an ancient, mass-ively heavy, newly steel-plated door.

Gauri Subbiah knocked at it. There was no answer. She knocked again. Still no sound from inside.

'Odd,' she said.

She looked at her severe watch again.

'Chagoo ought to have been here by now,' she said. 'Generally he comes at a very early hour. It is one of his duties to feed the rats also kept down here, the ones we have for testing vaccines.'

'Perhaps he is just only somewhat late?' Ghote suggested.

'No. He may be here already. He locks this door from inside. In case he has to move a snake from one cage to another. He should have heard me knocking, however. But perhaps . . .'

She turned back to the door and began thwacking hard at its steel plates with the flat of her hand.

There was no response.

'Very odd,' she murmured. 'But possibly he can't hear, if he is busy down at the far end where the rat runs are. And there are steel plates on the other side of the door as well.'

'Shall I beat on it also?' Ghote asked.

'Why not, Inspector? Your hands should be harder than mine.'

Ghote doubled his right fist and gave the steel sheet in front of him a ferocious tattoo of thumps.

Still no response.

'Well, he can hardly have failed to hear that,' Gauri Subbiah said. 'I suppose he can't have come, after all.

He may be ill. Or have had an accident on his way here. Or . . . or, something.'

But with each suggestion she had sounded less confident.

'All the same I do not quite like it,' she added.

'But, madam, why not?'

He felt obliged to put the question. Something in what she had told him about Chandra Chagoo had seemed somehow a little wrong. As if she might know more about him than she had said. Why, after all, had she jumped on the fellow as the likeliest thief of those ACE-i samples? Was it only because he worked in the basement where they were kept? Or could there be some other reason?

'I don't quite know why, Inspector,' Gauri Subbiah replied, with more hesitancy in her voice than he had yet heard.

Then she gave a little, rather choked, laugh.

'You will think it odd, Inspector,' she said, 'that a scientist should admit to having a premonition. But we are human also, you know. We have our weaknesses. Even nowadays I have to stop myself taking ten paces back if an unlucky black cat crosses my path. And, you know, I had a feeling just now, no more than a feeling, that Chagoo may be inside there after all and not somehow be able to respond.'

'But are you having another key to this door yourself?'

'No. I don't have one. As far as I know there are only three. We have to have tight security because of the snakes. If one of them should escape . . .'

'So who has keys?'

'Good question, Inspector. Chagoo has his, of course. When he is inside he lets in anyone who needs to enter. Professor Phaterpaker has a key of his own, because he says he sometimes has to come in to examine his rats at night. And there is a third one for emergency use.'

'And that is kept where?'

Ghote had asked the question automatically. But the moment he had done so he thought that it was as well that a detective, used to keeping logical track of things, should make himself aware of all the facts. If Chagoo had for some reason learnt his thefts were about to be brought home to him and was absconding, he might have left the basement locked like this to delay pursuit.

'Inspector, I am not quite sure where the third key is kept. Dr Mahipal, who has recently resigned from the Institute, had charge of administration. He would have known where it was – in whatever safe place.'

'I see. So, would it be possible to contact Dr Mahipal?'

'We may have to do that in the end. He has joined Grant Medical College, lecturing to first-year students. Or perhaps I could get him by phone at home. It is still early. But what I think I had better do first is to speak to the Director from the phone in Laloo's box.'

'Very good. And I think it would be better if I myself was to stay here.'

'You do, Inspector? You feel the same premonition as I did?'

'No, no, madam. A police officer cannot go by premonitions.'

'Even if a scientist can, Inspector?'

Gauri Subbiah gave him a smile with the barest hint of mischief in it, and whisked away up the stairs.

He stood there with his back to the heavy door.

If this Chandra Chagoo came late after all, he would have some sharp questions for him. And, as likely as not, find out in five minutes or ten that he was indeed the ACE-i thief.

And then . . . The Commissioner had said the culprit was not to be charged with the offence he had committed. His film world friends had to be protected. But why? Why should they get away with buying stolen goods? With accepting smuggled articles? Often in themselves illegal?

No. If Chandra Chagoo had stolen those specimens he would charge him with that offence. Indian Penal Code, Section 378, Theft, read with Section 14 of the Dangerous Drugs Act. Yes, by God, he would.

Dr Subbiah was taking longer than he had expected. What could she be doing? Perhaps Professor Phaterpaker had been able to tell her after all where the third key might be, and she was having difficulties to find . . .

His gaze wandered round.

A long rank of freezer cabinets on the wall opposite. Snake venom must be stored there, yes. In one corner some sort of machine for freezing same, by the look of it. All pipes and nozzles with a thin white glittering layer of frost on them. Must be why it is so nice and cool here. And, beside that machine, a sloping wooden shelf with a large book open on it. A ballpoint, secured by a length of greasy string, hung from a hook in the wall above. A register?

He looked at his watch.

Dr Subbiah must have been away ten minutes. More even.

He went across and took an idle look at the book.

Yes, as he had guessed, a register. Register of snake venom requisitions. *Date. Name of Person Requisitioning. Venom Type Required. Amount Supplied. Time Supplied.* The entries in crude, unformed letters. Chandra Chagoo's writing, no doubt.

He peered more closely.

Any entry for today already?

What date is it? Must be October the fourth.

There was no entry. But for October the third and for days before it there were entries in plenty. *Dr Subb*, in what must be Chagoo's badly formed letters. Daily demands going back – he flipped rapidly at the pages – right until August. Large quantities also. She must be a very-very hard worker.

'Inspector.'

Gauri Subbiah herself was standing at the foot of the stairs.

'Oh. Yes, yes. Madam, you are here.'

'And with a key. It seems the mali found it under a bush in the garden this morning. How it got there is a mystery. But that can wait. This is certainly the right one. I am only sorry I was so long getting it, but the mali had given it to Laloo, and Laloo is incapable of giving a simple answer to a simple question. Everything gets a whole history, with jokes.'

'Yes, I was watching the fellow telephoning to the Director. I could not help wondering then what it was he was finding to talk and talk. But, madam, have you no idea how this key came to be in the garden itself?'

'None at all, Inspector. As I said, a mystery. But perhaps we will soon find out.'

She went across to the Reptile Room door and inserted the key, a heavy iron object, evidently dating back to the earliest days of the old house.

She was having difficulty getting it to turn. Ghote wondered whether to volunteer to do it for her.

'Always difficult, as I remember,' she murmured. 'There's some trick... Oh, yes, that's it. Pull the door towards you.'

She gripped the big round doorknob with her other hand and leant a little backwards. With a loud scraping sound the key turned in the lock.

She hauled the door open.

Ghote let out an involuntary gasp. Not far from being a shriek.

There, only a few feet inside the room, lay the body of a man, face down. And sliding across his naked back was a vicious-looking, long, black-spotted snake.

'Russell's viper!' Gauri Subbiah exclaimed.

Chapter Five

At once, to Ghote's astonishment, Gauri Subbiah took a single rapid step into the Reptile Room, bent and seized the snake from the rear just under its head. A moment later she had risen to her feet with the creature hissing furiously in her hand, its long black body writhing and threshing.

'Madam, madam,' he shouted. 'What are you doing? It must be dangerous.'

Already he was trying to work out how he could come to her rescue. Get her out of the consequences of that rash act.

'No, no, Inspector. Not to worry. My father was a mali at a big house in Pondicherry, you know. He taught me how to handle these creatures.'

She turned towards a row of glass-fronted, dark-shaded cages where the shapes of other snakes, sleeping and still, could just be made out.

'Yes, look,' she said. 'The glass of that cage has somehow been smashed. But I can get this into an empty one.'

'But, madam, the danger!'

She laughed. Actually laughed.

'Oh, Inspector, wasn't I just telling you? A snake needs as long as one month to replace its venom once it is ejected. And I would be very surprised if this one has not used all it had on Chandra Chagoo there.'

'That is Chagoo then, madam?'

But he had known who it must be the instant he had set eyes on the man lying there face down, his head no more than a heavy thatch of coarse, grimy grey hair, his body clothed only in the greasy lunghi wrapped round his waist.

'Oh, yes, Inspector. That is Chandra Chagoo all right.'

She thrust, as she spoke, the head of the long, thrashing Russell's viper through the door of the empty cage. With a series of sinuous windings it rapidly disappeared into the dark interior.

Gauri Subbiah shut the door.

Then she turned to Ghote.

'So what we must be asking now,' she said, 'is *How did Chagoo come to be where he is? How did he die?* But that would be your business only, Inspector.'

'Yes. But, no. No, madam, this is not at all my business. This is just only a death due to circumstances unknown. As such it must be investigated by the local police. It is nothing whatsoever to do with Crime Branch.'

He felt an immense sense of relief. Up to someone else now to go into the mystery of the key found in the garden, to deal with the question of how the cage with the deadly Russell's viper in it had been smashed open. And, best of all, he himself could go to the Commissioner at once and report, almost certainly the truth, that the ACE-i specimens had been taken from the Mira Behn Institute by the man now lying dead on the floor here.

End of altogether awkward task. No need at all now to arrest anybody on some trumped-up charge just so as to keep the breath of scandal away from Asha Rani and her like. Everything one hundred per cent back to normal.

'But, Inspector,' Gauri Subbiah said with some sharpness, 'you are here itself. There must be questions coming into your head. You cannot just walk away from them.'

'Madam, you are wrong, I regret to inform. It is even my bounden duty to, as you have said, walk away. If I was beginning to ask questions here and now, I would be taking over proper role of whatever officer the police station for this area is sending. That would not at all be the right thing. No, I will contact them per telephone. But that is all I must do.'

'Well, I dare say you know your own business best, Inspector. But I can see you are no scientist. A scientist could not find themselves confronted by a situation like this without having a thousand and one questions in their head. And without asking them also.'

He felt it as a rebuke. But scientists were surely persons above the common level. *Truth Is God.* They worked under that motto. As for himself, it was Commissioner is God. Had not his orders been clear? Yes, find out the truth. *Ask questions, man, ask questions.* And then, when you have found out answer, make up some other charge so as to put your culprit behind the bars.

For one short moment he was tempted to say he would, after all, investigate this death himself. Send protocol to hell. Forget about informing Commissioner sahib that the case had been conveniently closed. Ask, ask and ask about that mysteriously missing key. Ask how the glass front of the snake cage had come to be smashed. Ask Gauri Subbiah even what the real reason for her seeming to know Chandra Chagoo would be behind the basement's locked door. Question her hard. Brush away as nonsense all that *ten paces back if an unlucky black cat is crossing your path*.

But, no. He was a police officer. He did work under orders. Not for him to question them. Not now. Not so long as he continued to be a police officer.

Facing the Commissioner in his immense ornate office half an hour later, Ghote found his account of how the ACE-i specimens must have been taken from the Mira Behn Institute quickly accepted.

'Very good, Inspector. Excellent piece of work. I will not forget it. I am seeing Miss Rani tonight. She has kindly consented to appear at a fund-raising tamasha for the Police Hospital. So I will be able to tell her she need worry no longer.'

'Yes, sir.'

But, making his way out, down the broad, red-carpeted double staircase, past the cold white marble bust of the British first Commissioner of the Bombay Police, past the little twin brass cannons at the entrance, the knowledge came to him beyond discounting that he would have been altogether happier if the Commissioner had questioned and questioned him. If every detail of what he had done at the Mira Behn Institute had been demanded of him.

But what answers could he have given? He had not even asked everything he might have done. He had grabbed at the easy way out. The fact that the Commissioner had grabbed it in his turn did nothing to quiet the worm of uneasiness within.

With downturned mouth and heavy-footed he walked across the stony compound to his own cabin, slumped down at his desk. And there confronting him – one more jab at the start of this bad day – was a bright white memo slip from Assistant Commissioner Dhasal. In one short sentence it informed him that the task of handling the smuggling air stewardess, Nicky D'Costa, had been assigned to Inspector Adik *w.e.f. today's date.*

Should he go to the ACP and ask, now that the Mira Behn Institute business was dealt with, to have Nicky D'Costa back in his own hands? But that would be pushing himself too much to the fore. Adik, newcomer to the Crime Branch though he was, had a fine reputation. Why should he not handle Nicky D'Costa as well as himself? Or better even?

And there was work enough for him to do. A Crime Branch officer's in-tray was never empty.

But, although the rest of the day's paper-shifting was satisfactory enough, and decidedly tiring, that night he lay long awake. Alternately, he cursed himself for not having pursued the business at the Mira Behn Institute in the way that determined Dr Gauri Subbiah had wanted, and then endlessly explained to himself how impossible that would have been. The pleasant evening he had spent at home – Protima had cooked his favourite masoor dal aur saag, the comforting solidity of lentils and spinach just lifted up with enough ginger – was wasted entirely. Not a single pleasant thought could he conjure up.

He woke earlier than usual. Unrefreshed.

Then, going eventually to eat his morning poories, his attention drawn by even noisier-than-usual arguing among the crows outside, he saw in the road once again the Commissioner's car, standing there spattered by a post-monsoon shower, still lightly falling.

He could scarcely believe his eyes. Am I dreaming, he asked himself. Is it hallucinations I am having now?

But at once those questions were answered. By a vigorous knocking on his door.

Nevertheless, he was still disconcerted to find that it was, just as on the day before, the Commissioner's driver who was there.

'Commissioner sahib is wanting? Once more?' he brought out.

'Ji haan, Inspector.'

'Very well, very well, I am coming.'

And once again his hair was uncombed.

'Ah, Ghote.'

The Commissioner sat back against the polished leather of the car seat.

'Step in. I wanted another word. Thought it best to

drop by on my way to Headquarters. Get in, man, get in. Don't stand there in the rain like an idiot.'

'No, sir, no.'

Ghote scrambled in, perched himself on the seat at a respectful distance, hoping the wetness of his trousers was not making a damp patch.

'Jadhav, walk.'

Jadhav, who had only just taken his place at the wheel, slid out again and went, left-right, left-right, left-right, away along the road, the shower darkening the back of his uniform jacket.

'Now, Ghote, this is what it's about.'

But the Commissioner immediately fell silent, seemingly suddenly at a loss to explain exactly what it – whatever *it* was – was about.

'Yes, well, you see,' he began again eventually, 'I was discussing this matter with Asha, with Miss Rani, last evening, and she was particularly anxious that no— What shall I say? No hint of scandal or anything untoward should get about concerning the Mira Behn Institute. She takes a personal interest in the place, you know. Donates funds, all that. And apparently there's some first-class work, absolutely A-1, being done there. As you may have observed yourself yesterday. It seems they have some sort of a research genius. A woman. From Pondicherry, I think Miss Rani said. And very rightly – mind you, very rightly – Asha does not want anything to cause any upset there. Apparently this researcher, the Pondicherry lady, is about to present a paper in one of the medical journals in the West, or she may even have just done so, a paper that will revolutionize . . . Well, will revolutionize whatever the exact subject of her research is.'

The Commissioner fell silent again.

'I understand, sir,' Ghote said, although there was a great deal he hardly understood at all.

'Yes. Well, in the circumstances Miss Rani wants— That is to say, I think the fatality you were telling me about yesterday, that fellow who had been making off with those samples, ought to be investigated rather more thoroughly. I don't want it left entirely to whatever station officer happened to be given the inquiry. Understood?'

Now Ghote had understood. But he felt he could not say that of course any wish of Asha Rani's was the Commissioner's command. He contented himself with a murmured 'Yes, sir.'

'Well, you're the chap who was on the spot at the time. Makes sense really for you to keep a watching brief. Dare say, in fact, it'll all come clear quickly enough. But best to make sure, eh? Best to make sure.'

'Oh, yes, sir.'

He stood there where he was as the Commissioner's car moved off. The shower drizzled to its end.

What am I to do now, he asked himself. Is Commissioner sahib once more wanting some nice answer? Or am I to sit on the head of whoever is the investigating officer and see he is truly asking the right questions? And at last finding out exactly how Chandra Chagoo was coming by his death?

A municipal sweeper wielding as his broom a big palm branch picked up from somewhere – how did he get that, he wondered – passed by, casually pushing the rubbish from the gutter in front of him.

And whatever fellow it is I am overseeing, he brought himself back to thinking, will have one hell of a task before him. One raising, as Dr Gauri Subbiah was saying, one thousand and one questions.

Why, for a start, had Chandra Chagoo been locked in that Reptile Room? Why had he not had his key with him to let himself out?

He checked himself.

How did he know the fellow's key had not been somewhere in that room? As far as he could remember, thinking about the body on the floor during the brief time he had seen it, there had been no sign of a key. There had certainly been no key on the inside of the heavy door as he had left to telephone the local police station. But Chagoo might have put it down anywhere. Anywhere at all in the big bare room with its caged snakes along one wall, its runs for specimen rats at its far end.

The thing was he had not looked. He had refused to investigate in any way. Even to ask the first necessary questions. But what if the station officer given charge of the case had also failed to ask about the key? Had failed to search the almost naked body before it was taken for forensic examination? Perhaps even no proper search of the Reptile Room had been made. Some officers at local stations were by no means as conscientious as they ought to be.

No, while he had still been there in that room he should have made at least some inquiries. Had he been truly doing his duty? Or had it been his duty, after all, not to go poking in his nose? Hard to answer.

Two boys going to play cricket, bats across their shoulders, came towards him, pushing and pulling at each other. Ved, he wondered abruptly, what should that son of mine be doing now? Is he also playing cricket today? Or should he have left for college? Why must it be the father who has to think of everything?

He looked at his watch.

Still too early for Ved to have gone as a matter of fact. Too early also to make his way out to the Mira Behn Institute? Would anybody except Laloo the chowkidar be at the old house? Would the officer investigating be on the scene? Or must he go first to Sewri PS? And was that even the appropriate station? Might not be. Area boundaries could be confusing.

But should be safe at least to eat something before setting off. Yesterday, in front of Asha Rani he had hardly been able to think what to ask his stomach was so much rumbling.

He turned to go back inside, almost getting bumped into by an earnest early-morning walker, striding out, looking straight ahead, white shorts creaking with starch round a too fat belly.

'Sorry, sir, sorry,' he said.

Instead, he secretly muttered, I should be asking you *Where the hell do you think you are going?*

And what about the key Dr Subbiah had eventually used to get into the Reptile Room? She had said that the

mali found it in the Institute garden. But where exactly
had that been? And when? At what time had Laloo
received it from him? And was it Chandra Chagoo's own
key or the emergency one? The one that no one seemed
to know where it was kept?

And, if Chagoo had somehow been locked in the
reptile room, why had he smashed the Russell's viper's
cage? A snake-handler must know that was the most
dangerous one of all surely? Had the man been drunk?

Why had he himself not thought to stoop at least,
grasp that mat of coarse grey hair, lift the fellow's head
and sniff at his mouth? He had hardly looked at him at
all, in fact , once the Russell's viper had been dealt with

Yes, Dr Subbiah had been right. There were a thousand and one questions to be asked. And perhaps some
of them he should have asked himself twenty-four hours
ago.

At the police station in Sewri he learnt that the Mira
Behn Institute inquiry was being conducted by one
Inspector Baitonde.

'He is at the Institute itself?' he asked.

'No, no, Inspector,' came the reply. 'He is here only.'

A little surprised that the fellow was not at the scene
putting questions, he asked where he could find him
and was told, a little grudgingly. Crime Branch officers
were never very welcome at local stations, with their
tendency to want answers to questions that someone
had neglected to ask, with their unnecessary demands
poking away at happy, everyday routine.

Baitonde turned out to be a tall, morose-looking man. Hangdog eyes. Thin in the face. A thickly drooping moustache, seemingly almost too heavy to stay on his lip.

Ghote introduced himself and explained, with some discreet omissions, why he was there.

'And how is it going, Inspector?' he asked eventually.

'It is one damn muddle. That is all there is to be said. How can anyone whatsoever make a decent report on something so full of doubts and difficulties?'

Ghote refrained from pointing out that an investigating officer's object should not be to make a decent report but to cut through the doubts and difficulties till the truth had been reached. Instead he asked just one of his thousand and one questions.

'Tell me, have you found out yet how it was this Chagoo came to be in that locked room?'

Baitonde's drooping moustache rose up a little as his face took on an expression of stone-like obstinacy.

'How can I be answering each and every problem that damn business is cropping up?' he said.

'But that must be one of the first questions to answer.'

'Oh, yes? And how many others are there also? Why should one be first rather than another?'

'Inspector, you must be starting somewhere. I was saying only that this is one of the first questions.'

'But who are you to say it, Inspector? How long have you been over at that place? No one there is wanting to answer one damn thing.'

'But have you questioned that researcher, Dr Sub-biah, who was finding the body?'

'Stuck up bitch woman. Why should I question her? If she was finding the body that is her own stupid fault.'

'But, damn it all, Inspector, whosoever is finding a body is absolute key witness. Is her name on your FIR only?'

'She was giving first information: her name is on First Information Report. Yours should be there also. You were with her when she was finding, no?'

He felt caught out. How could he say to this deliberately offensive fellow that he had quickly left the Institute after phoning through to this police station, because he did not want details of what the Commissioner had ordered him to do to come out?

'I was almost there, Inspector,' he answered. 'But Dr Subbiah was the one who found the body. You should have taken a full statement.'

'I am not here to be told who to question and what to ask. This is my case, Inspector, and I will question whoever I am wanting and ask whatever I am liking.'

'But you cannot see—'

And, with the irate question on his lips, Ghote realized he was simply being led deeper and deeper into a mire of recriminations. They would do nothing but make a confused situation yet more confused.

He took a deep breath.

Only one way to deal with a fellow like this. Stick to the main point. It was just only like dealing with some scallywag from the slums. Once you paid any attention to back answers you were lost. No, with that sort of badmash you had to hammer and hammer away with questions about exactly whatever it was they had done. Then, with luck, you got somewhere.

'No, Inspector,' he said, not yielding an inch, 'what I am wanting to know is how this Chandra Chagoo got into the Reptile Room there when it was locked itself?'

'How should I know what a straw-brain like that is doing?'

'A straw-brain, is it? And how do you know that, Inspector?'

'All of these fellows from the melon fields are more or less straw-brains.'

'Are they? And who told you that Chagoo was, as you said, from the melon fields?'

Baitonde looked down at the ground. Moustache registering one hundred on the despondency scale.

'No one, Inspector. Just thought.'

'Then I suggest we go over to the Mira Behn Institute ek dum and find out a great deal more about Chandra Chagoo.'

Grudgingly Baitonde got to his feet. But there was still some spark of cantankerous fire left in him.

'One thing I am knowing,' he muttered. 'The damn straw-brain was not having any key on him. I suppose you are thinking I am not at all knowing my work, because I am not some high-and-mighty Crime Branch-walla. But do you think I was failing to carry out a search of body before it was taken to JJ Hospital. Search of whole damn locked area also?'

He gave Ghote a glare that seemed to demand an answer.

Ghote sighed.

'I am happy to hear you know the procedures, Inspector. So on your list of objects taken from the body I will find no mention of a key?'

'List is not yet made. But when same is done no key will be there. If you want to know how that place became locked, then you can only go to the key the mali was finding under some bush at the back of the house. I am telling you no key was inside with the body. That room is not too difficult for searching. Not many of nooks and crannies, you know.'

For a moment Ghote contemplated asking Baitonde how long he had taken searching the Reptile Room and why, twenty-four hours after the investigation had begun, the written record of the search had not been completed. No doubt the answer was that the dead man was only *from the melon fields*, a person whose death did not merit very much investigation.

But better not say anything of that. No point in antagonizing, more than strictly necessary, a fellow he was going to have to work with.

'Very well,' he said, 'perhaps for time being we can assume it was Chagoo's key that someone took away after he was locked in the Reptile Room and threw down in the Institute garden. But have you checked where were the other keys to that room?'

'Other keys, Inspector?'

'Yes, Inspector. It is assumption only that, if Chagoo's key is missing and one has been found thrown down somewhere, they are one and the same. Not necessarily the case. I was not long at that place yesterday, but even I was finding out there are three keys to that

73

room. One is meant to be in the hands of the Director, Professor Phaterpaker. Have you asked him if he has it still?'

Baitonde gave him a glare.

'Why should I go worrying and scurrying to ask some damn silly question to such a Number One scientist?'

'Because, Inspector,' he answered, 'if ever the truth about Chandra Chagoo's death is to be found, it is vital matter to locate each and every one of those keys.'

Enraged by Baitonde's attitude, he had spoken with more vehemence than he had wished to. But, hearing in retrospect the words that had come out of his mouth, he realized that what he had said was indeed true. Chandra Chagoo had been found dead in a room that someone else must have locked. At the very least, the circumstances were curious. At the most, they might well amount to murder.

But, in either case, the chances were that something to the discredit of the Mira Behn Institute would emerge. And it was his task, on the direct instructions of the Commissioner of Bombay Police, to see that nothing reflecting badly on the Institute reached the light of day.

So, should he, in fact, take a leaf from Baitonde's book and let the matter of the keys drop? Should he simply let the fellow carry out such minimal inquiries as he was likely to make, and then report, once again, to the Commissioner that there was nothing at the Institute that need worry his friend Asha Rani?

'So, Inspector,' he heard himself saying almost at once, faintly appalled at the decision he was taking, 'what about that Key Number Three? The one for emergency use? It has got to be located. Did you do anything to find out even where it is meant to be kept?'

A sullen glint appeared in Baitonde's eyes.

'No, I did not,' he said. 'But if those keys are so important-important, why don't you yourself, Inspector, big-big Crime Branch inquiry, ask all those burra sahibs about them?'

'Yes, Inspector,' Ghote replied. 'First-class idea. I will go. But you also will come with me.'

Chapter Six

So half an hour later, Ghote, standing just behind the grouchy form of Inspector Baitonde, whom he had cunningly manoeuvred into being the one directly to face the Mira Behn Institute Director, saw Professor Phaterpaker take out a heavy iron key from a locked drawer in his desk.

Not, he noted, the drawer into which the Director had most probably shuffled his papers the morning before.

Waiting for Baitonde to rouse himself enough to ask whether Professor Phaterpaker could now bring to his mind where the third emergency key was kept, there flashed into his mind again the sight of the long, black Russell's viper slithering across dead Chandra Chagoo's naked back. Chandra Chagoo whose body was, even at this moment, under examination in the mortuary at the JJ Hospital.

'Thank you, sir,' he heard Baitonde eventually mutter. 'I am not having any more to ask.'

With a sigh he stepped in himself.

'There is one more thing actually, sir. The third key

to the Reptile Room, besides this one you are having and the one belonging to Chagoo?'

'Yes?'

'Can you tell us, sir, where it is likely this third key may be kept?'

'Ah. No. No, I cannot. I think I explained to you yesterday, Inspector, that the administration of this Institute was in the hands of a man, Dr Mahipal, who was assisting me in my research work also. Unfortunately he has seen fit to leave us. And I am afraid – Mahipal was lacking, you know, in that meticulousness one has a right to expect – he departed without informing his successor of all that he should have done.'

'I see, sir. And that successor is . . .?'

'Ah, well, as a matter of fact, no one has been appointed to that position. I had it in mind to offer it to Dr Subbiah, whom I believe you met yesterday. But she—That is, she should now have more time. She has recently completed a most important paper, one which I fully expect will bring this Institute a good deal of what you might call renown. It is for the journal of the Académie des Sciences in Paris. Dr Subbiah has a certain command of French, coming originally from Pondicherry, you understand. In consequence I have not liked to burden her with further duties.'

Ghote patiently waited till the end of all that before putting another question. One all the more sharply expressed for the long wait.

'But am I understanding correctly that you yourself, sir, are having no idea whatsoever where is this third key, vital to our inquiry?'

Professor Phaterpaker's spectacles had slipped down his long nose. With a gesture of spitting anger he pushed them up again.

'Really, Inspector, you cannot expect the Director of an Institute such as this to be acquainted with every petty detail of its workings.'

'Very well, sir. Then we must find Mr Mahipal, and put the question to him.'

But outside the Director's door – only just outside – Inspector Baitonde said, in an over-loud voice, 'To hell with your Mahipals and Bahipals. I am damned if I can see if this third key of yours matters one jot. The one the mali found is bound to be Chagoo's.'

Ghote considered.

Should he try to make clear to Baitonde the importance of getting the question of the keys totally clear? Make him see, as it seemed he had so far failed to do, that if Chagoo's key was the one found in the garden, rather than that Chagoo had hidden his own key somewhere in the Reptile Room for some reason – the sort of search Baitonde would have carried out might well not have revealed it – then his death could not possibly be the result of some extraordinary accident. It would be beyond doubt, murder. Someone would have deliberately taken Chagoo's key and locked him in with that deadly Russell's viper.

But this would mean going on to explain that it would be necessary to conduct the inquiry not simply with the object of finding out who that person was, but with a fearful added complication. The murder inquiry would have to be handled so that, if possible, no shadow of any sort fell on the Mira Behn Institute. The Mira Behn Institute under the protection, first, of the Commissioner himself and then of no lesser a figure than the heroine of heroines, Asha Rani.

So let Baitonde go off on his own now? Most probably straight to some restaurant or other for a cold drink and something to eat. Let him go, and then visit Grant Medical College himself and ask this Dr Mahipal about the third key? Certainly that would be a great deal easier than trying to put questions through this particular, sullen and uncooperative investigating officer.

He decided to take the easier way.

Main thing after all, he said to himself, is finding out truth of this key business. First step to finding out how Chagoo came to be lying dead there with that snake crawling over him.

'Very well, Inspector. Let me take charge of the keys inquiry. You, I suggest, may go and find out as much as is possible about Chagoo himself. We would hardly learn exactly how he was coming by his death unless we are knowing more about the man. Was he a drunkard only? That I have asked myself. Did he come to smash that snake's cage in one drunken fit? Much to learn there.'

'At least more sense in that than in key chasing,' Baitonde muttered.

Ghote took this for agreement.

How did fellows like Baitonde get to be where they were? Was it by bribery, in the hope of good pickings when they were bribed in their turn? Was it by chance itself? Or what? Impossible to find any answer.

At the high-towering, many-turreted Grant Medical

79

College, the peon who had been told to take him to Dr Mahipal found him in the staff common-room, waiting to give his first lecture of the day. A tall, thin man who might be any age between thirty and fifty, he sat hunched over the *Times of India* in a way that reminded Ghote of nothing so much as a saras, a long-billed crane.

He got awkwardly to his feet and offered a joined-palms greeting. But the gesture had to be taken as no more than a gesture because it was at once evident his right arm was so withered his hands could not, in fact, meet.

Was this, Ghote promptly wondered, why Professor Phaterpaker had found him less than perfect as a research assistant? Not adept at handling whatever apparatus had to be handled? If so, Professor Phaterpaker had said nothing about it. Perhaps out of delicacy? But, thinking of the Director behind his wide desk, delicacy of that sort did not seem a likely thing for him to have shown. So, another query. To be answered or not, as time would show.

'Dr Mahipal,' he said after introducing himself, 'I would not keep you long. But a matter has arisen where I think you could help me. Have you heard by any chance that the snake-handler at the Mira Behn Institute, one Chandra Chagoo, was found dead yesterday?'

'Killed by one of his own snakes,' Dr Mahipal said. 'Yes, there are three or four lines in the *Times of India* this morning. The words *Mira Behn Institute* caught my eye and I read the item.'

'Did you know Chagoo well?' Ghote asked, quickly

changing his mind about simply finding out where the emergency key to the Reptile Room was kept.

Possibly some useful information here. If Chagoo was a drunkard ... And quicker to find out here and now than waiting for Inspector Baitonde to produce some answers.

'No, I cannot say I knew him well,' Dr Mahipal replied. 'I spoke with him often enough, of course. He looked after the rats Professor Phaterpaker used in his research, and it often fell to me to check on their progress, so—'

He broke off, and sat in sudden silence. A deep frown on his face.

Now what has happened to him, Ghote asked himself.

'Please, Dr Mahipal,' he said after a moment, 'has what I was saying about Chagoo somehow caused you some problem?'

Dr Mahipal came to with a jerk.

'About Chagoo? No. No, no, Inspector. No, it was just that I was reminded – reminded of something else altogether. Something rather unpleasant.'

'I see, sir,' Ghote said, though he did not. 'So I am supposing you cannot tell me very much about Chagoo?'

For a moment or two Dr Mahipal considered. Then he spoke.

'Yes. Yes, Inspector, I think I can tell you something about Chandra Chagoo, though whether or not it will help you to discover how he came to die I cannot say. But the fellow was – I do not wish to speak ill of the dead – but he was downright rotten. I thought so even from the very first time I saw him. There was something about the way he looked at you that was venomous, as venomous as any of the snakes he took such pleasure in handling.'

'Venomous?' Ghote asked.

Dr Mahipal's unexpected attack on the dead man had aroused his curiosity. He hardly saw how this revelation, if it was true, would help him solve his mystery. But it sent questions buzzing round his mind like so many bees at a honey jar.

'You are saying Chagoo was a venomous individual? Please, can you give me one example of something venomous he was doing? Or was it just only your impression?'

'An example? Well, that is difficult. Perhaps the feeling I always had about the man was largely subjective. His way of looking at one in a sideways manner was . . . What shall I say? It was sly. Or worse than sly. It was as if he was always thinking how to take advantage. For instance, I found him, one night when I was working late, inside the Director's office, a place he had no conceivable reason to be.'

'I see, sir. And what explanation was he giving?'

Dr Mahipal blinked at the question.

'I—Well, I did not quite like to ask him, Inspector,' he said. 'I just waited there until I had made sure he had gone downstairs to the basement, and then . . . Well, then I thought no more about it.'

Extraordinary, Ghote thought. But then the man was a scientist. Perhaps he had better, more important, more abstruse things to think about.

'Yes, sir,' he said. 'That is perhaps something useful to have learnt about the man. But can you give me also other instances?'

Dr Mahipal stood and thought. Then he sighed.

'I think, Inspector,' he said, 'you would at least find others at the Mira Behn Institute would confirm my feelings about the fellow.'

'Well, I will ask,' Ghote said. 'But I was talking yesterday, before Chagoo was found, with Dr Subbiah, and she was telling something that does not altogether fit this picture you have drawn. Did Chagoo not offer, when Dr Subbiah was new at the Institute, to take her with him to his native village – Sitala, is it? – for the big Naag Panchami mela they are having there? That should be a kindly action, no?'

'Yes. You're right. Chagoo did take her there. But I think – I do not want to put words into another's mouth – I think, if you ask Dr Subbiah, she will tell you she went with Chagoo because the man had somehow blackmailed her into going. He wanted, I think, his fellow villagers to witness what élite people he was knowing in Bombay.'

'Blackmail?' Ghote asked sharply, scenting all sorts of hidden secrets that might or might not lead to an explanation of the snake-handler's death.

'Well, what you might call moral blackmail, Inspector. As I understood it from Dr Subbiah afterwards, he put it to her that she would be seen as unfriendly, a social climber, if she did not accept this offer. That was something she was very vulnerable to, Inspector. Although Gauri Subbiah is, to my mind, one of the finest scientists I have ever encountered, she is, or was in her early Bombay days certainly, to a large degree unsure of herself. She comes, you know, from very humble circumstances.'

'Yes, sir, I see how that could have been so. But, excuse me, I understand you too come from the harijan community. Why did Chagoo not invite you to Sitala also?'

'The harijan community?'

For an instant Dr Mahipal looked disconcerted. Ghote wondered if, in fact, he was going to deny his own lowly status within the layers of the caste system. But the hesitation was momentary only.

'My harijan status,' he repeated. 'I suppose Professor Phaterpaker told you about that. But there is an easy answer to the question you asked, Inspector. Dr Subbiah is a woman. It pleased Chagoo to have her, by whatever amount, in his power. That, if you like, is an example of his venom.'

'I see, sir. Then, please, do you think it would embarrass Dr Subbiah to confirm same? I am thinking it is important to learn as much as is possible about Chagoo. At present we are knowing almost nothing.'

'Then,' Dr Mahipal said, leaning forward in an even more crane-like way, 'is it that you are treating Chagoo's death as murder? No mention of that was made in the *Times of India*. But it hardly surprises me to hear it. There must be a good many people who would have liked to murder Chandra Chagoo.'

'Murder, sir? I was saying nothing about murder.'

But, he thought, at the back of my mind all along I, too, have been considering murder. Considering, or, more, refusing to consider. Just only accident is what the Commissioner will be wanting to hear. Asha Rani also. Myself perhaps most of all.

'I must make it clear, sir,' he said, speaking more vehemently than necessary, 'the circumstances of Chagoo's death have still to be explained to one hundred per cent.'

'Very well, Inspector, if you say so. But, nevertheless, I would find no difficulty in believing the man has been murdered.'

'When I am having enough of evidences I will agree with that or not,' Ghote replied, stiffly still. 'But, sir, what I was coming here to ask is about the keys to the Reptile Room at the Mira Behn Institute. I do not suppose *Times of India* was mentioning, but Chagoo was found inside that room, locked. Now, I am understanding there were just only three keys to the room. Is that so?'

'Correct, Inspector. Professor Phaterpaker always insisted on having his own. He sometimes went to check on his rat specimens late at night. Chagoo, of course, had one. He fed the rats and snakes in the early morning. And there was a third, kept in a safe place for emergency use.'

'And that safe place was where, Dr Mahipal? No one at the Institute seems to be knowing.'

'Oh, good God, I should have made sure somebody did know. But I left in such a— In such ... In such

85

a hurry, one way and another, the matter completely escaped my mind.'

Ghote would have liked, hearing this saras of a fellow hesitate so much over the way he had left the Mira Behn Institute, simply to ask if he felt keenly having to give up research to go lecturing unruly first-year students. To conduct research, surely that must be one of the most rewarding things anyone could do. To probe the unknown, and to bring back as answers new truths.

But duty called.

'So, sir,' he said, 'that third key would be where exactly?'

'In a cupboard in my office, the office that used to be mine, Inspector. The cupboard just above the working bench there. The key for that I did hand to the chowkidar, Laloo, when I left.'

'Thank you, sir. For once I am getting a clear answer to one question. Thank you.'

And there in the cupboard above the bench in what had been, until recently, Dr Mahipal's office, just where he said it would be, the heavy iron third key was.

Ghote stood there weighing it in his hand. Cheerful Laloo beside him, waiting for the little cupboard key to be returned to him.

'You kept the key to this cupboard here yourself?' Ghote asked him. 'You were not giving it to any individual whatsoever?'

'No one was asking, Inspector. No one at all.'

Laloo laughed merrily at this, for whatever reason. Or none.

So, Ghote thought, the two keys that were not Chagoo's are now accounted for. Neither could have been used to lock Chagoo in. So what does that mean? One thing only. It is a case of murder. Definitely. A case of murder. If Chagoo was left in the Reptile Room without his key, then that steel-plated door must have been locked by someone from the outside.

And, surely, it was not a drunken Chagoo but this person, whoever they were, who, before quickly leaving the place, had smashed open the Russell's viper's cage. Leaving the snake to do its work.

The suspicion that something of this sort was what had happened and been there at the back of his mind, a rain-loaded cloud waiting to burst, from the very beginning. But he had fought it away. How much easier it would all have been if Chagoo had died in some accident, and if that could be shown to have happened. A decent explanation to give. Something for the Commissioner to take to his *filmi duniya* friends. Any possible shadow lifted from the Mira Behn Institute. All well in the world.

But that was not the situation.

No, it was unmistakably clear now that Chagoo had been killed by whoever had locked the Reptile Room with his key and thrown it under a bush in the garden outside. But who? Who had done that? Who could have done it?

New questions to be asked. And perhaps now, not Gauri Subbiah's thousand and one, but a hundred and one. The matter was no longer a total mystery. It was a murder that had to be investigated. The questions now could be directed to one end. Arrows to find a single dangerous beast.

Chapter Seven

The first of my one hundred and one questions, Ghote said to himself, can perhaps be getting its answer here and now itself. From Laloo.

Laloo, standing there after relocking the cupboard where the third key had been kept, was jiggling about still with barely suppressed laughter. What about? About anything. Or nothing. But the fellow had been sitting in his chowkidar's glassed-in box very early the morning before. He had said, too, that Professor Phaterpaker sometimes worked late into the night. So presumably Laloo was at his post at that time, as well as first thing in the day. If so, he might well be able to say who had been here in the house when Chandra Chagoo had died.

With a single question the whole complicated business could be narrowed down to a fine point. The former Resident Medical Officer's house was within the compound of the Peerbhoy Hospital; a well-protected compound, high-walled, tall-gated. A hospital that attracted élite patients – every other well-known person reported as being ill went to the Peerbhoy – had to protect the privacy of such respected high-ups. So, if this reasoning was correct, Laloo might well be able to name everybody who had been inside the Institute at the time the snake-handler was locked into the Reptile Room.

Just ask.

'Tell me,' he said to the fellow, careful to make the enquiry seem so much idle chat, 'are you on duty first thing in the day and at night also? You were here very early when I was coming yesterday, and you were telling then that Professor Phaterpaker is often here very very late.'

'Oh, yes, Inspector. You are right. Many many times Directorji is coming late-late in evening. It is then, when I am unlocking for him, first the gate itself, and then the door, we are having some talks. In the night he is liking, as he is saying, to let down all of his hairs.'

Ah, the answer to one of those little questions that have been bothering me. That is why Professor Phaterpaker is on such good terms with Laloo but hardly can put a name to any other worker in the place.

'So,' he went on, 'you are here itself sometimes from the end of one day till the beginning of the next?'

'Always, Inspector, all the time. Laloo is a day-and-night fellow. I am just only dozing it on my bench when all is quiet.'

'Really? You sleep here in the Institute? Have you no home to go to?'

'Oh, Inspector, here is my home. What better could I be having? When monsoons are pouring down I am dry-dry. When it is hot-hot I am in cool only. One thing on wrong side only.'

'Yes?' he asked, intent on keeping the talk going. 'What is that?'

'Inspector, it is down below.'

'Down below?'

'Inspector,' Laloo said, pointing dramatically to the stairs to the basement. 'Do not go down there. Do not ever go.'

Ghote held back his amusement at the expression of horror on Laloo's face. An expression worthy of the simple idiot, staple of many a Bombay film.

'Why should I not go down? What is there to be afraid?'

'Snakes, Inspector. Reptiles. They are calling that place Reptile Room. It is because terrible-terrible snakes are there, crawling everywhere. With their poison-poison tongues going in and out, in and out.'

Should I explain about snakes' tongues, Ghote asked himself, feeling a twinge of guilt at how recently it was that he had learnt from Dr Subbiah that snakes' poison really came through the teeth. One thing, anyhow, he noted. Certainly Laloo cannot have ever been down to where Chandra Chagoo was bitten to death by the Russell's viper.

But Laloo's expression of hundred per cent terror had immediately lapsed into his seldom absent, meaningless grin.

'Oh, but, Inspector,' he said, 'rest of this place is very-very good. While there is canteen, I am never hungry. Never. Let me tell you, Inspector, what you must do in this life is to have a cook for a good friend.'

'I dare say, I dare say.'

He risked another question, still keeping a casual tone. Best not to let the fellow guess what it was he really wanted to know.

'A nice life you are having, isn't it? And I suppose also you must be learning many things late in the night that you would not get to know in the day?'

Laloo wagged his head, as much as to say *Of course, but do not expect me to admit it aloud*. Ghote accepted the confession.

'I bet it is more even than what Professor Phaterpaker has told you?'

And Laloo, grinning like a monkey now at the prospect of jokes and gossip to come, fell for the extended banana.

'Oh, yes, Inspector. Many, many things I am being told. If the burra sahibs are staying here after office hours, when they are at last leaving often they are liking to chit-chat. All, all. Burra memsahib also.'

Ghote experienced the temptation to hear as much of that gossip as Laloo liked to produce. But he stopped himself from adding the hint of a question that would unleash the flood. There was something more urgent to be found out.

'So who was here in this house late in the night yesterday?' he asked, trying to retain the idle note he had managed up to now.

Laloo's eyes lit up.

'It is when Chagoo was killed by one of those terrible-terrible snakes, yes?' he asked.

So much for softly-softly-catchee-monkey.

'Yes,' he agreed. 'When Chagoo died. What I am wanting to know is who was in this house then? In case, you know, someone heard something. Can anybody get in here without you seeing?'

'No, no, Inspector. One door only. Laloo is there. Yes, sometimes he is sleeping. But never-never leaving post. Not for shoo-shoo even. Holding in same till morning hour. So soon as any person is ringing at bell inside gate-pillar I am awake-awake.'

'And no one can get in except by the gate itself?'

'Ji haan, Inspector. No one, no one. High wall goes all the way round whole hospital compound. And front door here is locked also. One and only door of whole damn house.'

'Good. First-class. Then you can tell me what I am wanting to know. How many people were in this house when Chagoo died?'

'Yes, yes, Inspector. Answer is easy.'

'Yes?'

He waited. Was he actually going to get a list, even a short list, here and now, of all the people who could have locked Chandra Chagoo away to his death?

He was.

But it was to be a list he did not much like.

'Besides Chagoo, who had not left, three only were here. Directorji himself was here until just before it is midnight. Subbiah Miss was here also, until just after that. And Number Teen was Dr Mahipal.'

This last name was a surprise.

'Dr Mahipal?' he asked. 'But I thought he had altogether quitted the Institute? He has gone to Grant Medical College, no?'

'Oh, yes, Inspector. But he is sometimes coming back in the night. He was here then for two–three hours, leaving at one hour past midnight.'

'But why was Dr Mahipal coming back here? I am not at all understanding.'

'Oh, Inspector, he is saying there is research-research he is wanting still to do. He was leaving on computer here some figures he was needing. So in the night he was coming to steal back same.'

'Steal? I do not think you can steal a figure only.'

'Mahipal sahib is saying *Steal*, Inspector. Saying and laughing only.'

'All right, if Dr Mahipal likes to call that stealing then I am happy to agree.'

So here was the answer to the question he had wanted to put to Dr Mahipal but had felt to be too intrusive. It cast a light on the man. Plainly, after all, he was a dedicated scientist and not simply someone ready to earn a salary by passing on in his turn whatever knowledge he had. He wanted to continue his research, even to creeping back here in the middle of the night and making friends with Laloo so as to get data from the computer he had been using. So why had he resigned from the Institute so hurriedly?

Still, no time for side-issues. In his grasp now he had the names of three people who had been here in the house when Chagoo died. Only three people.

But such names. The impact of what Laloo had said began to sink in. Three people who could have, at some time before midnight, locked in Chandra Chagoo to his death. And each of them was – or in Dr Mahipal's case

94

had recently been – at the heart of the Institute. To arrest any one of them as a murderer would be to bring down on the Institute the utmost weight of publicity. And publicity of any sort was what he had been directly told by the Commissioner to keep at bay.

There was Professor Phaterpaker, distinguished head of the Institute. World authority on malaria vaccine, and, in the Commissioner's own words, *A first-class fellow.*

There was Dr Gauri Subbiah, the researcher who had just sent a paper to some respected French scientific periodical that was going to bring renown to the Institute. A special favourite of famous and influential Asha Rani.

There was Dr Mahipal, perhaps not quite as disastrous a person to have to arrest under Indian Penal Code Section 302, but still someone who had worked at the Institute and as an assistant to Professor Phaterpaker. Someone, too, who, sitting there alone like a hunched crane in the Grant College common-room, had seemed truly sympathetic. And who just had been revealed as a dedicated scientist, a searcher for truth.

Almost impossible to conceive of pulling in any one of them. But there they were.

Or were there perhaps – could there be? There must be – more than three?

'You say just only three people were here?' he demanded of Laloo. 'Is that true? Hundred per cent true?'

'No, Inspector.'

Laloo produced his belly-shaking meaningless laugh.

95

'No?' Ghote cracked sharply through it. 'Then who . . .?'

He felt a little leap of joy. Was this going to be release from the predicament he felt creeping towards him? Was he going to learn that someone else had been in the house that night? Some outsider, who would not cause too many problems?

He waited, tense, for Laloo's answer.

'Inspector, Laloo was here also, yes? So are you going to say I myself was putting Chagoo into Reptile Room, locking the door and throwing away key?'

Just Laloo. The idiot. As if it was likely . . .

He countered all this with another question. A slap of a question.

'How it is you are, after all, knowing what-all has happened?'

Laloo laughed again, almost as loudly as before.

'Inspector, Inspector, all are knowing. When something as much to talk as this is happening, all, all are talking, talking.'

'Yes, all right. I suppose so. So, now answer my question and no more of nonsense: except for yourself, the Director, Dr Miss Subbiah and Dr Mahipal, who else was in this house? Who else? Tell me.'

Laloo's grin disappeared.

'Inspector,' he said, 'no one. That is damn truth. No one. No one.'

Then one new question to ask. One that had to be put.

'So, Laloo, in the middle of the night you are asleep on your bench. Now, if anybody was coming down from the top of the house, you would hear them, yes? Wake a little, and see who it was?'

'Oh, no, Inspector. Someone come running-running down the stairs, clip-clop heels on the wood like a horse pulling a victoria only, yes, then I would be hearing OK. But, creep-creep, and not even Laloo will wake. If someone was trying to open door to go out, then yes. But creep-creeping inside house, no.'

'I see.'

So there it was. The almost unthinkable complication that had been coming up from behind him like a sly pickpocketing gang working some tourist – one to distract, one to jostle, one to lift the wallet – was there now in full. Was he really going to have to persuade Inspector Baitonde, officially in charge of the inquiry, that one of the three people that Laloo had named was responsible for the death of the snake-handler and should be arrested? If that was what had to be done, he knew well enough that the odium would slide off Baitonde like water from a duck's back. But it would stick to him.

For one moment he contemplated doing what, he guessed, Baitonde would have done if the business had been left to him. Pulling in helpless Laloo and beating some sort of confession out of him. Or leaving him in the cells as an undertrail till the storm had passed over. If it took years.

But there was here a truth to be discovered. And if that truth was, that for some reason, Professor Phaterpaker, say, had done to death Chandra Chagoo, then he would step in and see he was arrested. And endure whatever befell afterwards.

And the same went for Dr Gauri Subbiah. Or Dr Mahipal. Two people, though they were, whom he had begun to admire for the work they did. If he found it was one of them that had brought about Chandra Chagoo's death he would do his utmost to make sure they went for trial.

Into his bleak thoughts there came the ringing of a bell.

'Inspector, the gate, the gate,' Laloo jabbered.

'Very well, go down and open.'

He followed the chowkidar again, gripped by another fit of laughter, down to the hallway. The person at the gate – the bell had been ringing and ringing with brutal insistence – was Inspector Baitonde. Ghote went out to meet him.

'Oh, you are here, Ghote,' Baitonde said, as Laloo swung the tall gate open.

'Yes, Inspector, I am here. I have been questioning this fellow about who was inside this building yesterday night.'

Baitonde gave Laloo a glare rather than a glance. And got no cheerful grin in return.

'You should question-question in our Detective Room, Inspector. Where you can give out some good slaps and no one to hear.'

'Not needed. I have learnt all I am wanting to know. And more.'

He turned to the suddenly subdued chowkidar.

'You may get back to your post inside,' he said.

'And be quick about it, unless you are wanting my boot,' Baitonde put in.

They watched Laloo scoot away.

'Yes, Inspector,' Ghote said, putting plenty of sting into the words, 'I have learnt from that fellow some damn nasty news.'

'Then you should not believe,' Baitonde answered. 'That kind are always lying and deceiving. And if they are not, it is work of a moment to make them swear they were.'

'I do not think it is lying and deceiving this time. The fact is, Inspector, first I have found out exactly where those other two keys to the Reptile Room were last night. Both fully accounted for. So it is no longer in doubt Chagoo was murdered.'

'You are telling me some big news? Plain the fellow was murdered. Plain from the damn start.'

'All right. I had a strong feeling such was the case, yes. But until and unless those keys were located, there was a chance, small or big, that Chagoo's death was just only some sort of accident.'

'Crime Branch idea.'

Once again Ghote wanted to slap the fellow down so hard he would never get up again. He longed to remind him, and forcefully, that Crime Branch existed so that no-goods like him did not brush each and every case under the table. Or make stupid idiots of themselves when they did attempt to get at the truth. But, once again, he reined himself in.

'Never to mind that,' he said. 'Here is Fact Number Two. Inside this house at the time Chagoo was locked in the Reptile Room down there you could find just only three persons. You could find Professor Phaterpaker, the Director. You could find Dr Gauri Subbiah, who is about to produce a world-important scientific paper. Or you could find a very very respectable scientist, Dr Ram Mahipal.'

'You are forgetting that damn chowkidar, whatsoever his name is.'

'No, Inspector, Laloo was owning and admitting to me he was here also. But can you see him doing whatever was done to Chagoo? For one thing, he is dead scared only of going down into the basement when there are snakes in the Reptile Room. And then such a fellow is a leaf in the wind only, no?'

'Leaf is easy to tear with one hand itself.'

'No, Inspector. This business is too much of concern to certain VIPs, even VVIPs, for that sort of answer to be given.'

Baitonde's pendant moustache sank a little lower. An acknowledgement of a fact too solid to be brushed aside.

'Damn people from above who think they can ask and ask,' he said. 'Why will they not take *Kuch nahin* for answer?'

'Because, Inspector, such people get to their high places because they do not accept *nothing at all* as being good enough.'

'Then you can stick your nose up to them all you want, Inspector. I will stay happy where I am.'

'As you like. But, let me tell you, there is work to be done on this case. And done it will be.'

A long moment of confrontation.

But it was Baitonde who backed off.

'Oh, if it is some work only, I will do it. Might as well.'

'Good. Then, first of all, Inspector, what have you so far found out about Chagoo? You found some people to question, yes?'

'Oh, yes. Asking questions is damn fine work. If you are having to ask just only little people. One fist made, and answers come pouring-pouring.'

'So what answers came pouring for you?'

Baitonde heaved up his moustache.

'Fellow is staying—'

'Was, Inspector. Was staying. He is dead itself.'

'Fellow was staying, if you want each and every dot on i and cross on t—'

'I do, Inspector. When you are looking and looking for the truth you should not accept wrong answers. Even the smallest.'

He was making yet more of an enemy of this sullen idiot. But there came a time when nice-nice was a waste only.

'Very well, Chagoo stayed in a room in a chawl opposite Municipal TB Hospital.'

'Very good. Not too far from Mira Behn Institute. And he has got what family there?'

'None, Inspector. Oh, yes, he has a wife, some children also. But she is staying in his native place.'

'Village Sitara.'

'So you are knowing something about the fellow?'

'Something,' Ghote replied with careful ambiguity.

No harm in letting Baitonde think he knew more than he did. May take care then not to add to facts he has found. Easy-way-out fellow that he is.

'Yes. Well, Chagoo has this room, and he takes no notice of anyone and no one takes notice of him. I had to give out some kicks before I was getting inside.'

'So you saw inside his room? What did it tell you?'

'Not too much.'

Had he scared him now from giving even what information he had got hold of?

'But something, Inspector? An officer of your experience would see things some Head Constable (Investigation) would miss to one hundred per cent.'

Weighty moustache perking up.

'All right, the fellow must have had some left-handed business or other. I can tell you that. I do not suppose a place like this Institute would pay him too well. But there in his room was one nearly full bottle Peter Scott whisky. Was, I am saying. There no more.'

He gave a guffaw of a laugh.

'Plus also very nice radio. That is there still. Mine is as good. Plus TV with video, too heavy to carry – damn shame – and some very very interesting tapes for same.'

'What tapes, Inspector?'

Could they be something stolen from the Institute? Something valuable somehow?

'Jig-jig tapes, what else, Inspector?'

Quickly, to keep Baitonde from setting him down as altogether too innocent, he banged in another question.

'So, what do you make of all that, Inspector?'

Baitonde shrugged.

'Some side-line business, as I was saying.'

'No, Inspector, I think there would be a good deal more to it than side-line business only.'

Baitonde glared back at him.

'What then?'

'Blackmail, Inspector. I am happy to be betting that Chandra Chagoo was blackmailing someone here in this Institute. So now we are getting a smell of a reason for him to have been killed.'

Chapter Eight

Who had Chandra Chagoo been blackmailing? Professor Phaterpaker? Dr Gauri Subbiah? Dr Mahipal?

And what could he possibly have been blackmailing any of these three about? Ghote thought. Scientists. Truth-seekers. Oh, in the private lives they might have done something to lay themselves open to blackmail. Human weaknesses. You never could tell. Very, very respectable people could turn out to have scandalous sex secrets.

Did Professor Phaterpaker, for example, haunt the prostitutes of the Cages? But, even if he did, such a fact coming out would not be so harmful that he would kill to keep it concealed. What things about his personal life, his human weaknesses, would? None, surely.

As difficult, too, to see situations where either Gauri Subbiah or Dr Mahipal would be driven to such an altogether desperate action.

So who? Why? Which?

And the three questions, prodding at Ghote's mind like a naked sadhu's iron trident, produced an answer that, he saw in a lightning flash of revelation, might yet save him from this three-pronged dilemma.

Were there not, after all, some other people with access, just possibly, to the house of the Peerbhoy Hospital's former Resident Medical Officer? People, in fact, who might have among them someone Chagoo could have been in some way linked to?

Because the Mira Behn Institute was inside the big compound of the hospital itself. And in the hospital there would be not only patients – who could conceive of a patient getting up from his bed and going to kill the snake-handler? – but doctors and other medical staff and, most likely of all, lower-grade workers: cooks, boilermen, orderlies, peons, ward boys, sweepers.

Among such people, people much like Chagoo himself, there might well be one he had known. There might be one with some ordinary, everyday motive for killing him. Someone who for some reason owed him more than they could pay. A husband with an unfaithful wife. Someone Chagoo had had in his power whose life he had made miserable beyond endurance. A dozen reasons. Twenty. Thirty.

And if such a person existed, it was likely enough when they wanted to see Chagoo that he would let them into the Institute through a window somewhere, by-passing Laloo at the entrance door.

'Inspector,' he said to Baitonde, 'there is one angle we have not thought of. Peerbhoy Hospital.'

'What Peerbhoy Hospital? First you are saying three sciencewallas held in much respect have murdered that damn snake-handler, and now you are saying Peerbhoy Hospital. Is it one of the posh patients inside there –

rich must get better faster – you are accusing and abusing now?'

Ghote inwardly promised himself that one day . . .

'No, Inspector,' he said. 'But, think. Inside that building, in the same big compound as this one, how many people are there that a fellow like Chagoo would mix with?'

'How many? I do not— Oh, I am understanding, you are saying now Chagoo's murderer would be one of the little people there?'

'Yes, Inspector. Or at least I am saying it is more likely someone there murdered the man than that it was the work of a scientist from here. So what I am wanting is for you to go to the Peerbhoy and check on each and every one of such fellows. Did they know Chagoo? Were they on duty in the hospital last night? Could they have been absconding from duty for one half-hour only? Were they in any way Chagoo's enemy? Or the sort of friend who can turn into a deadly enemy?'

'So many questions? You are wanting me to go there and ask all these questions?'

'Yes, Inspector. That is what I am wanting. It must be done. In any report I was making I would have to state it has been done, together with name of officer in charge, yes?'

He looked hard at the sullen face, the hangdog eyes, the weighty, drooping moustache. In silence.

'Oh, hell with you, I am going, I am going. And God knows when you would see me again.'

If that was not for seven lifetimes I would not mind, Ghote thought. Except that I would very much like to hear you had found some first-class suspect there. Damn soon also.

One from there instead of the three first-class suspects I am having here.

Because I cannot be sitting idle and hoping this is some simple killing between Chagoo and whoever he is knowing among the Class Four staff at the Peerbhoy. I must be asking questions here at this Institute itself.

Or, first perhaps, at Grant Medical College. If Dr Mahipal will turn out to be the man I am wanting, he is the one who would cause less of problems.

'Oh, and Baitonde,' he called in the direction of the inspector's broad back moving reluctantly away, 'one thing more.'

Baitonde turned.

'More even, Inspector?'

'Yes, man. The report on Chagoo's body, from JJ Hospital, yes?'

'What of it?'

'Have you had? I would like to see.'

'Inspector, you know the bloody fellow is dead itself. I know he is dead. What point in having some damn Examiner telling us the same?'

'His duty, Inspector. And yours to receive his report. And mine to see it.'

Baitonde turned away, clumped off.

Ghote took that for agreement. Of a sort.

It was not until early in the afternoon that Ghote was able to see for the second time Dr Mahipal, kept busy giving the same lecture to successive new classes of first-year students – *Kindly pay attention . . . Questions. Questions . . . That is the path to take* – but he was waiting for him outside the lecture room as the students came tumbling out, boys with new untouched notebooks tucked under their arms, bright sari-wearing girls with the same notebooks, already part filled, clutched to their bosoms.

He stepped into the room as the last student, a plumply fat boy was saying to another, equally well fed, 'One bloody waste of time, yaar.'

Dr Mahipal was standing stooped behind the demonstration table at the foot of the rising rows of benches, looking even more like a dejected crane than when he had seen him in the staff common-room.

'They were telling that you would be here now and free, Doctor,' he greeted him.

'Oh, it is you, Inspector.'

The weariness in his voice was like a slow tide of grey mud.

'Yes. And I was wanting to talk some more. But if you have not yet had your tiffin, perhaps I could go with you. To eat somewhere not in the college. Outside itself.'

Was there a quick look of suspicion, of fear, at the suggestion? Was this the man who had, for some unknown reason, murdered the snake-handler, and who was now alert to what it meant if a police inspector wanted to talk in private?

Or was it just the man's quick response to an

unusual request? Just asking himself why it had been made?

'No. No, Inspector. I seldom eat lunch. So talk here, if that suits you.'

'Very well. Shall we sit?'

He gestured to the front of the tiers of narrow benches, shiny with generations of use. He would have to sit beside his witness there instead of facing him where he could more easily detect flickers of unease as his questions got tougher. But the man had looked so exhausted he felt he could hardly conduct this questioning standing, one opposite the other, across the wide, chemicals-stained demonstration table.

'Thank you. Yes, I am tired. To tell the truth, Inspector, I find the rows of faces I have been looking at for the past day or two a thoroughly depressing sight.'

He came round the long table and dropped on to the end of the first bench. Ghote sat down beside him.

But he jumped at the opportunity Dr Mahipal's remark had given him to begin the interrogation with some soft-soft questions.

'Why did you find those faces so depressing, Doctor?'

'Why?' Dr Mahipal smiled, just. 'Because I feel it my duty to impress on these would-be doctors of medicine at the start of their careers the need for a certain integrity, I suppose. And because, looking at those faces, I see nothing but desire.'

'A desire for learning, for finding out? But that must be good, isn't it?'

'If it was that sort of desire, yes, Inspector, it would be good. Very good. But it is nothing like that.'

'Then what is it?'

Dr Mahipal gave a little bitter grunt of laughter.

'It is a desire to be able to hang a certificate saying MBBS on the wall of some smart office somewhere and then begin raking in the rupees, Inspector.'

'But all of them? You are seeing such on each and every face?'

Dr Mahipal sighed.

'No, I suppose not. There must be some young people there with more of idealism, even if I have not seen it. And that is probably because I was not looking hard enough. Because I did not ask of every single face I saw in front of me what was in it to be seen. So put me down, if you must, Inspector, as a confirmed cynic.'

'Oh, Doctor, I am not thinking you are such.'

'That shows your good nature, Inspector. But I am a cynic. Or I am one now, I assure you.'

Ghote thought he saw a chink here to put in his first probe.

'You are now a cynic, you say, Doctor. Tell me, is that somehow the result of leaving the Mira Behn Institute?'

He saw at once that his tentative exploration had hit a nerve. A sore spot. Dr Mahipal's face, even seen from the side, had taken on an unmistakable look of grim distrust.

Was he going to lose him? Here so near the start?

'But I am asking what I must not,' he said hastily. 'Kindly do not think I am wishing to pry out your private thoughts.'

Dr Mahipal twisted on the bench to look him straight in the face.

'Then what are you here for, Inspector?'

A sudden sharply hostile question he much preferred not to answer. So he countered, as he had learnt to do in such circumstances, with a return question. As hostile.

'I may also ask that of you, Doctor? What for are you here? At Grant Medical College, trying to put into the heads of young people who do not want to know what it is to be a scientist? A researcher? An asker of questions who will not accept anything but the true answer?'

Dr Mahipal's head dropped as if the muscles of his neck had suddenly been severed.

From a face looking plungingly down at the floor his answer came.

'What am I here at Grant College for? Because I could not stay one day more at that place, if you must know.'

Gold.

Gold?

Perhaps.

'That place? The Mira Behn Institute? And why was that, Doctor? Why?'

Slowly Dr Mahipal's head came up again. But he did not now look Ghote fully in the face.

'Why should I tell you, Inspector?'

It was a question not expecting any negative answer.

'I will tell you why, Dr Mahipal. Because, as you were stating this morning itself, the man Chandra Chagoo was murdered. I have proof of that now. So all who were in any way connected with the fellow must answer what questions I am choosing to ask, yes?'

A silence.

'Very well, Inspector, put your questions.'

Ghote could at that moment have asked where exactly in the Institute Dr Mahipal had been at the time Chagoo was locked in the Reptile Room with the Russell's viper. What in reality his relations with the snake-handler had been?

But some instinct told him to say something different.

'I have asked my question already, Doctor. Why did you leave the Mira Behn Institute? When we were talking this morning and you were mentioning the rats you and Professor Phaterpaker were using in researches you were suddenly breaking off. At the time that made me somewhat wonder why. Now, I am thinking it was because there was something wrong concerning those rats. Rats in the Mira Behn Institute basement, and looked after also by one Chandra Chagoo. Was it because of something wrong about those rats that you left the work, meaning so much to you? Were you under some cloud itself?'

'Me?' Dr Mahipal shot back, suddenly straightening up on the narrow bench. 'Myself doing something wrong? You could not be more mistaken, Inspector.'

'No? Then who was doing whatever wrong thing it was? Was it Chagoo? Or who?'

'Isn't it obvious?'

'But you must tell me,' Ghote answered, fencing a little.

'Professor P.P. Phaterpaker then, Inspector. Professor P.P. Phaterpaker, so-called world authority in malaria vaccines. That is the man who was doing wrong.'

'What wrong? What is this?'

But he got an answer he little liked. The shutter of obstinacy rattling noisily down in front of Dr Mahipal's face. Shop closed. No more buying, no more selling.

'Doctor, I was asking,' he tried again, nevertheless. 'You say the wrong that caused you to leave the Mira Behn Institute was Professor Phaterpaker's. But what wrong it was?'

For several moments he thought Dr Mahipal was going to resort to total silence. But at last he turned a little towards him.

'There is a story in Premchand,' he said. 'You know Premchand, the great Bengali writer, Inspector?'

'Yes, yes. We police are able to read, you know. I was seeing that film also. *Chess Players*. Quite good.'

'All right. Well, in one of Premchand's stories he says *What does a thief get by killing another thief? Contempt. But a scholar who slanders another scholar gets glory*. But I did not want that sort of glory, Inspector. If I was ever to get anything like glory, I wanted it to be for what I had discovered. For what I myself had succeeded to find out about the human body and what different substances will do for it.'

Ghote thought for a little.

'Nevertheless, Doctor, already by what you have just said you have slandered your fellow scholar, Professor Phaterpaker. So, however much you are not wishing for that sort of kudos, you are too late.'

113

'Yes. I should have held my tongue. I should have held my tongue just now, and I should have held it when I came to realize what exactly Professor Phaterpaker was doing. But I could not. All my life I have—'

He broke off.

'Yes, Doctor? What have you done for all of your life?'

The man beside him on the narrow, shiny bench produced a sound something between a sigh and a groan.

'Well, let us say, Inspector, that it was my firm belief always that science was sacred.'

'And it is not?'

Ghote felt a small, seldom considered pillar of his existence beginning to crumble.

'No, Inspector. At last I have finally learnt that scientists are all too human. Damn it, it was not as if I did not have evidence already. Evidence, if not in front of my eyes, at least in my ears. One cannot work in a scientific environment for long without hearing tales of the truth being betrayed. Oh, there are famous examples even. In Russia there was Lysenko, the agricultural scientist who took control of all such work in the Soviet Union. His falsifications were on a massive scale. But I thought that case was a political affair. An exception. In Britain there was one Sir Cyril Burt who also produced made-up data. But he was a social scientist, and I said to myself that his was only a semi-science.'

'But they were not one hundred per cent exceptions?' Ghote found he could not help asking.

The pillar was flaking away faster.

'Once I told myself that they were,' Dr Mahipal replied with a twisted smile. 'Once I used to believe a historian of science called Bronowski – American or British I don't know – when he said there is a contract between all scientists that each one can depend upon the trustworthiness of all others. He was saying science as an institution depends upon that. And I was believing it. In the past I somehow thrust aside what I very well knew, that we in India regard exams as obstacles to be got over even by outright cheating. Especially by outright cheating. I persuaded myself that, once exams were behind, truth came in once more.'

Ghote felt a cold sinking percolating down through him, washing away a hundred vague but cherished beliefs.

'But, Doctor,' he burst out, 'is it you are saying one and all scientists in India will be cheating? No exceptions?'

There shot into his mind then a picture of the laboratory up in the roof of the Mira Behn Institute and of the grave-faced young scientist he had found quietly absorbed in her work there. And had soon afterwards accompanied to the basement of the old house to find Chandra Chagoo lying dead, face down, on the floor of the Reptile Room with the Russell's viper slithering across his naked back.

'Doctor,' he said. 'No exception? Not— Not even, for one example, Dr Subbiah, your former colleague?'

Dr Mahipal lifted his head a little.

'Oh, yes, Inspector,' he answered. 'One exception is there. Others also, no doubt. Many, even. But you are right to pick out Gauri Subbiah. There is a scientist who is doing wonderful work. She— She has, which is important, quite extraordinary manual skills' – Ghote thought for an instant of the marvellously deft way she had dealt with the Russell's viper – 'but also she never falters in paying the closest attention to every detail of her work, and that is something, you know, requiring very great self-discipline. But, above all, Inspector, Gauri has courage. Perhaps you don't think of that as a quality necessary to someone working quietly away in a laboratory. But it is. To be a truly great scientist you must have the sheer courage to speculate, to be able to think of hypotheses that have not been envisaged by anyone before you, to ask the unaskable.'

Dr Mahipal's saras-crane, peering face had taken on an altogether new animation. Ghote could see the flush of blood underneath the skin.

'Yes,' the delicate, almost ghost-like saras of a man went on, 'if I say I am envying her, it is because I wish I had been gifted with only one half of that quality. Of what makes a scientist into a true discoverer. So, no, Inspector, Gauri Subbiah is no cheat. She has no need to be. Fraud and Gauri are as far apart as sawdust and salt. Yes, shining exceptions can be found.'

His voice sank suddenly away.

'But once,' he said, 'I was believing the exception was the researcher who was stooping to fraud. Now I know better. Yes, I know better.'

Ghote felt, despite the shining exception of Dr Subbiah, he still had to plunge into the deep-sucking morass Dr Mahipal had mapped out in front of him. He had been told, after all, even if in no more than a broad hint, that Professor Phaterpaker probably had something to conceal. Something evidently more dangerous to his reputation than any gossip about visiting prostitutes in the Cages.

'But what is it exactly you were saying and stating about Professor Phaterpaker, Doctor?' he asked. 'You are telling me definitely that he also is a cheat?'

Dr Mahipal jumped to his feet.

'I am saying nothing,' he shouted back in sudden anger.

'No. No, you have said too much. You cannot keep silent now.'

A thin, cheerless smile crept on to Dr Mahipal's face.

'But, yes, Inspector,' he said. 'I can keep silent. At least I have now learnt that.'

Ghote stood in his turn.

'I am requiring and requesting you to state exactly what it is you are alleging that Professor Phaterpaker has done.'

'Why don't you ask him? Ask him, Inspector.'

'I am asking you.'

'And I am saying nothing.'

'Dr Mahipal, may I remind. Under Section 179 of the Indian Penal Code it is an offence to refuse to answer a public servant authorized to question.'

This at least seemed to strike home. The harijan scientist looked suddenly less confident.

Ghote recalled the man's humble origins which Professor Phaterpaker had spoken of so scornfully. They would colour his reactions to police questioning, no doubt. Here was no rich man's son used to treating the police with contempt.

'Once more, Dr Mahipal,' he said, 'I am asking what it is you are alleging Professor Phaterpaker has done wrong.'

A silence. Lasting only two or three seconds.

'Very well, Inspector, if you tell me I will be committing an offence by not answering your question, then I will answer. You are wanting to know what I suspect Professor Phaterpaker has done? Then request to examine the raw data, as we call it, that he has been using for many years. That was the request I made. And to me he answered *You know what you are implying? It is altogether monstrous. Monstrous.* Then he would say no more. I felt he was treating me as my mother used to do when I was a child and I kept demanding something she did not like to answer. A rap on the head and *Who told you to be asking questions?* So there and then I decided I must leave the Institute, whatsoever the cost.'

Chapter Nine

Professor Phaterpaker. If what Dr Mahipal had said about the Mira Behn Institute Director was true, then he did have something to hide. Something that would damage his reputation a great deal more than any number of visits to the prostitutes of Kamatipura becoming public. And – the thought entered coldly into Ghote's head as he left Dr Mahipal, looking now even more exhausted than when his class had spilled out of the lecture room – such dubious actions were something that Chandra Chagoo, in charge of the rats the professor used in his work, might possibly have got to know about.

And, if he had, would that have been reason enough for Professor Phaterpaker, distinguished Professor Phaterpaker, to want to get rid of the man? Even by murdering him? Or, at least, by contriving to leave him to the mercy of the Russell's viper?

Very likely it would.

So he would have to go to the Director once more and put to him the sort of questions he would put to any common murder suspect. Unless, when he got over again to the Mira Behn Institute, he found Inspector Baitonde there with the names of some Peerbhoy

Hospital workers who had known Chandra Chagoo. Or, a notion too pleasurable even to allow into his mind, with one of them already dangling at the end of his big fist.

Nor was Professor Phaterpaker going to be an easy suspect to question. There had been times in his early morning talk with him the day before when he had been abruptly and inexplicably furious. He had, apparently, been yet more furious when Dr Mahipal had approached the matter of his *raw data*. And the fury of people in influential positions, if they felt themselves to be wrongly suspected of even the least serious of crimes, was something to be avoided.

Unless it could not be.

As it could not be now.

And at the Institute there was, as he had expected, no sign of Baitonde. Was the fellow actually doing what he ought to be? Asking and asking at the Peerbhoy? Or had he sloped off to some illicit bar, or a brothel even? But, no. After the open threat he had put to the fellow he must at least be doing something towards questioning the Peerbhoy workers. Even if, so far, without result.

So, Professor P.P. Phaterpaker.

He found the Director, neat in his starched, high-collared white atchkan, at his big desk, a scatter of papers in front of him. The green cotton-backed blinds at the windows – no shower-bearing cloud was now hiding the sun – were throwing over the whole big room, with its sombre surround of ranked wooden filing cabinets, a dim, underwater-like light.

He cursed inwardly.

Conditions not at all good for catching a tiny change in expression when an awkward question was suddenly put, or a sudden rising of sweat on the back of a hand.

He felt a little downwards lurch of depression. And fought it away. He was going to need all his confidence in the minutes ahead.

'It is most good of you to see, Professor,' he began.

'Not at all, not at all, Inspector. We must always do what we can to help our police get to the bottom of a mystery.'

'Well, you are right, sir. Chagoo's death is one damn great mystery.'

Professor Phaterpaker slowly pushed his spectacles back up his nose to their most comfortable position.

'You have my sympathy, Inspector. You have all my sympathy. I have given this matter some little consideration, and for the life of me I cannot understand how the man's death could have come about. A mystery. A perfect mystery.'

Now, Ghote thought. But damn this dim, undersea light.

'No more altogether a mystery, sir,' he shot in. 'Chagoo was murdered. Definitely murdered.'

But, if there was any change of expression in the face of the man who might, just possibly might, himself have murdered the snake-handler, it was not to be made out.

'Murdered, Inspector?' came the calm reply. 'And how is it you are now so sure of that?'

He gathered himself together.

'Well, sir,' he answered carefully, 'you will remember

121

I had to come to ask you about the key you have for the Reptile Room, and you were telling me there were just only two others, the one Chagoo himself had, and one kept for emergency use. Now, with some difficulties I was able to locate this third one. Dr Mahipal had left it in a locked almirah in his room, and had forgotten to inform anyone.'

Professor Phaterpaker shook his head sadly.

'Slipshod,' he said. 'I do not like to say it of any colleague of mine, or ex-colleague perhaps I should call him, but the fellow was slipshod. Definitely.'

Unfair, Ghote thought at once. After all, it was the Director himself who had failed to nominate a successor to Dr Mahipal in his administrative responsibility. How could the key be officially handed on? But, on the other hand, there was no reason why Professor Phaterpaker might not be right about Dr Mahipal's efficiency. Whatever the man's idealistic ideas, he might not be very accurate in his work. So had he in fact been dismissed from the Institute, rather than quitting on his own volition? And if that was so how much of what he had said could be trusted?

'Then, sir,' he asked cautiously, 'was such the reason for Dr Mahipal going as just only a first-year lecturer to Grant Medical College?'

Professor Phaterpaker's slippery spectacles dropped suddenly half an inch down his nose.

'Well, Inspector,' he said after a moment, 'I can hardly give you a direct answer to such a question. But – shall we say? – that I leave you to draw your own conclusions.'

The obliqueness of the reply made Ghote reconsider. Especially coupled with the thought that it must have been a sudden flush of sweat that had caused the descent of the spectacles, for all that he could see nothing of it in the dim greenish light.

'I have understood Dr Mahipal was leaving of his own accord,' he said sharply. 'Is that, then, not true?'

Again there was a tiny pause before Professor Phaterpaker answered.

'Ah, well, Inspector,' he said eventually, 'you must understand that these matters are never altogether clear-cut. There is a difference, I agree, between a man resigning his post and a man being – what shall I say? – kicked out. But sometimes the two states may draw close together.'

'In this case itself, sir?' Ghote persisted. 'I would like to get the matter altogether clear because Dr Mahipal was one of the three people with keys to the Reptile Room.'

Spectacles jabbed back up.

'Inspector, am I to understand that you think anybody, anybody, who had a key to that place might have— Might have been responsible for the death of that wretched man?'

'Sir, what else is there to think?'

'Why, surely— Surely it could be that . . . Inspector, there must be dozens of other people who could have got down there and done that thing. Hundreds.'

'I do not think so, sir. Kindly let me explain whole situation. Chagoo was found in the Reptile Room early yesterday morning, by myself and Dr Gauri Subbiah.

He had died, apparently, from the bite of a Russell's viper after somebody had smashed open the glass front of its cage. The key Chagoo had always in his possession was nowhere to be found in the whole basement. But it was found – and I was going to some troubles to prove that it was Chagoo's own key – it was found under a bush in the garden here. So, sir, it must be plain that, unless Chagoo for some reason had let into this house some fellow known to him, he could have been sent to his death only by a person already inside. As you must know, sir, there is one only door to the house, and Laloo, the chowkidar, guards that day and night.'

'But— But— Inspector, I myself was here the night before last. Did Laloo tell you that?'

'He did, sir.'

Professor Phaterpaker sat back in his big chair.

'Well, I am glad to find that Laloo, despite his sometimes frolicsome manner, is efficient in his duties,' he said. 'And, of course, you can hardly suspect myself of— What was it? Going down to the Reptile Room, smashing the glass of that snake's cage, locking the wretched Chagoo in and leaving him to his death?'

A quickly flashed, assessing look from behind the heavy spectacles.

'Sir, I regret I am bound to consider each and every possibility.'

Professor Phaterpaker looked at him at length and in silence.

'Are you indeed, Inspector?' he said at last. 'Then I suggest you consider the possibility of myself being a common murderer with my friend the Commissioner of Police.'

And, if Ghote had found it hard till now wholly to see Professor Phaterpaker, first-class fellow, as a murderer, after this blatant threat he began to consider the possibility more seriously.

'Sir,' he said, 'you have twice referred to Chagoo as a wretched fellow. May I ask why you call him as that?'

'I ... er ... A figure of speech only, Inspector. A mere figure of speech.'

'I am not altogether agreeing, sir. Why should you use such a figure of speech about this particular individual? Sir, what dealings did you have with Chagoo?'

'None. That is— Inspector, I very much resent the line of questioning you have seen fit to adopt.'

'Nevertheless, sir, these are questions that must be put. And must also be answered.'

Professor Phaterpaker behind his desk, its large white blotter showing up almost luminously in the green dimness, gave Ghote a glare like a baleful frog.

But at last he replied.

'Very well, Inspector, let me admit that my relations with the man Chagoo were not always of the easiest. He was, to put it in a nutshell, an unpleasant individual. I had as little to do with him as possible.'

'But in the nature of your work, sir, since you are making use, as I understand, of rats for your experiments—'

'Rats? Rats?' Professor Phaterpaker broke in with evident irritation. 'Why are you harping and harping on rats, Inspector? A scientist in the discipline I practise does rather more, you know, than count up numbers of rats. A great deal of my work is conducted far, far from this Institute. I go out into the mofussil, Inspector, and supervise the administering of my vaccines to the poor people in distant villages, people year after year at the mercy of malaria. They are somewhat more important to my work than your rats.'

'Yes, sir,' Ghote said, a little abashed. 'But, if I may come back to Chandra Chagoo, is it not true that when you are here inside this Institute you were seeing more than just only a little of him?'

'A little? A lot? Where do you draw the line, Inspector?'

No, this time his philosophizing questions were not going to work.

'It is not so difficult to draw such a line, sir. Did you see Chagoo on most days? Yes or no?'

Spectacles pushed up once more. But not with as furious a jab as sometimes.

'Inspector, a great deal of my research involves testing various vaccines on rats. It is a customary way of evaluating theories. And so, yes, I suppose a day seldom passed without my having to inspect the specimens. Unless I felt it was something I could entrust to Dr Mahipal, whose duty it was, besides his own research, to assist me.'

'Despite this slipshod work you were accusing him of just now?'

'Well, perhaps I was hasty there. No doubt on occasion Dr Mahipal did fail to be as precise as is desirable, but then . . .'

A wave of the hand. Vague as a puff of air in this humid weather.

Ghote countered it. Almost with a stinging slap.

'But *then* you are saying. But then what, sir?'

Professor Phaterpaker failed for a moment to answer. Then, with a little cough that shook the jut of grey-white beard on his chin, he replied.

'Well, Inspector, since you press me, do we not all at times cut a few corners, as I may say? I don't suppose Mahipal was immune to such human weaknesses. I don't suppose you are yourself, Inspector, come to that. After all, your work can in some ways be paralleled to that of a scientist. In both we ask questions and hope to find answers. And, I am sure that, once or twice in your lifetime at least, you have accepted an answer that might not be the whole truth?'

'I am hoping that such a thing has never occurred, sir,' Ghote snapped back.

Whether it had or not was something he was not going to ask his conscience at this moment. Not if it allowed Professor Phaterpaker to slide out of his troubles. And by accusing an absent junior colleague.

'From what I have seen also of Dr Mahipal,' he went on, 'I do not believe for one moment he would falsify any results of experiments. It was a subject we were discussing this afternoon itself.'

'Was it indeed, Inspector? And may I ask why you were hob-nobbing, yes, hob-nobbing, with a person no longer a member of this Institute?'

But the question simply gave Ghote further grounds for feeling that Professor Phaterpaker, however much of a world authority on malaria vaccines he might be, had something to hide.

But what? What?

'I regret, sir, details of a police investigation cannot be disclosed to all and sundry. However, I was asking you a question.'

'Were you, Inspector? And if you were, let me say, it was in a manner showing very little respect.'

'If so, sir, I much regret. But there are matters for which I must have answers. One of such being, why were your relations with the Institute's snake-handler so bad as you have indicated? Was he mistreating the rats you had under experiment? Or what it was?'

But now Professor Phaterpaker sat back in his chair.

'Yes, Inspector,' he said, almost smiling. 'Yes, I am afraid that you have hit on what I might call a sore spot. I did have occasion, more than once, to suspect Chagoo of interfering with my experiments, either by over-feeding the rats or in some other ways. I never was able to get proof. But, of course, my suspicions did affect my attitude to the man. You asked me why I called him a wretched fellow. There you have your answer.'

All right, Ghote thought, somehow I seem to have let you off my hooks. I have given you a chance to provide an answer that cannot be checked. But, all the same, as you provided it, you were building up some first-class lies.

The very way Professor Phaterpaker had first called Chagoo a wretched fellow, had then gone back on that and finally admitted his dislike, or worse, of the snake-handler, told him he was lying, clearly as if each of his words had been marked with a heavy crossing-out. There was the air of relief he had been unable to conceal when he had at last arrived at his *There you have your answer.* There had been, too, those roundabout expressions like so much cotton padding, *On what I might call* and *I am afraid that.* Every sign of a liar.

The distinguished scientist. A liar. But why was such a man telling lies?

Into the lengthening silence that had fallen in the green-gloomed room, there came a harsh buzz of a call from the outer office.

Professor Phaterpaker reached for the key on the intercom with a rapidity that betrayed once more his relief.

'Yes, Miss Chinwala?'

'Inspector Baintonde is here, sir. He is saying he is wanting urgently to speak with Inspector Ghote.'

'Then let him come in. Let him come in.'

No request, Ghote noted, to himself as to whether he was willing to have any interruption. But he hardly resented that. Baitonde was back from his inquiries at the Peerbhoy. Was he bringing news that there was a man over there who had suffered somehow at the hands of Chandra Chagoo? A suspect there could be no difficulty in putting into the cells?

The door burst open and Baitonde came striding in.

'Yes, Inspector?' Ghote snapped. 'What it is you are wanting?'

A big sneering smile spread round Baitonde's huge moustache.

'Some good news, Inspector. You said urgent-urgent. So I am bringing same ek dum.'

Was this it?

'Well?'

'Been over to Peerbhoy Hospital, as per instructions. Found one easy answer.'

'Yes, man, yes?'

'Night-securitywalla at Peerbhoy is tip-top fellow. Damodar Singh by name. He is keeping one eye on each and every worker. No bloody shirking under him.'

'Well then?'

'Workers, nurses, doctors even. That fellow is damn well knowing if only a mosquito is moving.'

'And what it is he was telling? What?'

'He is damn one hundred per cent certain no one was leaving his post last night. All doors locked in hours of darkness. No one whatsoever getting out. Doctors, ward boys, no one.'

Ghote felt his hopes – but had he really ever believed he would get out of his troubles so easily? – go clattering to the ground like a frail pavement hut in a monsoon gale.

'And you believed him, Inspector?' he asked. 'You believed this on the word of just only one man?'

But he knew he had put his questions altogether too feebly. The fact of the matter was that, however much Baitonde was – in Professor Phaterpaker's phrase about Dr Mahipal – a cutter of corners, he was equally endowed with cunning. He would never risk making a claim which, with a single question, could be shot to pieces. No, if he said there was a really tough night-security man at the Peerbhoy, and if that fellow was ready to swear no one on the staff had left the building during the night hours, then that would be the case. No question.

'Oh, yes,' Baitonde answered now, with a grinningly odious swagger. 'I am believing, Inspector. Believing-believing. You may ask also. But you will not be finding anything of different. So, there is one job done, and I am off-duty hundred per cent, isn't it?'

'Oh, yes,' Ghote answered. 'Yes, go home, man, if that is what you want.'

'Well, go where some fun is,' Baitonde answered. 'That is more like what I am wanting.'

And, with a thunking slam of the door, he disappeared.

Ghote sat where he had been on one of the chairs ranged in front of Professor Phaterpaker's desk. He did not so much as look up at the man he had been questioning.

A grim iron cage had seemed suddenly to have clamped down on him.

Only three suspects to Chagoo's murder now. And, once again, he was faced with asking himself which of the three people who had been in the Institute building when the snake-handler had been locked in with the Russell's viper had turned that key in the heavy door's lock. Had tossed it away under a bush in the garden.

Professor Phaterpaker? Dr Mahipal? Or Dr Gauri Subbiah?

Chapter Ten

In the silence that followed Baitonde's crashing departure Ghote told himself that, whether or not Professor Phaterpaker was the person who had left Chandra Chagoo to his death, it was going to be difficult indeed to break down such a persistent evader of questions. Unless he was himself totally confident that neither of the other two people in the house when Chagoo had died had conceivably been responsible, he would not have enough conviction to probe and probe till he had exhausted every last subterfuge. Dr Mahipal he had already interrogated, if without coming to any clear conclusion. But there remained Dr Gauri Subbiah.

And he did not want even to have to consider Gauri Subbiah as a murderer.

Oh, yes, yes, he thought, there had been nothing to stop her going down, in the dark of that night, to Chagoo in the Reptile Room. How exactly she could have disabled him long enough to get hold of his key was another matter. But there would be ways. Dr Mahipal had praised her *quite extraordinary manual skills*. And look how cleverly she had dealt with the snake on Chagoo's back.

What reason she might have for killing Chagoo he could not fathom. But he was afraid he might find a reason. A reason showing her in a very different light from the one he had come to see her in.

Since his single encounter with her, he had to admit, she had risen and risen in his estimation. Partly from what Dr Mahipal had told him about her. About her power of asking the unaskable. The mark, as he had said, of the truly great scientist. Partly even from his memory of Asha Rani's praise, ridiculously extravagant though that had seemed, and from the almost reluctant tribute Professor Phaterpaker had paid her.

But, above all, what had stamped this impression of her on his mind had been that first glimpse he had had of her at work in her laboratory. Solitary, single-minded, steady. Gaze fixed unwaveringly on the screen in front of her, hand click-clicking at the fat red buttons of her counting recorder, white coat shrugged over plain green sari, the thick dark schoolgirl plait of hair running down it.

No, like it or not, Gauri Subbiah had become for him the ideal of what a scientist could be. Endowed with nothing but the clarity of thinking which Dr Manipal had spoken of and a resolute, unfazed determination – the daughter of a mali and a maidservant, after all – she had by asking and asking wrested answers from the intractable unknown mass that confronted all researchers. That confronted all humanity.

What sort of answer she might have found was beyond his comprehension. What exactly her researches had led to he was incapable of doing more than hazily guess at. But he knew they had led to an extraordinary success. Her paper, which even Professor Phaterpaker had said would bring renown to the Mira Behn Institute, was on its way to distant France, or had even already arrived there. It would be published in some highly distinguished scientific journal. To make then its full impact on the whole world. From the lowest beginnings she had triumphed.

No wonder he wanted nothing to take away from that.

'Well, Inspector,' came Professor Phaterpaker's sharp voice from the other side of the wide desk, 'I take it you have no more to ask me.'

With a weary sigh he addressed himself again to the stony, beard-jutting, bespectacled figure.

'I am sorry, sir, for that interruption. But, yes, there is more to ask.'

Professor Phaterpaker looked at him with a growing gleam of anger behind the glasses which, once again, he now pushed irritatedly up the slippery length of his nose.

'Am I to understand then, from what I was hearing your fellow officer saying, that you have discarded the notion that the person who – what shall I say? – disposed of Chagoo might have been some badmash employed at the Peerbhoy who he himself had let in?'

'You were hearing Inspector Baitonde's report equally with myself, sir.'

'So it follows that you are sitting there now thinking to yourself once more that I may be a murderer? The Director of the Mira Behn Institute? A scientist – I do not hesitate to say it – known for his work throughout the world? Inspector, have you any idea how many papers of mine have been printed in the journals? Here in India? In America? In almost every country that has a reputable medical or scientific establishment?'

'No, sir.'

What other answer to make to such a battery of questions?

'Well, I will tell you, Inspector. I happen to have published no fewer than two hundred and thirty-seven papers, some together with various colleagues, some with the assistance of my juniors, many exclusively under my own name. Two hundred and thirty-seven papers. And you are accusing me of murder?'

'No, sir. I am not at all accusing. I am simply stating one inescapable fact. A fact which perhaps you, as a scientist, should accept as being just only that, one fact. That in this house on the night Chandra Chagoo, snake-handler, was murdered there were present, besides the chowkidar on duty at the door – a fellow utterly scared of any sort of snake – three people only. Yourself. Dr Mahipal, who had come to retrieve certain research figures from his computer. And Dr Gauri Subbiah.'

His reluctance even to pronounce that last name hung from him like a convict's chains. But the name was there. Part of his inescapable fact.

And now Professor Phaterpaker seized on it.

'So you are saying, Inspector, that you believe a woman, a woman like Dr Subbiah, a scientist who is likely with the publication of her paper to become, in due course, though I say it, as distinguished as myself, you are saying that she is no more than a crude killer?'

'Sir, I—'

'Let me tell you, Inspector, just what a reputation Dr Subbiah is about to acquire. She has been researching a whole new spectrum of angiotensin converting enzymes, a powerful inhibitor of hypertension. Using the venom of our Indian Russell's viper, hitherto considered to be impossible as an inhibiting agent, she has with a series of experiments of dazzling elegance – dazzling – produced findings which will surpass both in effectiveness and in cost all previous therapies in this field to the extent of almost seventy per cent. Do you understand the importance of that? For Dr Subbiah's repute? For the repute of this Institute? For the repute of Indian science, and I may add for the very considerable revenues which will come to our country from the exploitation of Dr Subbiah's discovery?'

'I am grateful to you for telling, sir, but neverthe—'

'No, Inspector, let me add one thing more. I have not hesitated over the past two years, since I saw the possibilities of Dr Subbiah's research, to put the whole resources of this Institute behind her. Why, when I was at a conference in America and happened to hear that a team of scientists there was obtaining Russell's viper venom from a snake-worshipping village in Bengal, I undertook myself to send Dr Subbiah's just-completed paper to Paris with all possible speed. Yes, Inspector, I stayed in this house late on the eve of the Independence Day holiday supervising the faxing, the faxing, of a preliminary copy in case her work was beaten to the post.'

He leant back in his chair with something of the air of a puffed-up frog.

'Sir,' Ghote tried to take command again.

'No, Inspector, I fear you do not at all understand. Let me tell you I ordered a considerable part, a very considerable part, of this Institute's, alas, scanty resources to be devoted solely to that one effort. I have sacrificed, without hesitation, resources I required for my own work. I have put in jeopardy, you may say, my own career. That is the extent to which I have backed Dr Subbiah. And now you tell me you intend to arrest her on a charge of murder? Ridiculous, Inspector. Every bit as ridiculous as the thought of arresting myself.'

Ghote, head down under the barrage of words, saw now what it was Professor Phaterpaker was attempting. He was simply trying to thrust the blame for Chagoo's death on to the man he had forced to resign from the Institute. On to Dr Mahipal, the convenient scapegoat.

And, he thought suddenly, a whole lot of what he had said about devoting resources away from his own work to Gauri Subbiah's must be sheer invention. The new equipment she had been using had been the gift of the film community led by no lesser a star than the nation's idol, Asha Rani. Asha Rani had told him so herself. The Commissioner had confirmed it.

Was there some saying in English about *Blinding with science*?

He felt a rush of revulsion for the man on the other side of the big desk. So many hundred papers in science journals all over the world, yes. But, if Dr Mahipal was to be believed, something of a faker also. How many of those papers had been fully based on accurately obtained results? On figures that could be entirely trusted? What had the man done with his raw data? His work was on malaria vaccines: that would mean surely that the success or failure of what he had sent for field trials could be assessed only by recording the changes in the incidence of malaria out where they had been conducted. Not much difficulty in going to villages in the remote mofussil and producing figures that said just what you wanted them to?

He rose stiffly from his chair.

'Sir', he said, 'I do not think it is profitable to discuss this matter any further at the present. I may have to come back, however. Kindly remember that.'

Outside on the landing, though he had firmly intended to mount the stairs at once to see Dr Subbiah, he found his resolution melting away.

No, he needed to collect himself.

He turned and tramped down the stairs, so unseeingly he could well have tripped and gone tumbling to the bottom.

In the narrow hallway of the old house, dark, despite the temporarily bright sunshine outside, he stood still, wondering what to do, where to go.

Laloo was in his box, but he seemed to be asleep or half-asleep. Had he been awake the night before, having one of his long gossiping conversations with Professor Phaterpaker, perhaps discussing the event of the previous night? Or had he been talking even with Gauri Subbiah? He had said once that when the house was deserted, still and silent, in the dark hours he chatted at length with the burra memsahib. It would be typical of that dedicated worker to come back to her laboratory at night.

But on the night Chandra Chagoo had died, had she come in for an altogether different purpose? No, no. Do not even think about that.

He tapped furiously on the glass of Laloo's box, and, when the fellow had come to from his doze, bustled him out to unlock the gate almost at a run.

There was, on the pavement opposite, he saw as he stood there getting his breath back, an aged Muslim bonesetter, flowingly white-bearded, a little round white cap on his head – not very clean – who had set himself up under his sun-greyed hole-pocked black umbrella beside a lamp standard. On a couple of dark dirty-looking mats were laid out the trappings of his trade, black-rusted tin boxes, a big old mortar rayed with dark cracks, a large long-handled pestle. Propped against the lamp-post a battered painted board had on it, half obliterated with age, blood-red pictures of a man with a crutch and a man with his arm in a sling. Above them the figures *Rs20, Rs15*. Stale promises of instant cure.

Hundred per cent different sort of medicine from the Mira Behn Institute, he thought. Plenty of cheating there. If perhaps some cures sometimes. But then how much more guaranteed are full scientific treatments?

Even the day before he would never have asked himself that question. Now after what he had heard Dr Mahipal say in the Grant College lecture room and after confronting Professor Phaterpaker the doubt had darted, thorn-sharp, into his mind. There to stay.

139

No, he had been right. He could not possibly bring himself to go and interrogate Gauri Subbiah just now. He must have time to think. To push aside, if he could, the image of the dedicated scientist. To replace it with one of a person capable of locking in Chandra Chagoo with that poison-darting Russell's viper.

Chapter Eleven

Incapacitated by his gloomy thoughts, Ghote was still unseeingly staring at the old bonesetter when his view was interrupted by a cluster of women going by in the roadway, chattering hard to each other. In a moment he had placed them. No saris, but dresses. Some in unrelieved black, most in rich purples and dark reds, splashily flower-decorated. And, as they had got nearer, he heard they were speaking loud English. From the Bombay Christian community or perhaps from Goa. Yes.

Then, by the bunches of tightly bound flowers many of them were carrying, he realized where they must be going. Not far away there was the big old European Cemetery. This noisily chattering band must be on their way there from the nearby bus depot. The flowers would be to place on the graves where Christians buried husbands, wives, mothers or fathers.

Sewri Cemetery. But that should be the very place he wanted now. Somewhere quiet where he could think. He could find a shaded spot with no one nearby, sit for a little and get straight in his mind what he had to do about Gauri Subbiah. What it was his duty to ask her.

What he might not need to pry into. If there was anything.

A few minutes' walk trailing behind the mourners – a heavy grey cloud was temporarily hiding the sun, another shower before long? – brought him to the gates in the ornate railings surrounding the cemetery, as tall as the wall of the Peerbhoy Hospital compound but, rusty and broken here and there, an altogether less formidable obstacle. He followed the group inside – they were hurrying a little now, anxious about the closing hour – past the guards, bamboo lathis idly twirling, wide khaki shorts flapping.

Tombstones of every shape and size rose up in front of him like a petrified forest. Many leant crazily to one side or another, dark with age and littered at the foot with broken stone fragments. Others glinted in the still bright light, hard and shining in heavily carved marble, white and green and pink. Asphalt paths, worn and pot-holed, led this way and that further into the grasses-thick, wide area of the cemetery. Wandering onwards in search of his quiet spot, he glanced idly at the names on the graves as he passed. Fernandez, Morenas, Afonso, da Silva, D'Costa.

He stopped stock-still.

Nicky D'Costa, the air stewardess. How pleased he had been, little more than a week ago, when he thought he had managed to make her more frightened of himself and what he could do than she was of a seldom-seen Abdul Khan. Frightened enough to give him, when the time came, something that would put that notorious gang boss, her occasional lover, into a cell. *No, frankly,*

Inspector, it'll take a better man than you to put paid to Abdul Khan. The Commissioner's words when the whole Mira Behn business had begun came swimming up into his mind like black oil rising to a sun-glittering surface.

Was Inspector Adik handling Nicky D'Costa as carefully as she ought to be?

He wished he knew the Crime Branch newcomer better. One slip in security, and Abdul Khan would not hesitate to see such a danger to himself was got rid of.

But he had been given his orders. Silly Nicky D'Costa was no longer his business. Brilliant Gauri Subbiah was.

Suddenly hot, he marched off, battering at himself with internal rage.

But before long he came to a halt. He had put off the moment of that necessary interview with Gauri Subbiah. A self-granted breathing space. But that was so as to have time to think. To work out clearly what exactly he should ask. So no more shirking. Find somewhere to sit, sit down there, and get to work.

He realized he had in his furious marching come into an older part of the huge cemetery. This was where the British in those long ago days had buried their dead. Here the names that caught his eye were Hobson, Yule, Birdwood, Keatinge, Rivers. The tombs were much more ancient, little temple-like structures, with here and there spindly trees growing from cracks in their stone-work, long stone slabs with urns on them or, almost unrecognizable under layer after layer of monsoon greenness, stone-carved winged creatures of some sort drooping in sad, sad attitudes.

Angels, yes. Christian angels.

But over there was just the sort of place he had been looking for. A patch of soft dry ground under an old gnarled tree, a tamarind. In the deep shade of its wide spreading branches he could sit in comfort – the threatened shower had passed – and with few people coming to this neglected corner he would be quite undisturbed.

He settled down, back resting against the time-crusted trunk.

So . . . Dr Gauri Subbiah. Was it truly possible that, two nights ago, she had gone down those stairs from her laboratory under the roof of that old British-style house? Had gone into the Reptile Room in the basement? Had met Chandra Chagoo there, had talked with him for a little and then had seized her opportunity and – yes, this would be it – had struck him on the head with some heavy object?

In the short time he had actually been in the Reptile Room, scarcely more than a couple of minutes, he had not been able to get anything like a good look at the thick tangle of coarse grey hair on Chagoo's head. He had been too concerned with Gauri Subbiah holding that twisting, threshing snake to have had eyes for anything much else. There could well have been a bloody contusion that he had not seen at all.

Here he came to a stop. Something neglected. He had not yet had the report on the body from the Examiner at the JJ Hospital which would have confirmed and described that injury. Baitonde was meant to be seeing to it. He would need a reminder. Another one.

But could Gauri Subbiah have dealt Chagoo a hard

enough blow? Well, it would not necessarily have required great force. Especially delivered by someone knowing enough of anatomy to strike at the best place.

But then what about Professor Phaterpaker? And Dr Mahipal? The same reasoning clearly went for each of them. All right, the Director was old, but he was not totally feeble. And he would know as much about the best point to aim for as Gauri Subbiah. Or Dr Mahipal.

Then, while Chagoo was unconscious or incapable of resisting, had Gauri Subbiah actually taken his key, turned and quickly smashed open the Russell's viper's cage? And at once flicked out and locked in Chagoo to his death?

Surely not really possible?

But then into his mind's eye came again the sight of her grasping the Russell's viper just behind its head, holding it, wriggling and jerking, firm in her grip. Yes, she certainly would not have hesitated to let the venomous creature out of its cage and leave the Reptile Room before it had time to attack her rather than the half-unconscious snake-handler.

But why could she have wanted to do that? There seemed to be no reason. There she was, at the high point of what was going to be a wonderfully successful career, with this paper on ACE-i derived from Russell's viper venom just recently sent, Professor Phaterpaker had said, to France.

So why should she risk ruining all that by killing Chagoo? No possible reason. And yet, seen from the point of view of capability and nothing else, Gauri Subbiah must be his most likely suspect. Professor

Phaterpaker was probably in fact too old to move as swiftly as the murderer would have needed to. Dr Mahipal, with that withered arm of his, was not the most active of men, even if he could perhaps have delivered the necessary blow to Chagoo's head left-handedly.

So what he would have to find out from Gauri Subbiah, if he possibly could, was what there might have been in her relations with the unpleasant Chandra Chagoo, as Dr Mahipal had described him, that could have made it necessary for her to end his life. So necessary she would risk everything to do it.

'It is Inspector Ghote.'

He looked up, startled.

Gauri Subbiah was standing there, regarding him with that steady gaze of hers. For a moment he thought he had actually conjured her up as a vision, so intently had he been thinking about her. But, no, she was real. Standing there, straight as a lily stem, wearing today a simple cotton sari in a different shade of green. Banana-leaf green, he thought Protima would have called it.

God, he thought, a flush of sweat springing up all over his body, must I question her here and now itself?

'Inspector, sorry. I seem to have caught you by surprise. Are you doing what I occasionally come here to do? To think in the quiet?'

He scrambled to his feet.

'Yes, yes. I was thinking itself. Yes.'

On her rather solemn features a slight smile appeared. Sun from behind a cloud.

'But what were you thinking about, Inspector? A promotion you are hoping for? What to buy your wife as a Diwali present? Or was it what you have come to the Institute to investigate? Professor Phaterpaker told me you have, after all, been put in charge of inquiries into Chandra Chagoo's death.'

'Yes. Yes, madam. Or, rather, no. I am not altogether in charge of inquiries. That is the duty of one Inspector Baitonde from Sewri PS itself. He would be coming to see you before long. There are questions he will have.'

'Questions, Inspector? What questions?'

He wished she had not asked. But he did his best to find a simple reply.

'Well, for example, madam, since you were inside the Institute perhaps at the time Chagoo died, he would have to ask what time you were leaving that night?'

'Oh, yes. Well, there will be no difficulty in providing him with an answer to that. I make a point, however busy I am, of never working after midnight. I need to be fresh for the following day. So I was leaving, as Laloo can perhaps confirm, at just after that hour.'

'I see. Thank you, madam. I will let Baitonde know. I am working closely with him, as Crime Branch officers do in important cases.'

'So Chagoo has now become an important person?'

'Yes. No. That is, madam, the Mira Behn Institute, as you must be knowing, has many influential friends in Bombay, and the Commissioner was considering that the investigation of Chagoo's death should be supervised by an officer from Police Headquarters.'

'I see.'

She smiled again, as if she was storing away this

piece of information about the workings of Bombay Police.

Quickly, before she could use what she had learnt in order to ask other possibly embarrassing questions, Ghote, now more in command of himself, put in a question of his own.

'But, madam, you also? You have come here just now for thinking?'

And the question, though it had not been intended to put Gauri Subbiah into a predicament in any way similar to his, seemed to have been just as upsetting.

The little whitish scar across the tip of her nose darkened.

'Yes. That is, no. No, I have not got any particular problem to solve at this moment, Inspector.'

She smiled again, more brilliantly.

'No, nothing like the problem I actually solved sitting just where you were. It was here, under this very *imli* tree itself that there actually came into my head the idea of the chemical process that would neutralize Russell's viper venom. What Professor Phaterpaker has taken to calling my great discovery.'

'Oh, madam. It was here? Under this tree itself? One day there must be a plaque put up.'

She laughed.

'No, Inspector, I hardly think what I discovered, though it may well bring crores of rupees from the West into India, is deserving of any plaque.'

He wondered, all the same, whether he should ask her next what it actually was she had come to this spot to think about today. Her work on her discovery was

over. Her famous paper gone to its French medical journal. So what did she have to work at now?

But to ask that would almost certainly lead him, he
thought, into interrogating straight away this one of the
three people in a position to have killed Chandra
Chagoo. And he had decided it was not the time or
place for that. All right, he had, in what he had been
pondering, fixed more or less firmly in his mind a line
of questioning to begin on. But he was not ready yet.
He still needed to step back, to take a more distant view.

Yes, tomorrow would be the right time to question
her.

So now he launched into a safer topic.

'Please, madam, I am not fully understanding what-
all is done in research such as you are undertaking. Can
you be explaining? It is an altogether interesting subject.'

'Well, what exactly is it you want to know, Inspector?'

He blinked and considered.

'Kindly tell, then, what is happening after an idea,
such as the one you were having under this tree only,
is coming into your head. What is the next thing? And
the next? And the next?'

She smiled again, with the smallest hint of gentle
mockery.

'You are asking a great deal. However, let me see.
Yes, take that moment when I had my inspiration under
this tamarind. What did I do next? Let me think. Ah,
yes, I remember. I went home to my evening meal.'

'It was at this time of day itself also? I am glad to
hear. It makes this moment all the more to be

149

remembered for me. But what did you do, when you had taken your meal? Madam, you are married?'

'No. No, Inspector. If I had married, I suppose I would not be a scientist at the Mira Behn Institute. I would be in Pondicherry still, cooking for whatever husband I had. But now I take that meal at the hostel where I stay.'

'Then I must be pleased you did not marry. India itself must be pleased.'

She blushed. The tiny scar on her nose pink now.

Ghote felt a little ashamed at having caused her embarrassment.

'But, please,' he said hastily, 'what was happening next? Next day itself?'

'Oh, I woke up. I went over in my mind what I had thought, and I found it still made sense. It had been no daylight dream. So I went into the Institute. I decided what experiments would confirm this hypothesis that had come to me. I made a long list of all the questions I would need to ask.'

Again there came her quietly serious smile.

'I believe I thought then of what my mother used to say to me so often. *When little girls ask too many questions their ears are dropping off.* But mine I still had. So I made another list. Of the apparatus I might need, and I sent down a requisition slip to—' A moment of hesitation. 'A requisition slip to Chagoo for Russell's viper venom. And by the end of that day I had begun the first of my experiments.'

'And one by one they confirmed this theory you were having?'

'Yes. But that was over many weeks, months even, you know. And it was not out-and-out confirmation, but, rather, that enough of the experiments came out right for me to be sure what I had hit on was the truth.'

'I see. But, tell me please, those results that did not confirm your theory, what did you do with the venom you had used? Do you dispose of such? Forget it was ever existing?'

A look of shock – it could be nothing else – appeared on her face.

'Certainly not. No scientist, no reputable scientist, would do any such thing. There might be very good reasons, nothing to do with the validity of the tests, for a freak result. But you should preserve it if necessary, and declare that result. Absolutely.'

'Very well. Excuse me. I did not mean to be insulting.'

'No, no, I'm sure you did not. Very few laymen understand how a scientist works. Ought to work.'

Ghote asked himself now, in a quick flick of inner interrogation, whether he should pursue that *Ought to*. Was Gauri Subbiah perhaps saying she knew a scientist who was not altogether reputable? Could that be the distinguished man Dr Mahipal had almost accused of some sort of fraud? Professor Phaterpaker himself?

But to press her about that would do nothing, surely, to contribute to the inquiry he was avoiding pursuing at this moment. No, stick to asking for merely interesting information.

Might come in some day.

'So it was many experiments you were making?'

'Oh, yes. As many as a hundred major ones. The chemistry involved is very complicated.'

'I see. But then when enough of experiments are done— But how long were these one hundred taking, please?'

For a second time a chance question seemed to give Gauri Subbiah trouble.

'I— I do not really know – er – Inspector.'

Then she recovered herself.

'Of course, I do know really. It is just, you see, that a scientist, or one like myself certainly, will think, not in terms of how long a series of experiments has taken, but of how many were necessary and what percentage of the individual tests provided the expected answers.'

'Oh, yes, yes. That must be so.'

'But, I suppose, my work took me some fourteen months at least, even using my new apparatus Miss Asha Rani and other members of the Bombay film community had given.'

'Ah, yes.' He had hardly followed. But a little politeness would make sure he still kept clear of the interrogation he did not want to embark on. 'So, after all the work on experiments, was it a matter then of just only writing the paper that was sent to that French medical journal?'

'Yes, that's so,' came the brief answer.

'Thank you. This is altogether most interesting to me. So how long did it take you to write your paper itself? I am afraid I was saying you *just only* had to do it. But I suppose it may be a Number One difficult task?'

'Well, sometimes a paper is hard to get down in

writing, yes. Though, in fact, this one did not take too long. I had it all in my head as I was working, you see.'

'Ah, yes. So how long it was?'

He hardly knew why he had asked that. But, once again, it proved to be a question that seemed to upset the young scientist.

'It took— I don't know. Why should— Oh, well, yes, it took some time. Some time. Two weeks, three. I don't know.'

'But then the great day was coming? Professor Phaterpaker was telling he himself sent a fax to Paris. For speed only. And he was having to stay late one night to do it, before all was closing down here for Independence Day holiday.'

'Yes, yes. That was it. It gave him a lot of pleasure to take charge of that.'

For a little they stood there in silence. In Ghote's mind there was a picture of Professor Phaterpaker triumphantly supervising a specially kept-back Miss Chinwala, busy feeding the Institute fax machine. The same picture, he supposed, must be in Gauri Subbiah's mind at this moment as well. Perhaps seen as the actual beginning of her rise to worldwide fame.

'So when your paper was received,' he asked at last, 'what is happening there in France?'

'Well, the procedure is more or less the same everywhere. Whatever journal you have submitted a paper to sends it out to what are called referees, for a process known by the name of peer review. They are scientists of as high a reputation as can be got, who are in some way expert in the field. If eventually they approve, then your paper is published. That is the waiting stage mine has actually reached. I should hear the verdict before too long.'

'But what if it is a no?'

Gauri Subbiah smiled.

'It will not be, Inspector. I do not want to boast. But I know that the theory is good, even very good, original and elegant, and that my experiments validate it. So it will be published.'

'And when it is, in this very well-regarded journal in France, then there would be no more problems?'

'Well, in the end there will not be. But there is a long way to go after that before the full commercial uses of what I have discovered can be exploited. But, I hope, I will not have very much to do with that.'

'Because you will be wanting to continue as a pure scientist, is it?'

'Yes, exactly, Inspector.'

He thought he saw a tiny shade of something pass across her face then. A small turning-away of that steady gaze.

What had caused it? If it had really been there. Some secret doubt, after all, about what she had discovered? But that could hardly be.

A mystery.

'Well, Inspector, I was interrupting the thinking that you were doing under this *imli* tree. Forgive me. I will leave you in peace now.'

She smiled, turned and walked away. A little more rapidly than he might have expected. Thick schoolgirl plait of dark hair swinging.

But it was not in peace that she left him.

Had he been wrong, he asked himself furiously, not to have pressed her, when he had her in front of him, with iron-hard questions about Chagoo and what had happened in the night hours at the Institute?

And what had those hesitations of hers about reputable scientists meant? Had there been something there concerning Professor Phaterpaker he should have gone more deeply into? And, worst of all, what about that moment of doubt her face had betrayed just before her somewhat abrupt departure? Did it mean . . .

He refused to let it mean anything.

But as he brushed the crumbs of dry earth from his trousers and prepared to leave in his turn, he saw in the distance a solitary champak tree standing against the sky, pointing upwards like a thick finger. He saw it, indeed, as a finger, held up in strict warning to himself. Inspector Ghote, tomorrow stamp on your feelings about this star of scientific light. Do your duty.

Chapter Twelve

Ghote, on his way home, could not help contrasting the comforts that awaited him with those at the hostel Gauri Subbiah must by now have reached. For her only what food the hostel cared to provide. For him a meal almost certain to include some particular favourite, one of the dishes that in answer to persistent questioning he had at various times admitted to Protima that he especially liked. At home, too, he would be able to talk over the day's doings, both his own and Protima's and young Ved's. Gauri Subbiah, he imagined, would have no one to talk to, would have to go to her room and read the evening away.

But, at home, he found he was not to be as contented as he had expected.

'What it was Commissioner sahib was wanting you to do today?' Protima asked, as she unbolted the door to his tap on the outer latch. 'You were leaving so soon after he had spoken with you in his car.'

At once the first earth-cracks appeared in the smooth grassy maidan he had seen himself traversing. He would have liked to have replied with a full account of everything that had happened to him since that early hour.

On the day before he had, without a second thought, told Protima all about the missing ACE-i samples, about his meeting with the superstar Asha Rani – Protima had been very impressed – as well as about the faint feelings of doubt that had come to him after speaking to the distinguished Professor Phaterpaker. And then he had described that shocking moment of discovery when Gauri Subbiah had at last unlocked the door of the Reptile Room.

Protima would expect to hear an equally full account today. But at once he foresaw a difficulty. In these home-coming chats Protima never hesitated, if she thought it right, to tell him what he ought to do. She did not play the detective, but if some question of behaviour came to the fore she would make her views known. Decidedly.

So, over the years, he had learnt to suppress anything he thought might give rise to a difference of opinion. And the day before, for that reason, he had carefully omitted saying anything about Nicky D'Costa and the way her case had been abruptly taken away from him and given to Inspector Adik.

Now, as he sat in his chair while Protima knelt taking off his shoes and socks before bringing him the easeful delight of having his feet pressed, he had a nasty feeling that, when he came to tell her about his meeting with Gauri Subbiah in Sewri Cemetery he would be unable to keep silent about that gravestone with the name *D'Costa* on it. No reason at all why he should mention it. But, even because of the very lack of reason, he felt sure it would somehow spill out.

And the coming need for carefulness at once upset the flow of his narrative. He sped it on. He skipped altogether Inspector Baitonde's irritating lack of interest in his duties, something he would by no means have done in the ordinary way. It was putting such frustrations into perspective, with Protima's eager agreement, that was the best part of their talk. He hardly succeeded next in making it clear why there were only three people who could have got into the Reptile Room to end Chandra Chagoo's life. And when Protima said she did not understand the business about the keys he snapped at her.

'Oh, it is too difficult to make clear. You must take my word. There are some things only a trained detective may understand.'

'It does not seem to be so difficult to me. It is just only you are not fully explaining.'

'I have told and told. If you are not able to understand, what more can I do?'

'But—'

And then she bit her lip.

As plainly as if the words had been written above her head in letters of red neon flashing on and off like an advertisement for shirtings high over Bombay's skyline, he realized she had deliberately stopped herself from asking even one more question. She had sensed his inner doubts about what lay ahead in the investigation, and she was drawing back from all further probing.

At once he felt an overwhelming rush of affection towards her.

He leant forward and put a hand on the nape of her neck as she knelt there. And then the words came.

'Oh, I am sorry, sorry. You see, I am worrying there is something where I have done wrong. Or where I have not done what is right.'

Then he told her all about Nicky D'Costa. How at Sahar Airport he had spotted her as a smuggler. How he had threatened her with charge-sheeting, and had withdrawn the threat on condition she let him know when her occasional lover, Abdul Khan, could be caught red-handed in some plainly criminal act.

'It is Abdul Khan, the big ganglord? In the papers each and every day?'

'Yes, yes.'

'Then you were doing right to let that girl go free.'

But then he had had to go on to tell her how the Commissioner had swept the business out of his hands, and how when he could have asked ACP Dhasal to be given it back he had failed to do so. And at last he admitted to the faint suspicion he had that tough Inspector Adik might insist Nicky D'Costa brought in information about Abdul Khan sooner than was reasonable.

And, again, Protima did not ask him a single question.

Nothing about whether he could have refused to let the Commissioner take Nicky D'Costa out of his hands. Nothing about whether he could from the very first have asked ACP Dhasal to let him switch duties with Inspector Adik. Nothing about whether he ought to have gone to Adik and put the case for going softly-softly.

Not one question to make him feel yet worse, though

she must have had dozens buzzing in her head. She was a wife in a thousand. In twenty thousand.

Next morning a reason yet again to put off for a little longer interviewing Gauri Subbiah came to him. He ought first to check on Inspector Baitonde. Had the fellow, for instance, got hold of that Examiner's report on Chagoo's body? Had he done anything else to advance what was after all the case he was nominally in charge of?

And, of course, the Sewri Station House Officer told him – with a half-concealed grin – Baitonde was 'not in his seat'.

'But it is late only. Where is he? Has he left already on enquiries?'

'Oh, Inspector, I am very much thinking he has not yet left his bed itself.'

'Then—'

Exasperation silenced him.

'Very well, I will wait only.'

And wait he had to. For almost an hour.

Then when Baitonde, brushing at his heavy-hanging moustache as if at the beginning of the day he was preparing himself for action, did come in he failed entirely to provide any answer to Ghote's sharp 'Good morning, Inspector, and where is it you have been?'

'Ah, it is you, Ghote bhai,' he said instead. 'You have solved deep, deep mystery at Mira Behn Institute, yes?'

'No, Inspector. And no help have I had from you itself.'

160

'But, yes, man, yes. I was finding out that no worker at the Peerbhoy could have come to the Mira Behn in the dark of the night, no?'

'Well, yes. Yes, you were doing that.'

For a moment he thought of asking the fellow if there was any possibility that this was not the case. But he decided against. What he had thought when Baitonde had come barging into Professor Phaterpaker's office with that information still held good. It would be so easy to check with the securitywalla at the Peerbhoy that even Baitonde would not have risked inventing his evidence.

No, no Peerbhoy worker could have left the premises to go to meet Chandra Chagoo in the dead of night. So there remained just those three people inside the old house. Professor Phaterpaker, Dr Mahipal and— And Gauri Subbiah.

Abruptly, without stopping to invent some task for Baitonde to do, he said he had to get over to the Institute himself.

When at last he approached once more the laboratory at the top of the old house he found, thanks to the frustration Baitonde had left in him, that he was almost glad the moment had come to tackle without fear or favour the young scientist.

Standing at her door, knuckles ready to knock, he had one momentary vision of her. Schoolgirlish almost, with that single long, thick plait of hair down her back, straight standing, and, above all, with that quietly grave look in her eyes. For an instant his old disinclination even to put any question to her that hinted that she

161

might just possibly be responsible for leaving Chandra Chagoo to the mercy of the Russell's viper swept back on to him.

Then he straightened his shoulders, knocked sharply at the door and went in without waiting for an answer.

He had expected to find the young researcher at work. But he had not expected her to be so deeply immersed that there was a long silence before she responded at all to his 'Good morning, madam'. With her momentous paper safely sent off, he had thought she would be taking things somehow more easily.

Yet, now he came to think of it, when he had come to the laboratory before she had been equally hard at work.

'I am sorry to be interrupting, madam,' he said at last, loud-voiced. 'But there are some— That is to say, I must— There are questions I must ask you. I must. In place of Inspector Baitonde. Yes.'

Gauri Subbiah turned away from her VDU – she was again using the counting device with the two fat red knobs – and, with a sharp indrawn sigh, swung round on her tall stool to face him.

'Well, I suppose I must give you your answers,' she said. 'But, Inspector, the less time you take the happier I shall be. I must tell you that. You see, I have a mountain of work I am needing to get done.'

Should he ask her why? But, no, if for whatever reason she had all that work in front of her, then the least he could do would be to keep strictly to questions about Chagoo and his inexplicable death.

'Yes, well, madam,' he said, 'what I must first of all explain is that from my inquiries till date I have ascertained that on the night that Chandra Chagoo was killed just only three people were inside this building.'

He saw the look of quick understanding in her eyes.

'And I was one of them,' she said.

There was no hint of a question in the statement. Ghote accepted it for what it was.

'Yes, madam. You were. And I must be telling you also that inquiries have shown the key you collected from Laloo the chowkidar, the one the mali had found in the garden and given to him, was Chagoo's own.'

Again she seized on the implications to the full.

'You're certain of that, Inspector? It must be an important piece of evidence. It can only show Chagoo's death was not some extraordinary accident. If his key was not somewhere in the Reptile Room, then it must have been taken from him. And by someone who then locked him in, although—'

'Madam, yes. I myself personally am satisfied the only two other keys to the Reptile Room were in their places after that door was locked. So the key the mali found was definitely Chagoo's own. And, madam, that is meaning murder has been committed.'

She looked at him. Steadily.

'If you say so, Inspector, then I agree such must be the truth of the matter. I may be wrong, but I do not think you are the sort of person to allow evidence to go unchallenged.'

He felt a glow of delight. This young but very

successful scientist was putting him in a place almost parallel to the one he had given her in his mind.

'Well, madam, I am hoping I am such an investigator, yes,' he said. 'But you are understanding the situation to the full? Three people only in this house that night, and you are one of those.'

Again a quick frown of doubt.

'But, Inspector, excuse me for questioning what you have said, but have you considered that someone might have entered illegally? I know there is only the one door to the house and only Laloo can let anyone in. But, Inspector, there are windows. And I have seen once the old mali taking out water for the garden through one of them.'

'Yes, madam, you are right to question everything,' Ghote answered, rejoicing that he too had asked the question Gauri Subbiah had, and had his answer. 'But I must remind you that this house is in the compound of the Peerbhoy Hospital, which is altogether security-guarded. No one, with sole exception of personnel from the Peerbhoy itself, could have come near even to one of these windows.'

'But, Inspector, at the Peerbhoy there must be—'

He interrupted her.

'No, no, madam. Let me inform you Inspector Baitonde has checked that. He is satisfied that no member of the hospital staff, either high or low, was getting past night-security man there.'

'I see. But you, Inspector? Are you satisfied also? If you are, I am happy to accept that three of us only could have entered the Reptile Room that night.'

Ghote felt another small jab of pride at having been preferred in the eyes of this scientist to Inspector Baitonde. But he had to tell her the truth.

'Madam, I also am satisfied.'

Still her doubts had not ended.

'Three people only, Inspector, you have said, but are you not forgetting Laloo? He was there also. You will excuse me for asking, but I am used to questioning anything in any way unexplained. It is the scientist's habit.'

'The detective's habit also,' he answered. 'And, yes, madam, I have taken into account Laloo's presence. But, no, he is not the man to have done what was done in the Reptile Room that night. He is altogether too scared of snakes ever to go down the stairs there. Nor was he having anything of motive.'

Gauri Subbiah considered for a moment.

'Yes, Inspector,' she said, 'I think I must agree. I had forgotten Laloo's absurd fear of all snakes. Nor is he man enough to have murdered a vicious individual like Chandra Chagoo.'

Ghote seized on that.

'A vicious individual, you are saying? Kindly state whether you are having evidence for this. I remember you telling that he once took you to the Naag Panchami festival in his village. Surely that was not a vicious act?'

He felt quietly pleased. Without his having to ask a single question about Gauri Subbiah's relations with Chagoo he had landed fully in the heart of the matter.

'Evidence, Inspector? What sort of evidence do you expect? I do not think I can produce for you one plainly vicious act the man did. But I can tell you plenty about what he hinted at.'

'Then, please to tell.'

'Yes. Well, about Chagoo taking me to Sitala when I had not been in Bombay more than a week or two and Hindi and Marathi were, as they say, so much Greek to me. You've got a good memory, Inspector. Well, from the way Chagoo behaved when we were in Sitala I very soon gathered that this was not altogether an act of kindness. He was wanting to let one and all know that in the big city, whoever his companions had been in the village, he was now having as a friend a full researcher at the Mira Behn Institute. If he told someone I was such once, he was telling them a hundred times.'

'Yes. I understand. So afterwards you were no longer friendly with him?'

It was a question he had not wanted to ask. It was the beginning of a trail that might lead to an answer as to why Gauri Subbiah could have needed to end Chagoo's life. But it was a question, he knew, he had to put.

'You are wondering whether I came to hate the fellow, is it?' she said. 'To hate him so much I would want to kill him?'

Altogether blunt. And she was waiting for him to answer.

He swallowed.

'Madam, a police officer investigating has to put each and every question that may throw light on the crime under investigation. He has to do it.'

'Of course. I understand. I only wanted to get it clear

what exactly you were asking. But now I can answer. No, Inspector, I did not hate Chagoo. I did not – to answer the question you have so far hesitated to put – go down from this laboratory to the Reptile Room and kill him. I did not at any time leave this room until I left the Institute altogether. On the other hand, yes, I did dislike Chagoo. To the extent of never asking him for anything I required, extra supplies of venom, anything, unless it was strictly necessary. But, let me assure you, I was too much occupied with my research really to bother my head about the fellow. Perhaps you don't understand how obsessed a researcher can get when a problem defies them. I assure you almost nothing else occupies one's mind.'

'Oh, yes, madam. I am very well able to believe such.'

After all, he thought to himself, am I not obsessed with one problem myself at this moment? Who killed Chandra Chagoo? Why did they kill him? Unpleasant, even vicious, though it was plain he had been, did any one of the three people able to get to him there in the Reptile Room have a real interest in leaving him to his death at the fangs of that snake?

But, he saw now, there was yet another question he must ask. A question as blunt as the one she had asked him. Yes, she had told him, with apparent frankness, what her feelings about Chagoo had been. But was she telling the strict truth? The whole truth?

'Madam, this also I must ask. Chandra Chagoo, did he at any time attempt to have with you sexual relations? Of any sort whatsoever?'

He looked her full in the face. And saw the tiny crossways scar on the tip of her nose go suddenly more sharply white.

So had he hit . . .?

But after a half-second of hesitation she answered.

'No, Inspector. No. I dare say Chagoo had what you were calling sexual relations with women here in Bombay. He went back to his wife only once every year, as far as I know. But, whatever he might have liked, I can promise you, I never gave him the least chance to suggest anything like that. Distant. That is the word for the relations between Chagoo and myself. Distant, in every way.'

'Very well, madam,' he said, noting sadly in the back of his mind that he must still find someone to confirm what she had told him with that momentary reluctance. 'I am happy to leave a so unpleasant subject. And I am not able to imagine you had any other dealings with the man outside the ordering of venom supplies and similar requests?'

He felt the interview must be near its end. One or two similiar tidying-up questions and he could, with a good conscience, leave her to her mountain of work. But the answer he got now surprised him with its sudden vehemence.

'No. No.'

A look of darting resentment at the question. Gradually draining away.

'No, Inspector, what dealings with him could I have?'

'Well, I am not able to say, madam. I was just only,

as is the saying, dotting each i and crossing every t. Asking, perhaps, the last hardly necessary question.'

She smiled.

'Inspector, forgive me. I am not— You see, I am afraid I am not my usual self. Chagoo's death, whatever I felt about the man, has upset me. A murder in this house itself. I was doing my best not to let it interfere with my work, but I cannot deny that I have found myself thinking about it again and again. When I should have been concentrating on the answers coming up on my VDU I have instead been asking and asking myself what on earth can have happened that night.'

Once again he was tempted to enquire how it came about that she was still as busy as she had been before she had sent off her famous paper.

'I understand, madam,' he said. 'The murder of someone well known to you, even if he is a man you are disliking, cannot be other than distressful. But let me ask one last thing.'

'Yes?'

'You were saying you have been asking yourself how Chagoo's death can have happened. Please, has any answer occurred to you?'

If Gauri Subbiah was not the person who had left Chagoo to the mercy of the Russell's viper, then perhaps it was worth learning if someone as ferociously intelligent as she was had had any ideas about who could have killed him. He would never in the ordinary way have consulted a witness about a task that should have been his own entirely. But when the motive for the crime was so mysterious, and when it had occurred in surroundings he knew so little about, perhaps it was right to make an exception.

A slight smile flitted across Gauri Subbiah's grave face.

He got the impression from it that the very thoughts that had just passed through his head had come into hers. Why, she must have asked herself, should an inspector from Crime Branch consult a woman almost young enough to be his daughter, from right across the other side of India as well, about the case it was his duty to investigate?

'Inspector, I am sorry to have to tell you that, however successful I may be in scientific research, I find I am not at all successful at being a detective. No idea whatsoever has come to me about who could possibly have killed Chagoo. Or why, beyond the fact that he was not at all a pleasant individual, anyone should need to kill him.'

Have I obeyed the warning finger I saw in that upwards-pointing champak tree in Sewri Cemetery, Ghote asked himself, slowly making his way down the stairs from Gauri Subbiah's laboratory.

Yes. Yes, he answered, I think I have. I have asked Gauri Subbiah all that I should. All right, I must dot last i and cross last t by asking someone whether there were any signs that Chagoo was harassing her in a sexual manner. But I am sure answer will be no.

So that is over. It is not Gauri Subbiah.

Abruptly he felt enormously hungry. He looked at

his watch. Not much too early for tiffin. All that questioning of someone he was all the time wishing to have the right answers had taken it out of him more than he would have thought possible. No wonder there was a hollow feeling in his stomach.

Outside the Institute he realized that, just along the road from where the old bonesetter still squatted under his holes-pierced umbrella – had he had even one customer? – there was an eating place. *New Gentleman Hotel* the sign above it proclaimed. Without asking himself whether it was Class Two or Class Three or even lowly Class One, he hurried across.

But his stomach was not to be filled as soon as he had hoped. He had almost reached his destination when a commotion in the lane running down beside the hotel caused him to halt.

A man had come running and shouting out of the side door. He was holding out in front of himself a big frying-pan from which there billowed clouds of thick black smoke. The hotel cook. There could be little doubt this was what the oldish man with a brahmin's thread running right to left across his bare chest must be. But what made Ghote stop and stare was the person who came hurrying after the cook. None other than Dr Mahipal.

No reason, Ghote thought, why Dr Mahipal should not have been in the place. When he had been at the Mira Behn Institute this may well have been where, when he ate lunch, he would go. But why had he come hurrying out of its kitchen in the wake of the cook and his burning pan?

171

He waited to see if he could find out.

The cook quickly succeeded in extinguishing the worst of the blaze by turning the pan over and letting its contents fall to the muddy surface of the lane. Now he set about beating out with the back of the pan the few flames that had sprung up from the hot mess. But, as he did so, he directed at Dr Mahipal, hovering indecisively in the rear, a stream of furious t-spitting Marathi.

'Talking, talking. On, on, on. Asking this question, asking that. Never stopping. How can a man keep watching his work when you are all the time talking and talking?'

'But, Pitaji, there are things I had to ask you.'

Had he caught the words correctly? Pitaji? *Father*? Yes, there could be no doubt. Dr Mahipal had called the cook Father. But how could a harijan, an untouchable, have a father who was, like almost all cooks who had to handle food, a brahmin? Was the cook no brahmin but pretending to be such? But why should he do that? Or was Dr Mahipal no harijan?

Stepping quickly out of sight of anyone in the lane, Ghote thought that, yes, here was a possible answer. In all colleges some seats were reserved by law for the Scheduled Castes, often more than there were applicants for. So had Dr Mahipal claimed to be a harijan so as to get a seat? It would not be the first time a member of a superior caste had masqueraded as an untouchable in order to set foot on the first rung of a ladder that might lead to . . . To a researcher's post at the Mira Behn Institute?

Ghote stood lost in thought, his hunger of a few minutes before forgotten.

If Dr Mahipal – that lower-caste name was probably not his real one at all – was passing himself off as a harijan, one thing was certain. Professor Phaterpaker had no idea of it. Otherwise someone as ready to mud-sling against the man, as he had been in order to divert suspicion from himself, would have been quick to point to the offence.

And offence, he realized thinking of the further implications, it certainly was. A crime even. If it had been exposed, the researcher could well have lost his post at the Mira Behn Institute long before he had come to resign it. Nor would he then have been able to step at once into a lectureship at Grant Medical College. Professor Phaterpaker would have seen to that.

So the fellow was in a distinctly vulnerable position. And who was the very man he had himself pointed out as someone who would take advantage of any such information? Chandra Chagoo. So Dr Mahipal – call him that – might well have had a reason for getting rid of the snake-handler. Very possibly he—

'Why, it is Inspector Ghote.'

The man himself. No doubt he had waited just inside the lane for a few minutes, recovering from the abuse his father had showered him with. And now he had stepped out, once more a respected lecturer at one of Bombay's premier colleges. Happy to greet this police inspector he had, by chance, encountered.

But the police inspector was hardly happy to meet him.

Chapter Thirteen

'It is you, Dr Mahipal? You itself?'

Ghote knew a moment after he had shot out these words that he ought – unless he was going to reject the name Mahipal altogether – simply to have expressed mild surprise at this encounter. But he had been too overcome by what he had just worked out to hit the right note.

Could this, after all, be the very man he wanted? Here? Now? In front of him? Was it this crane-like creature with his withered arm who had been blackmailed by Chandra Chagoo? And had killed him? He was certainly one of the three people only who, it seemed certain, could have done that.

But how to find out if this was truly the case? What to ask to bring it all to light?

He ducked any immediate answer. And found an altogether different question.

'Ah, Doctor,' he said, recovering a little, 'you are just only the man to be helping me. There is something I was wanting to find out, and you may be the one person best able to tell me.'

He was given a fleeting, apparently friendly smile.

'If I can do it, Inspector . . .'

'Well, it is this. It is about your colleague, your former colleague I should be saying, Dr Subbiah.'

'Yes?'

'I am thinking, from what you have said about her before, you were perhaps the person in entire Mira Behn Institute who was knowing her best?'

Dr Mahipal considered for a moment. A hypothesis. Test it.

'Yes,' he said at last, 'I think you could say I know Gauri Subbiah as well as any colleague – or, if I must say it, ex-colleague – of mine at the Mira Behn. But, please do not expect me to tell you anything about her she would not like me to have said.'

Ghote experienced a momentary hesitation. Could it be that the man who had gone back into the Mira Behn Institute to retrieve, so he had claimed, some figures from a computer there was not the murderer of Chandra Chagoo? Was this careful answer of his an indication that he had some secret reason to think Gauri Subbiah might be Chagoo's killer? And was he determined, if so, to shield a friend?

Was he himself at this moment on altogether the wrong track? Had he missed something about Gauri Subbiah in the tense interview he had just emerged from?

But, wrong or right, here was a track he had to follow, if he could, to its end.

'Nevertheless, Doctor,' he said, looking the man straight in the face, 'It is your duty as a citizen to give a police officer authorized to inquire all assistance within your powers.'

He saw a tiny tightness in the face looking down at him.

'Well, what is it you think you have the right to ask?'

Ghote wagged his head.

'To tell the truth,' he said, 'it is, yes, a somewhat embarrassing question. But it is one it is my bounden duty to find the answer for.'

'Very well.'

'Then let me ask it straight out. Can you tell me if Chandra Chagoo was in any way sexually harassing Dr Subbiah?'

And the former researcher broke into laughter.

'Chagoo?' he spluttered out at last. 'Harassing Gauri? No, no. You have got it entirely wrong. Nothing like that at all, nothing at all.'

'You are one hundred per cent certain?'

'Inspector, neither sexually nor in any other way was it Gauri Subbiah that man was harassing.'

Ghote, at a pitch of alertness, took immediate note of the form of words Dr Mahipal had used. Unintentionally, no doubt. Did they mean he saw Chagoo as harassing, if not sexually, someone else? Was he talking about himself in fact? If in his mind there had not been another thought, different, blacker, there like a stone block not to be rubbed away, would he not have said simply *No, Chagoo was in no way harassing Gauri Subbiah*?

So was what had been revealed to him when he had seen the researcher being abused by his brahmin father right after all? Had the man been blackmailed by Chandra Chagoo? Was he himself truly now looking at Chagoo's murderer?

'Then,' he slammed out, 'if Miss Subbiah was not the person Chagoo was harassing, who was it? Was it you itself, Doctor? You and no other? I will tell you, that is what I am thinking.'

The tall man in front of him seemed to shrink even more into a crane's stoop.

'What— What do you mean? I do not at all understand.'

'I think you do. I think you are understanding very well.'

'You— You are saying that Chagoo . . . Inspector, are you saying Chagoo was in some way making my life a misery? That— That he was harassing me? Even blackmailing me for some reason? Have you got it into your head that— You are thinking I was responsible for his death?'

'Was he blackmailing? Answer yes or no.'

The saras swallowed, and swallowed again.

'Yes or no?'

'Inspector, no. No, no, no. I deny it absolutely. What could that man have to blackmail me about? What could he?'

Ghote looked at him implacably.

'About the fact, Dr Mahipal, if such is your true name even, that you are not of Scheduled Caste origin. That you are not and never have been a harijan, and that nevertheless you were beginning your academic career by claiming and pretending to be the same.'

'Yes.'

A single hardly breathed syllable. Yet it was as much a confession as if it had been a lengthy statement made under interrogation in a detection room somewhere, taken down in shorthand, signed and acknowledged.

Ghote treated it as such.

'Very well,' he said, 'I do not consider it necessarily my duty to make known your deceit, unless it proves material to a case in court. But will it prove material? Will it, Dr Mahipal?'

'Inspector, how can I convince you that, however you were getting to know my secret, that man Chandra Chagoo never did?'

'Not by just only stating and swearing such,' Ghote answered.

'But, Inspector, what more can I do? As a scientist I know that it is easier to prove by experiment that some theory does or does not hold true, that it is or is not so, than to prove in any way something for which you have no theory. If— If I was wanting to show a possible new medical treatment was effective or not, I could, if conditions were suitable, test it experimentally on rats, and—'

For an instant he broke off. A look of anger flitted on to his face. To be at once pushed down.

'I— I could test— Test such a treatment on whatever animal was suitable. On rabbits, on chicks, on any such. But if I did not know what it was I wanted to ask, if I had only a blank in my head, I could do nothing.'

Ghote wondered how well he had followed. But he pressed on.

'Nevertheless,' he said, 'Chagoo was working at the Mira Behn Institute, and until recently you were also. He was well knowing you, Dr Mahipal. He could have come into contact, by chance, as I was myself doing just only ten minutes back, with the cook at this hotel who is your father, yes?'

Dr Mahipal's face sank yet further into gloom.

'I suppose that is possible, certainly,' he answered eventually. 'But— But, Inspector, believe me, even if Chagoo had known my secret and was blackmailing me because of it, I could not have brought myself to kill him, not even an individual like Chagoo. I am not the man to do it. I would have paid. Paid, Inspector. Paid and paid whatever was necessary.'

Ghote thought he could perhaps believe this. After all, was this not the man who had lacked the courage to press the Director of the Mira Behn Institute to answer his doubts about his research? The man who had left the work he loved rather than question and question a superior who had, in his own words, treated him like a mother giving her child a rap on the head for going on asking and asking?

Yet in his own work over the years he had come across plausible rogues enough to make him ready to be as distrustful as any police detective in India. For all the apparent sincerity of this brahmin harijan's protestations, he might still be a clever pretender.

But something the fellow had poured out in his spate of denials had triggered a different thought. He took it up.

'Very well,' he said. 'I will accept what you have said.

For time being only. But there is one matter I would like to hear more of from you.'

The look of relief on Dr Mahipal's face was as comical as the circus clown's when he finds he has luckily caught the juggled ball.

'Yes, yes, Inspector. What is it? Anything you are wanting to know, I will tell you if I can. If I possibly can.'

'Then it is this. When you were talking just now about the way a scientist is working, in the example you were giving you came to mention rats. And for one moment only you were stopping. Stopping and thinking of something else. Yes?'

For an instant it looked as if the man was going to deny this. But it was for an instant only. Then a gleam of bitterness came into his eyes.

'I was thinking of something else, yes,' he said. 'You were quick to see it. But— But, Inspector, it had nothing to do with myself and Chagoo.'

'No? I am thinking it might well have something to do, however, with the real reason Chagoo was killed. He was, after all, the in-charge of the rats in the Mira Behn Reptile Room, equally with the snakes that are there.'

A slow-growing look of obstinacy began to show itself again in the face in front of him.

He did not let it grow more.

'Answer, please. Why did the mention of using rats for an experiment cause you to stop in what it was you were saying?'

'Inspector, I do not wish to answer.'

'Nevertheless, I am insisting. Why, Doctor? Why?'

180

'But— But if I answer it would seem as if I was accusing some other person so as to escape from the charge you have threatened me with.'

Some other person? Who could that be? Surely only Professor Phaterpaker, the man Dr Mahipal had already accused, or half-accused, of perpetrating some fraud. The man, too, who had not hesitated to attempt to point my inquiries in the direction of none other than Dr Mahipal himself.

'You will answer,' he said. 'You must. Now, why did you stop what you were saying and denying at the mention only of the word *rats*?'

Dr Mahipal licked at his lips.

'Inspector, must I answer?'

'You know well you must.'

The look of obstinacy was still there. Then it dissolved.

'If you say I must . . . Then— Then, Inspector, what made me come to a stop then was the thought that Professor Phaterpaker, yes, Professor Phaterpaker, may have removed from his experiments rats that were not confirming the results he wanted. It was because I suspected this that eventually I tried to question him, as I told you yesterday. When I was refused any answer. It was then I told him I would not work under him one day more.'

'As I had thought.'

Leaving the former Mira Behn researcher standing there outside the New Gentleman Hotel, Ghote strode off, busy weighing up this revelation and its implications. So Professor Phaterpaker's fraud, if he had truly committed any fraud, had been concerned with the rats in the Reptile Room at the Mira Behn. The room where Chandra Chagoo kept watch over the specimen rats. Where, too, he had met his death from the fangs of the Russell's viper.

One thing only to do, then. To go and question once more the professor, person of influence though he was, overbearing figure behind his wide desk though he was, the Commissioner's *first-class fellow* though he was.

He set off with straight-shouldered determination.

Only to realize he still had not had anything to eat.

Can I go hungry all the time I am putting questions to that man? he asked himself. Just only until I am getting home to Protima and her cooking? No, no, I cannot. Oh, if I was chasing some badmash or lying in wait in ambush somewhere, as I have done and done again, then I could go all day and all night with not one piece of food to touch my lips. But now? Now, when what I must do is to think and think and then ask and ask. Ask just the right questions also. Now I must have food in my stomach.

And, no sooner had he reached this important decision, than there came to his nostrils an odour of cooking. He looked round. There, a few yards down the next side lane was a stall. He approached it almost at a run, asking himself what would most satisfy his raging hunger.

He need not have bothered. The stall, a mean affair of two thin and twisted boards propped on rickety trestles, was offering at this late hour no more than three sad-looking left-over samosas.

Should he eat them at all? Gut-probing indigestion awaited him surely if he did. But if he turned away there would be only the continuing torments of hunger. Obsessing every corner of his mind. He would be entirely unable to concentrate. And concentration was absolutely necessary now.

How else could he frame those questions which might lead the Director of the Mira Behn Institute into betraying himself as the murderer of Chandra Chagoo?

'Give me just one,' he said to the vendor, a young man in a shiny patterned grey shirt, sucking in desperate puffs from the last half of a dark, acridly smelling beedi. 'No. No, make it two only. Oh, hell, I will take all.'

He picked up the first of them. Grease oozed on to his fingers. Nor was there much heat left in the flabby object.

He bit. Chewed. Swallowed. Finished it. Took the second. Even less warm. Even greasier. Bite. Bite. Bite. Down at last.

The third and last he rejected after one mouthful. But at least his stomach felt full now. Heavily, ominously full.

He turned away as the young vendor grabbed at the remains of the last soggy samosa and pushed it whole into his mouth.

He almost groaned aloud. At the prospect of internal discomfort to come. At the thought of the boy in his sweat-stained grey shirt, perhaps hungrier even than himself and not having had daring enough to give up the faint prospect of getting a few paisa for his wretched wares. But most of all at the thought of having to question Professor Phaterpaker once more.

And then it began to rain.

Chapter Fourteen

Ghote swore.

He wanted nothing so much at this moment as to be able to walk along very slowly going nowhere while in his mind he thrashed out a series of cunning questions to put to the Director of the Mira Behn Institute. Questions that would go from whatever innocuous subject he could find as a starting point, bit by bit on to some mention of Professor Phaterpaker's research, and from there to some telling question about the experimental rats, in their runs, sharing with the snakes the Reptile Room in the Institute basement.

And then moving on to asking why Professor Phaterpaker, the man with those hundreds of scientific papers to his name, had falsified his results. And from there, in one bound, he would go to Chandra Chagoo and ask how the snake-handler had come to know enough to blackmail the eminent Mira Behn Institute Director.

Till finally he would be poised to demand what the professor had done to shut Chagoo's mouth.

But the rain was getting increasingly heavy. No question of strolling along under such a shower as this.

So where to go? What to do?

Should he go back across to the Mira Behn, not so far away? Take shelter there? Yet what if he encountered Professor Phaterpaker? Would he not feel obliged then to begin his attack? To catch the man outside his home ground, without that wide desk between them? That would be just the right circumstance to produce the seemingly simple friendly remark he had seen as the beginning of the interrogation.

But what was that remark to be? His mind was blank.

No, the risk of botching the whole operation – of course, Professor Phaterpaker might be at work up in his big room and never emerge – was too much to take.

The rain was falling in great weighty drops now, each one separately splashing on the surface of the road. In a couple of minutes he would be soaked to the skin.

Sewri Police Station. That would do.

Run there as fast as he could. It was not so very far. And, while there, one thing at least to be done. Once again ask that idler Baitonde where the Examiner's report on Chagoo's body was. Damn it, he ought to have seen it long ago.

He set off sprinting along fast as he could go, past the tall open gate of the Mira Behn on the far side of the road, past the old bonesetter, huddled under the umbrella with as many holes in it as stars in the sky. Now the rain was as fierce as at the height of a full monsoon burst, spearing down in long silver shining rods, bouncing up knee-high from the roadway.

Ahead of him, like a sudden growth of mushrooms, umbrellas had sprouted in dozens, black, blue, red, yellow, patterned and plain, glistening and shining with the water already streaming off them. Less well-prepared citizens in this post-monsoon time held folded newspapers over their heads or briefcases too small to be any real use and scuttered here and there for shelter, laughing at their predicament, saris and shirts already beginning to cling. Dodging between them, with the wet now deeply soaking the whole top of his shoulders, he ran on, cursing.

Blood Sputum Semen Are Examined Here. A garish noticeboad caught his eye at the entrance to a yard-wide lane where a cluster of people, doing their best to keep out of the sudden downpour, were cheerfully exchanging comments. How different the research into those any-or-all body fluids was from Professor Phater-paker's world-renowned work on malaria vaccines.

But which, if he was right, was the greater cheat?

Damn the rain.

He swerved hard to avoid an umbrellaless woman making her way at a timid run towards him, the red from the kum-kum on her brow running in a scarlet trickle right down her nose.

Bloody Sewri PS, further than he had thought. He ought to have gone into the Mira Behn and risked being unprepared if Professor Phaterpaker had come down from his office.

And had that full-stop hesitation of Dr Mahipal's at the mention of rats misled him after all? It might have done. Mahipal, whatever his true name was, could in fact be no more than a disgruntled dismissed employee.

He came to a big intersection where a portly traffic constable, up on his little round stand, had erected above himself his outsize umbrella, fastened at waist and shoulders by stout straps. He darted across and stood sharing its cover for a breath-catching moment or two, pondering the doubts that had abruptly struck him.

Turn round, run back to the Mira Behn? He could get no wetter. Or go on as he had been, giving himself time to prepare properly to tackle Professor Phaterpaker?

He swung round to face the way he had come. And another bright-painted notice on the far side of the road confronted him. *Foolproof Cures for Secret Diseases – Kidney Stones, Warts, Stammerings, Night Blindness*. No lack of promises there. A medical man, of a sort, who would never bother with questioning and questioning his patients, except perhaps to find out how much he could ask in payment. Claims and assertions his whole stock. Someone very different from scrupulous, diffident Dr Mahipal. Who had surely told him the truth. Or had he?

But Gauri Subbiah, the promises she had made for her new ACE-i, or the promises Asha Rani, Professor Phaterpaker, Dr Mahipal, everyone had made on her behalf, were they perhaps as much flights of imagination as those of this quack doctor? No. No, they must not be. Gauri Subbiah must be as much a sign of hope as he had believed. All right, let the distinguished Director of the Mira Behn Institute be a common cheat. Let Dr Mahipal be a man too weak to ask the questions he ought to. But Gauri Subbiah must not in any way betray his trust.

He turned again, waited till a much-soaked victoria

had clopped by, its horse bedraggled, its driver hunched under a small sheet of plastic, its two bright-saried passengers endeavouring to shelter under a big piece of stiff brown paper taken from one of their purchases. Then he plunged out into the rain once more.

Not in the direction of the Mira Behn Institute.

Two minutes later, as the downpour began pattering to a halt as suddenly as it had started, he was climbing the steps into Sewri Police Station. To come face-to-face with a clean, dry and grinning Inspector Baitonde.

'Ghote bhai, what it is you have been doing? Run-run-running after some damn clue in all that rain? You are soaked to skin itself.'

'Yes,' said Ghote, 'I know.'

He shook the wet off like a half-bald pi-dog.

'What you are wanting, bhai,' Baitonde said, 'is one good damn hot cup of tea, yes?'

It was. Ghote wished at that moment for nothing else. But he did not at all want it at the hands of his deplorable fellow officer.

'No. No, I am not needing such. I would be dry in one moment only. And I have looked in just to ask you one thing itself.'

'Ask. Ask. But slurp some tea at same time. Come in, come in.'

And Baitonde held wide the door of his cabin.

Ghote went in.

'Sit, sit. Peon.'

Baitonde shouted in a voice that could surely be heard in every corner of the station, and at the same time gave the round bell of his desk a series of mighty thumps.

A peon appeared like lightning, looking apprehensive.

'Tea. Tea, you idiot. Damn quick also or you will be feeling my boot.'

'Ji haan, Inspector.'

The fellow disappeared.

'But sit, Inspector. What for is there to stand? Sit, sit.'

Ghote squelched down on to one of the chairs in front of Baitonde's desk. Baitonde went round to the other side, flung back his own chair, crashed down into it, stuck his legs up on the clutter of discarded documents and open newspapers on the desk.

'What I am wanting to ask,' Ghote said, deciding he must accept Baitonde's offer of tea with what good grace he could, 'what I was wanting to ask is: have you by chance got that Examiner's report on the post-mortem?'

'Post-mortem? Post-mortem? What damn post-mortem it is?'

Ghote sat up straighter. The wet trousers under him emitted a sucking sound.

'The post-mortem on Chandra Chagoo,' he said with some returning sharpness. 'We ought to have had sight of it long before now.'

Baitnonde was now busy extracting some last remains of his lunch from between his big yellow teeth.

'Damn Examiner,' he muttered almost inaudibly.

'So the fellow at JJ Hospital has been delaying and delaying?' Ghote asked.

'Oh, God knows. Either he is—'

He broke off to explore more deeply behind his molars.

'Yes? What it is?'

'Inspector . . . Ghote bhai . . . Why all this hurrying-purrying?'

'Because, Inspector, there may be something in that report which would help us find out just what was happening to Chandra Chagoo.'

'That we are knowing. He was getting to be dead.'

Baitonde took his finger out of his mouth long enough to laugh very loudly at his own joke.

'Yes. Chagoo is dead. But have we still any real idea how he was coming by his death?'

'One bloody great snake was doing it, Inspector. You were telling yourself. Seeing also.'

'Yes, yes. But that does not at all explain the exact events down there in that Reptile Room. If we were knowing just exactly what had happened, it might be altogether plain who was there with Chagoo, who smashed the glass of that snake's cage, why it was done only.'

'Inspector, who cares? Fellow is dead. Someone killed, all right. But we are well knowing the fellow was one out-and-out blackmailer. Better dead, I am saying.'

'No, Inspector. Very well, I would agree there are some people whose end is almost welcome. But in this case it is not so much the man who is dead that is mattering, but the man we may have to charge with killing him. Someone high, high up at one important medical research establishment.'

'Man we must charge? You are forgetting woman

191

also? Yes, if we must send someone from there to Thana Gaol to swing at end of a rope, best to be the woman.'

Leaning back in his chair, Baitonde rubbed his hands together with vigorous enjoyment. Ghote jumped up. His wet trousers clung for a moment, released themselves.

'Inspector,' he barked out. 'Kindly get in touch with Examiner at JJ Hospital ek dum. I am going now to Mira Behn Institute itself. There are questions I am wanting to ask.'

But walking back through the streets, softly steaming now in the sun – as were the shirt on his back and the trousers stuck to his calves – even though he demanded of himself again and again just what likely excuse he could produce to start his conversation with Professor Phaterpaker, no answer came to mind. Over and over he imagined that conversation sliding beautifully into becoming an interview, the interview becoming an interrogation, the interrogation becoming – was it possible? – a confession.

Was it really possible, though, that the distinguished Director of the Mira Behn Institute, a scientist known in distant countries for his research into malaria and the life-saving vaccines that prevented it, could be the man who had loosed that Russell's viper on to the good-for-nothing Chandra Chagoo? But surely it was every bit as impossible that Dr Mahipal, a scientist too and a man of little courage, should have done that.

Or, worse, worse, worse, how much more impossible was it that Gauri Subbiah, that figure of hope, that worker in the field of science who by her persistent investigation had already brought succour to thousands and thousands all over the world— No, be accurate. Who would bring help once her paper for the journal of that French academy had been assessed, agreed to, published, admired, translated into action. How altogether impossible that she should prove to be a common criminal to be one day hanged, as Baitonde had delighted in suggesting, in Thana Gaol.

Three impossibilities. And yet logically one of them must not be an impossibility.

For a moment he longed for there to be another world than this, a different *duniya*, parallel in all its circumstances to the here-and-now, save that somehow in it a wholly other series of events had taken place. Where Chandra Chagoo had simply been killed by someone entirely different from those three inescapable suspects in the world as it was. By Abdul Khan even. There was someone who would very likely have a reason to get rid of the snake-handler. After all, the man had been supplying him with the ACE-i samples he had passed on to his rich customers for champagne cocaine in the *filmi duniya* and elsewhere.

But there was no different *duniya*. He wished there was. It was a notion he had often let run in his mind, particularly on any occasion when he had happened to escape possible death, either in the course of duty or even just by stepping back from the road edge at the last second. What if there was a parallel world in which a dead Ganesh Ghote had not died? Where his life would carry on, with Protima not a widow, young Ved not suddenly fatherless, with whatever investigation he was engaged on not needing to be handed over to a brother officer because his own life had been suddenly ended. Or there might be thousands, lakhs, crores of different *duniye*, each taking a new path where what had happened in the old world had not taken place.

But when at last he reached the Mira Behn Institute he was still as far from a way forward as he had ever been. Nothing even halfway plausible as a start to the process of questioning Professor Phaterpaker had come to him.

He rang the bell at the tall gate, waited for cheerfully smiling Laloo to come and unlock for him, followed him back up the tarred path, stepped into the dark entrance hall, saw with half a glance that on the In/Out board the wooden slider against Professor Phaterpaker's name had been fixed securely at *in*, and set foot on the first tread of the broad polished stairs.

Where, at the head of the flight, stood Professor Phaterpaker himself, large red notebook tucked under one arm.

'Ah, good afternoon, Inspector Khote.'

'It is Ghote, sir. Ghote.'

'Yes, yes, of course. Forgive me, Inspector, but when one is deeply absorbed in a piece of research other things tend to fly out of one's mind.'

Wait. Could that casual excuse be just what he needed as a way in to his much imagined progression? The chain of questions and answers that would end with the solution to his mystery?

He was quick to grab the chance.

'You are at work on some research just only now, sir?'

Professor Phaterpaker gave a deep sigh.

'Just only now at work, Inspector? Alas, it is not just only now. It will be tomorrow. It was yesterday. It will be for many, many tomorrows. You can have no idea of the demands the profession of science makes upon one. If it is one's dharma to be a researcher, then one cannot keep out of one's head those thousand and one questions that one's subject confronts one with. I am even now on my way to examine the rats in my current series of experiments.'

'Rats? Rats? You are going to examine your rats?'

Ghote knew he was jabbering in a ridiculous way. But the suddenness with which his planned long round-about approach had been short-circuited had thrown him into confusion.

He gulped in a breath, and recovered himself.

'Then, Professor Phaterpaker, I also would like to examine your rats.'

Oh, kudos to me, he thought. I have succeeded to ask now the very question – however little of question it was – that may tell me what I am wanting to know. If the professor is seeing it as just only some curiosity on the part of a passing police officer, then he will invite me to watch these rats of his. And I will begin to think he cannot have been blackmailed by Chagoo over them. But, if he is not at all answering with one simple invitation, then . . .

Then I will begin to think I am on right tracks.

'No, Inspector, quite impossible,' Professor Phaterpaker replied in a voice muted by restrained fury. 'You—

You evidently do not comprehend the delicacy of the work I undertake. Of the work any scientist of repute undertakes. A newcomer peering and prying at my specimens might well cause them not to eat. Not to eat as they normally would, that is. It would be a factor seriously affecting my results. Upsetting very delicate experiments.'

One waterfall of excuses only.

So now one more question for you, Professor Phaterpaker.

'Impossible for myself just only to watch you counting and numbering your rats? But what effect, then, is having on them the death of the man who was daily feeding same? Tell me that.'

His shotgun question produced a sudden look of blank dismay on the face with the ever-slipping spectacles and the little jut of chin beard.

'Professor,' Ghote ground out, 'I have a number of questions I must put to you. Shall we go up to your room?'

He glanced meaningfully at Laloo in his box, ears so plainly like a cockroach's it was almost laughable.

'No.'

The reply banged out.

Professor Phaterpaker looked all round. Then he leant forward and addressed Ghote in a hardly audible murmur.

'I would not wish my colleagues – there are fearful gossips among them – to see a police officer marching me to my office when it is known to all that a murder investigation is taking place.'

'No, sir? Then where may we go? I must have answers to my questions. And now itself.'

For a long minute the Director was silent. Thinking, dodging, rejecting, thinking, twisting. But then his voice suddenly boomed out, benefit of Laloo and any other listener.

'Yes, of course, Inspector. You want to see how a scientist goes about things, the come and watch me observe the behaviour of my rats. Come. Come.'

And he took Ghote by the arm and bustled him down the stairs in the direction of the basement.

Once again Ghote confronted the steel-plated door of the Reptile Room.

Abruptly a wild premonition surged up in him. Beyond the door would he find, in another parallel world, in a different and black *duniya*, Chagoo's body lying there once again, the Russell's viper slithering over his bare back.

Chapter Fifteen

Professor Phaterpaker tugged from the pocket of his long white atchkan his personal key to the heavy door of the Reptile Room, inserted it into the wide keyhole, pulled the door as much as he could towards himself, gave the key a single thunking turn, drew the door back.

The floor of the big room was bare. Nothing at all out of place to be seen in the clear light coming through the narrow fixed windows at the top of its outer wall. At the far end the long glass-topped runs for the experimental rats stood silent and untended. Nearer and to the side were the snake cages, their occupants torpid in sleep. Ghote relaxed. A causeless premonition. Everything was as it ought to be. Even the cage once housing the Russell's viper he had seen writhing across dead Chagoo's back was just as it was before, its glass front smashed.

But abruptly a thought occurred to him.

It was absurd, but he had never examined the scene of the crime. As he had as a matter of course in every murder case he had been involved in, coming in at, or very near, the start. No body to look at now, of course. No doubt it was still at the JJ Hospital, while the Examiner was taking his time in compiling his report. Unless – perhaps more likely – that necessary document was already somewhere on Baitonde's desk buried under the day before yesterday's copy of the *Afternoon*, opened at the sports pages.

He went over to the smashed cage, conscious that at the far end of the room Professor Phaterpaker was hovering indecisively by the rat runs, now noisily alive with the creatures' scamperings. Plainly no thought of counting the specimens or of feeding them had entered his head. So let him stew. A little longer waiting for questions would make him all the more ready to answer.

Nothing much to see looking at the broken cage. The large hole in the glass, thinner than he had imagined, was down at the bottom. One good blow with a heavy object would have been enough to make it. And why should glass on such cages be especially thick? They ought not to be in any danger of being accidentally broken.

On the cage floor there still remained droppings of the poison-bearing creature that had once been there. The creature that had at last sunk its channelled tooth into Chandra Chagoo, injected its deadly poison.

The thought put it into his head to ask himself what must actually have happened when Chagoo had become victim to that second-hand way of shutting his mouth. Each of his three suspects was not unlikely, when you came to look at it, to have adopted such a sideways method.

Professor Phaterpaker – standing there still looking down at the scurrying rats – was as indirect a person as any he had met. Look at how he had tried to point the finger at Dr Mahipal without any word of plain accusation. This way of disembarrassing himself of Chagoo, if indeed the fellow had known too much about him, would appeal to his mind, as well as being physically easier than attempting more direct action. Equally, Dr Mahipal, with his withered arm, might seize on such a method of murder, if what he had said about preferring to pay and pay a blackmailer was not actually true, especially as – he had said as much himself – he would revolt from the thought of inflicting death. And Gauri Subbiah? A woman's way of killing, this, surely? It made her, in a way, the prime suspect still.

So whichever of them it was – could it really be Gauri Subbiah? – who had left Chagoo to the snake's venom must have first smashed the cage's front and counted on this enraging the creature to the point where it would attack.

So how exactly had the glass been smashed? Hardly with a bare fist. Not with that long black vicious snake just the other side of it.

He glanced round, and saw the tall wooden stool on which Chagoo must have sat when he was not busy feeding the rats or milking snakes of their venom. Yes, easy enough to pick that up by one of its legs, swing it hard and bring it crashing into the glass of the cage. Anyone could have done it with one hand.

But which of them had? He would not let himself answer. Certainly not until he had put his questions to the man standing beside the rat runs, the white atchkan lined with creases on its back from where he had been sitting in his tall chair behind his wide desk.

And now what must have happened when Chagoo had died was much clearer in his mind. First, Chagoo would have been put temporarily out of action. Had the stool served a double purpose? A blow from it sending Chagoo to the ground? Very likely.

He went over and looked at the stool more closely. There was, certainly, a long, newish scratch on one side of its grease-darkened top. Was that from when it had smashed open the cage? Likely enough. And, there at the edge, could that be a small dark bloodstain? Must get it put under the microscope. And must check also against that Examiner's report, whenever it was coming to light. See if whatever mark there was on the dead man's skull fitted the shape of the stool top.

Why was I not looking when we had just only discovered the body? Not my duty then, yes. But all the same . . .

Then as soon as Chagoo had been knocked senseless the culprit – which of them? Which? Which? – would have smashed open the cage and the Russell's viper, awake and angry, would have slid out, dropped down to the floor looking for someone, something, to vent its anger on. And as it had descended whichever of them had broken the glass must have turned, snatched the key – unless Chagoo had left it in the door on this side – and hurried away leaving the soon to be stirring blackmailer to his fate. The steel-plated door locked behind them. The heavy key tossed, at whatever convenient moment, under some bush in the garden.

Where the old mali, turning it over and over wonderingly in his earth-grubby hands, would have erased all traces of fingerprints. If Laloo had not completed that process.

But who had eventually thrown away the key? Who? Dr Mahipal? Professor Phaterpaker, still beside his rats but with his shoulders straighter now? Or . . . Or Gauri Subbiah. Say it. Think it.

No. Do not.

He swung round and marched over to the rat runs.

The sectioned compartments, each neatly labelled. *Injected 14 September - Not Injected Controls Only - Injected 28 September - Healthy, Post 21 September - Malaria Detected 21 September.* The animals in them, some busily sniffing and prying, others lethargic, lying on their sides, panting.

'Now, if you please, sir, I have certain questions.'

'Questions, questions. Oh, come now, Inspector, curiosity killed the cat. Isn't that what they say?'

Damn. Had he left him too long?

Or under that playful note was there an undertow of sharp concern? Of fear even?

'Sir,' he said uncompromisingly. 'It is not cats. It is rats. Rats I am wanting to talk, and what has been done with them.'

The faint smile the Director had succeeded in calling up vanished away.

'Inspector,' he said, his voice rising, 'am I to understand that somehow you have come to believe that— To suspect that these rats . . .'

The bluster abruptly faded.

'Yes, sir, these rats. I have very much come to suspect that there have been times when, in one way or another, you have interfered with the same. Moved some from one of these sections to another. Even perhaps you were taking away dead creatures when their expiring provided evidence that was not fitting whatsoever theory you were having. And I am believing also that Chandra Chagoo may have come to know this.'

Up went the spectacles at the end of a long forefinger. But this was no petty irritated jab. Rather, a long, thoughtful, playing-for-time gesture.

'Inspector,' the reply came at last, 'how shall I put this? Yes. Let me say that I think I see the misapprehension lying at the root of what you have been thinking. Forgive me if I am wrong, but I believe that fundamentally you harbour an altogether too idealistic notion of the scientist's way of life.'

'Sir, it is rats we are talking. Not at all way of life.'

'No, Inspector, I am prepared to come to the rats. But, first, I would like you thoroughly to understand my position. I think then you will be happy to dismiss from your mind any notion that I might have been responsible for— For the death of that fellow.'

A wave of the hand in the direction of Chagoo's tall stool, as if the man himself was still sitting on it. For a moment Ghote wished that was so. A different *duniya*. One where the snake-handler had never been left to his death in this locked room. One where he would not have to arrest under Section 302 as distinguished a man as the Director of the Mira Behn Institute.

Or, perhaps, a scientist as full of promise as . . .

But the thought had caused him to lose by the tiniest degree the pressure of his questioning.

'Yes? Yes, sir?'

It was the best he could produce now.

Professor Phaterpaker smiled again. Not much of a smile, but a smile. Ghote cursed himself. A man under full interrogation should be far, far from smiles.

'I wonder, Inspector, if you could bear with me while I go back in time? Back as far even as the redoubtable Sir Isaac Newton? You know whom I am speaking of?'

'I am speaking of rats, Professor. Not at all your Newton-pewtons. Famous scientist, apple falls on his head, theory of gravity, yes?'

'Yes, Inspector. But I will stay with him, if you don't mind. Because, you see, even a hero of science like Newton was capable, as I learnt in my casual reading not long ago, of falsifying his results. Falsifying them, Inspector. As, I freely admit, it could be said that I too have done with some of mine. Newton, let me explain, was in contention with the great German philosopher Leibniz over his theory of the universal application of the force of gravity. And apparently, in the end, in order to hammer home his victory, the great Sir Isaac went so far as to alter his original calculations. He had stated that the proof of his theory depended on a certain exact correlation. He simply made that correlation exact, despite lacking any figures that showed it to be so. Isaac Newton, Inspector, the great father figure of science.'

'Very well, sir. Since you are saying it, I will accept. But I am not at all seeing how Newton and apples and some German philosopher somehow make all OK what you have done here in this very room, cheating itself over these rats. With Chagoo perhaps one day coming to know what you were doing.'

'But what I am trying to tell you, Inspector, is that cheat— No, not cheating. But rather it is a certain massaging, as we say, of figures. It is the occasional choosing of experimental results that confirm a theory while discarding those that do not. Let me tell you, any such small fudgings, if not wholly accepted in scientific circles, are at least expected. We scientists are human, after all.'

For all that what Professor Phaterpaker was saying only reinforced what Dr Mahipal had told him earlier, Ghote found it hard to accept. *Truth Is God*. Were not those words written above the Institute's noticeboard in the very entrance of the building, however faded the paint had become?

Yet if truth should be a god from whom you could if you wished melt away parts that stuck out uncomfortably, did this not mean Professor Phaterpaker had done nothing to cause the whole scientific community of India to pelt him with shoes? If what he had done would bring him no great disgrace, did he have any reason after all to get rid of Chandra Chagoo?

He did not.

'Very well, sir,' he said, 'you are admitting you have been massaging, as you said, fudging also, with these rats. But I am not thinking you were explaining to Chagoo there about your Newton and your Pewton. I am thinking Chagoo could very well have seen you had transferred certain rats from one compartment to another, or taken control specimens and put them in as having been injected with your new vaccine, or whatever it was you were dong. He, too, even if he was just only, as they are saying, from the melon fields, was able to count, to read and write also. I have seen the register he was keeping just outside. And I am believing he one day said to himself: the burra sahib Director of this Institute is cheating only. And then he would have thought, yes, how much will he give for this-all not to be told to each and every scientist in this house?'

Professor Phaterpaker smiled.

Ghote experienced a sudden sinking of doubt.

'To each and every scientist in this house, Inspector? Think what it is you have just said. There are not so many scientists here. They are, each of them, aware that they owe their position, their well-paid and highly respected position, to myself. And they are also, as I have been trying to explain to you, scientists who very well know that on occasion research is carried out, shall we say, not to the highest standards, even in the hands of an Isaac Newton. Inspector, do you think that, if that man Chagoo had told his tale to every single scientist under this roof, the facts would not be, as they say, brushed under the carpet? Do you think I would have had anything very much to fear?'

The man was right.

Ghote felt a curdling of depression settling inside himself. He knew he ought to be solidly pleased to have unearthed as much as he had of the truth. But that truth, if it was truth, seemed now to have freed Professor

Phaterpaker from suspicion. And left – Dr Mahipal seemed suddenly altogether unlikely as Chagoo's killer – only Gauri Subbiah there to be investigated, trapped, charged.

No, that must not be. To hell with logic, police procedure, everything. He could not be at the end of his trail now. He could not be.

And then it burst in upon him that perhaps he was not. Had he let the wily Director confuse him with that half-confession to fraud?

Was his fraud perhaps an altogether more serious matter than some minor falsifications in the particular experiments he had been conducting with these rats?

Because he himself when he had first met the distinguished Director of the Mira Behn Institute, as he had climbed those wide stairs up towards him, had been greeted with that unexpected and inexplicable question *Do you have any scientific training?* What did that mean but that he was being asked *Are you an investigator trained in scientific method? Can it be that you are coming here to question all that I have done over the past years?*

There cannot have been any suggestion at that moment of simply some hanky-panky work about the rats here. No, surely the man had been afraid, if only momentarily, that his systematic cheating over many years might be exposed. The practised skill with which he had thrust his papers into a drawer in case a quick glance might betray some half-finished green ink additions or red ink crossings out bore that out. And that sudden change when it had become clear he had

come to the Institute only to ask about the stolen specimens of Gauri Subbiah's ACE-i.

And it was actually possible, too, that Chagoo had
got to know more about the Director than his mere
fudging of his current data. Dr Mahipal had, after all,
caught him one night in the Director's office. Very well,
Chagoo was uneducated. But he could read well enough.
And he was cunning. What was more certain than he
had been poking and prying in the wooden filing cabinets lining every wall in the Director's office. It would
not take much intelligence to question alterations in
green ink, crossings out in red.

Yes, far from the Director being out of the count,
the time might now be almost in sight when a charge
of murder could be made.

Risk all on a single dice throw? Something he would
never do in the ordinary way. But if Professor
Phaterpaker was not the person who had left Chandra
Chagoo to his death, then in all likelihood Gauri Subbiah
was.

Yes, a single throw.

'Professor Phaterpaker,' he said, 'what you have been
telling may or may not be the true case. But there is
more. In the course of inquiries here in this house I
have learnt that Chagoo has been late in the night inside
your own office. And, Professor, what could he have
seen there? Those many hundred scientific papers you
have had printed in journals worldwide, in your files
are there originals that differ from what you in the end
sent out?'

At the mention of Chagoo's presence in his office

Professor Phaterpaker's face betrayed more than he would have wanted. A glistening of perspiration on that long nose. Calculation behind the spectacles.

Ghote leapt in.

'Am I right, Professor?' he demanded. 'Has your cheating-cheating been happening for many, many years itself?'

'No.'

But it was a shout of desperation reverberating through the big basement room.

'Sir, yes. Yes, isn't it? Yes? Yes? Yes? You have done more than just only cheat with these rats. You have changed and altered your papers. You have invented and concocted, I am thinking, men and women in the distant mofussil, where you were stating you were doing such good works, and used them for your figures only.'

And Professor Phaterpaker broke.

'It is yes. Yes, I admit it. But . . . Oh, shall I ever be able to make you understand? Shall I ever make anybody understand? My fellow scientists? The newspapers? Anybody?'

He looked wildly round, slipping spectacles now almost off the end of his nose.

'Inspector, if I tell you how it was, how it was from the very beginning, is there any chance that it can be kept from becoming the common gossip of all Bombay? All India?'

'Sir, you have not yet fully told what it is.'

A grunt of a laugh.

'Have I not, Inspector? At all events, you seem to

209

have guessed the greater part of it. Ferreted out in two days the secret I have kept for years.'

Ghote felt a tiny flame of pride, deep in the darkness of his innermost being.

But he did not allow it to grow. There were more important matters to hand. His duty. To find out to the last detail the truth of what was before him.

'Sir, all you may do now is to give me the full and frank details, without more of twisting and prevarications.'

'Yes. Yes, that is what I wanted to do. What I want to do. To explain.'

'Then, sir, explain.'

Professor Phaterpaker looked down at the rats scurrying to and fro or lying half-dead in the runs at his side.

'Where did it begin?' he said. 'Yes. Yes, I can answer that. It began more than twenty years ago when I was a comparatively young man with my way to make in the world of research. I was working then under a very well-known scientist – he is deceased, but I still need not give his name – and one day he got to know that some research team in the UK, working in the same field as we were ourselves, was near a breakthrough, in much the same way as I learnt when I was at a conference in America early this year that Dr Subbiah's work on ACE-i was possibly in danger of being forestalled. We needed, in those distant days, only some two or three months to complete our field trials. But it began to look as if we would not get half that grace. So my chief proposed to me, under an oath of secrecy, that I should supply him with the figures required.'

He sighed and ran his hand along the top edge of the rat run beside him.

'Oh, he wrapped it up very prettily, my chief. After all, he said, we know the figures are going to be there as soon as our last results come in, so there is no grave harm in a little anticipation, is there, Phaterpaker? What could I do, even if I was not certain those figures would prove to be there? Well, I could have done what that gutless fool Mahipal did with me just a month ago. I could have backed down and quit my post. I was half inclined to do so. I even felt, if you will believe me, a certain sense of guilt. Guilt that a fellow scientist, and one then much further advanced on the ladder of achievement than myself, should be contemplating falsifying figures. That might have been enough to make me simply back away. Or – and, Inspector, I very seriously considered this at the time -- I could have denounced my chief. I could have done. But I was alto- gether bewildered. If I was going to make public his wholly unjustifiable request to me, how should I go about it? How should I proceed? There was no laid- down path. Nor is there now.'

Slowly the slipped-down spectacles were pushed back up.

'And then, too, I balked at throwing away a career that till then had been, though I say it, full of promise. So in the end, well, I simply provided the figures I had been asked for and kept silent. And we beat the British team to it.'

'And that is your full explanation, sir?'

Professor Phaterpaker produced a bitter smile.

'No, Inspector. No, it is not. You see, I saw then that the principles I had held, the principles I had been brought up to hold ever since I took any interest in science, were not as sacrosanct as I had thought. And after I had obtained, largely as a result of the success we had then achieved, a grant for some research of my own, when the occasion arose I did not hesitate to omit, for instance, the two results in ten that contradicted the hypothesis I was working on. And before long I learnt, all too easily, to go that one step further and take only the two results in ten that confirmed a theory.'

He looked up.

'If a snake is mistaken for a rope, great danger attaches to him who catches it. Isn't that what they say, Inspector?'

Ghote did not think that was a question requiring an answer.

'Sir,' he said, 'are you attempting to say that you have done nothing that many scientists in your position have not already done? Are not also doing today?'

'No, Inspector,' Professor Phaterpaker said, humbly enough. 'No. I wish in a way that were so. I wish I could think I have been doing nothing that almost every researcher does. But I know that is not the case. Oh, I dare say, here and there in the world there are men who have indulged in malpractice as consistently as I have come to do. I am sure, too, there are more of us who have at one time or another fudged a result, out of ambition, out of vanity, out of even mere carelessness.

212

Or out of vindictiveness towards a researcher who has challenged them, or from the mere desire to speed things up. I am sure there are more of us who have sometimes erred than there are those who have never in any way done so. But that is as far as I will go.'

Ghote thought for a little.

'Yet,' he said at last, 'the fact is remaining that for many years you have been producing results that are all the time flawed.'

'Not quite all the time, Inspector. Grant me so much. I am a scientist, you know, I am capable of following scientific methods. I have not always needed to massage my facts.'

'But of those many hundred papers you were telling you had contributed to worldwide journals most were achieved by false means. Yes or no?'

'I— I would not like to say how many, one way or another.'

He produced again his bitter little smile.

'One forgets, Inspector, how often it was necessary to improve things. Yes, forgets. The man who was secretly horrified when he was first requested to produce imaginary figures forgets now when and where he has done the same thing himself. But you know why I produced so much work? Why I had to? Why I sent paper after paper to the most obscure journals in the most obscure places in the world? It was so that I would not be found out. They gave me screens to hide behind. It is as simple as that.'

He turned away from the still scurrying rats, to

which he had addressed most of his long defence, and looked Ghote full in the face.

'Well? And what are you going to do about me now?'

'Sir, it is not so much a question of what I would do. It is a question of what Chandra Chagoo was doing.'

'Well, yes, I suppose it is. Inspector, I begin to admire your way of keeping and keeping to the point. You ought, after all, perhaps to have been the scientist that I feared you might be, coming in order to investigate my work, the first time I saw you.'

Ghote would have liked to have stored away that piece of flattery. He refused to let himself think about it.

'Sir, I was asking and demanding, and I ask again now. Had Chandra Chagoo come to know that you were for so long a cheat and a liar?'

Professor Phaterpaker took the harsh question like an exhausted swimmer facing the last overwhelming breaker.

'Yes,' he answered at last.

'He knew? He was confronting you also?'

'He was, Inspector. In his altogether cruder way, he too was confronting me, if only with the heaviest of hints.'

'And so . . . so did you take recourse to the one measure left for you?'

Another pause.

'No, Inspector. No, I did not.'

'No? You can prove same? I am telling you: you will need and need to.'

'Well, I do not know that I can wholly prove it. But I can at least tell you what happened.'

'Then tell.'

'For some time I had been aware, as it happened, of the thefts from this very basement, from those refrigerated cabinets out there, of supplies of Dr Subbiah's ACE-i. And it was apparent to me that one person only could have been responsible. Chagoo. However, I lacked any real proof, and in any case I was reluctant to give the fellow his marching orders. He was such a skilful handler of the Russell's vipers, whose venom Dr Subbiah needed in considerable quantities in order to complete her research, research that was going to add enormously to the renown of this Institute. So I was waiting to deal with Chagoo at least until Dr Subbiah's paper was completed.'

'Yes, sir?'

'Well, it was quite simple, you see. Chagoo had, as they say in the thriller films, something on me. And I had something on Chagoo. We had a showdown. In this very room as a matter of fact, late one night. And eventually we agreed to a truce.'

'A truce?'

Thoughts came and went in Ghote's head. Upheavals, reversals.

'So what are you telling,' he said slowly at last, 'is that you had no need at all to kill the fellow, yes?'

'Precisely, Inspector. No need whatsoever.'

Chapter Sixteen

So was it now two only, Ghote asked himself as he left Professor Phaterpaker still looking down at the scurrying rats. Was it now just only Dr Mahipal and Gauri Subbiah?

If what Professor Phaterpaker had said was true, then he had had no reason to kill Chagoo. And, thinking back to his first interview with the Director, certain oddities of his might well have been due to his secret knowledge that Chandra Chagoo had indeed stolen the ACE-i specimens. He had seemed very much put out when the thefts had first been mentioned. His spectacles had slid sharply down a suddenly sweat-slippery nose – that had been the first time his trick of pushing them back up had struck him – and he had snapped out an aggressive question of his own before launching into a long defence of the work of his institute. Then, even more significantly, at the suggestion that a Class Four employee was likely to be responsible for the thefts he had sat in silence for so long that he himself had been on the point of repeating the question he had asked.

Surely Phaterpaker must have been wondering then whether his arrangement with Chagoo was going to come to light. But if at some time during the night before he had left Chagoo to be killed by the Russell's viper, he would not have needed to be anxious.

So, yes, Ghote was almost certain now that Professor Phaterpaker, whatever crime against science he had committed, had not been responsible for Chagoo's death.

But then, too, it was highly doubtful if Dr Mahipal was guilty. Too weak. Too weak altogether. There was evidence enough to show him equally as blameless in this as Professor Phaterpaker. The simple fact was that Dr Mahipal would have paid any blackmail Chagoo demanded, if the fellow had actually hit on his lie about his Scheduled Castes origin. Yes, paid and paid.

Which left Gauri Subbiah.

Who had admitted she much disliked the snake-handler, but had claimed she did not hate him. Nor did it seem she had reason to hate him, reason to kill him. Yet . . . Yet there were tiny unexplained, half-explained things about her that might still mean she did have some strong reason to end Chagoo's life. And that was something she, far more than either of the other two, could have done in the way it had been done. A snake did not put any fear into her. She would not have hesitated to watch the angry Russell's viper slither out of its cage before leaving it to do its work. Or had she even held the creature while it sent the venom through its tooth into Chagoo's unconscious body? It was possible. That way his death might never have been classed as murder.

So what to do next? Who to question? Only one answer.

But, no. Number One priority, after all, was to get Chagoo's tall stool scientifically examined. On one of its legs there might still even be the fingerprints of whoever had swung it up and broken the snake cage's glass. All right, fingerprints on that would not be clinching evidence. All three suspects had good reasons to have been in the Reptile Room at various times. They could, if challenged, produce at least some excuse or another for having taken hold of the stool. Reasons perhaps not very likely, but in the hands of a sharp Defence pleader, when the case came to the courts, they could be made to look plausible enough. But nevertheless the prints of one of those three on that stool's legs would confirm in his own mind what exactly had happened.

Should he set about straight away obtaining specimen prints from each of the three possibles? It would be easy enough to do. Arrange somehow to offer a cold drink, and make sure the outside of the glass had been scrupulously cleaned first. Most likely Gauri Subbiah would hold a glass delicately between two fingers and pour the drink – a Limca? A Fanta? – into her mouth without letting the glass touch her lips. Coming from the more hidebound South, she would have been brought up to think about the ritual purity of any vessel she drank from, whatever her nowadays scientific view. But even so, the clear print of a forefinger and a thumb should be enough to match whatever there might prove to be on the stool. Or Professor Phaterpaker, and Dr Mahipal as well, could be asked on some pretext or other to look at a photograph, equally wiped free of any other prints beforehand.

But what if the prints on the stool leg turned out to be too smudged to be identifiable? Or if there were none on it at all?

That brought about a sudden spiralling descent to reality. The reality long fought away. The fact that the only truly possible candidate as Chagoo's murderer now was Gauri Subbiah.

He ought, a low inner feeling told him, to go back to her this minute. To press her with new, sharper, more penetrating questions.

But what could those be? Surely he had asked everything there was to ask?

No, damn it, he would leave it for a little. There were other things he had to do. He could . . . He could . . . He could go down to Headquarters himself with that stool. It was a hundred per cent urgent matter to get it to the fingerprintwallas. And it was altogether best to give such urgent instructions personally. Otherwise mistakes could be made.

Yes, clear enough. Bounden duty to go down to Headquarters now itself.

But, an hour or so later, coming away from giving his careful instructions about just what to look for on the stool – 'And examine the top also, not for prints but for some scratches that could have been made in smashing one glasspane' – he almost bumped into Inspector Adik crossing the compound.

Stocky, round-faced but unsmiling, business-like in the very way he walked.

'Hah, Ghote.'

'Inspector. How is it going?'

He did not mean to refer to Nicky D'Costa in particular. Just to make a general enquiry, not expecting much of an answer.

'You have not heard, Inspector?'

At once he knew that what he had not heard was for certain something about Nicky D'Costa.

'No. No. What it is?'

'Your D'Costa girl. Found this morning. Out at Worli Seaface. On the beach there. Throat cut. Throat cut, in the end.'

He knew what was implied by that *in the end*. But he was not going to ask for details.

For a moment he let his mind dwell on the girl as he had last seen her at Sahar Airport. Pretty face blotchy with tears. Air stewardess sari still, despite her distress, bright and smart. And in her widening eyes the tiny beginnings of relief that prison might after all be avoided.

But he thrust the inner picture into blankness. Pity you never could afford.

But rage you could.

'How the hell did it happen, Inspector?' he burst out. 'How the hell did you let it happen?'

Adik gave a shrug of his slightly too fat shoulders.

'Stupid girl trying to find out too much when she was sleeping with Abdul Khan,' he said. 'Something like that. I had told her she was not doing enough. I had had not one good word out of her.'

220

'But— But, Inspector, you had just only begun to run her. Two days only.'

'And you, Inspector, how long had you been running her? And what had you got out of her? Damn all. You can go softly-softly only so far. Girl like that will take you for one hell of a ride if she is let. I was telling her. Twenty-four hours, and, unless I am hearing something hard about your Abdul Khan and what it is he is now planning, it is one damn charge-sheet for you.'

'But, damn it, man, don't you know what sort of a badmash is Abdul Kahn? Give him one hint only he is betrayed, and he will strangle with bare hands itself. How could you risk such?'

Adik shrugged again.

'How could you, Inspector?' Ghote shouted at him. 'How could you? I am asking. Asking.'

Adik looked him straight in the eye.

'Questions, questions,' he said. 'By now you should have learnt, Ghote, there are some questions that do no damn good. No damn good whatsoever.'

Ghote wanted to hit him.

But, luckily for his whole career, other thoughts intervened. How would it help to strike a fellow officer? Would it alter Adik one jot even? Would it make him a different man?

He turned on his heel and marched out into DN Road, stood there on the broad pavement looking sightlessly across at the frontage of the huge Crawford Market building, at, high up near its roof, the stone carving of ryots groaningly at their ploughs.

The father of Rudyard Kipling. He had carved them.

His own father had told him that the first time he had
ever visited Bombay.

Abruptly he wheeled round and re-entered the
compound, went straight over to the winding stone stair
to the Assistant Commissioner's cabin. Up at a sharp
trot. Just one moment to peer through the square little
window in the cabin door to make sure the great man
did not have anybody with him.

No one.

He knocked.

'Come.'

He went in, stamped across to the wide sweeping
desk with its variously coloured telephones, its ornate
inkwells holder, its piled papers under their heavy little
paperweights.

'Ghote? Yes, what is it, man?'

'Sir, I am just learning the air stewardess, Nicky
D'Costa, has been found with her throat cut, signs of
torture also.'

'Yes. That's quite right. Our friend Abdul Khan
doesn't hesitate when he thinks someone has been
asking too many questions, whether in his bed or out
of it.'

'Then you are certain her death was Khan's work,
sir?'

'His work? No doubt about it, Inspector.'

'Then, sir, are we this time pulling him in? This time
he has gone too far?'

The Assistant Commissioner shook his head. Even
produced a tight, angry little smile.

'No, Inspector. We are not at all pulling him in.'

'Not, sir? Not? But why it is? Why? Why? Why?'

'Inspector, I can understand your feelings. The girl D'Costa was your discovery, and it was a pity she had to be put into other hands. But I must remind you: you do not bombard a senior officer with questions. Understood?'

For a long moment Ghote could not bring himself to answer. He wanted to demand when was the right time to question a senior, if it was not now, when a woman under police care had lost her life in abominable circumstances. But at last he took a deep breath and provided the answer expected of him.

'Understood. Sir.'

'Very well, Inspector. Now let me tell you why we cannot pull in Abdul Khan for this. For one simple and good reason. Khan was at the time of the girl's death a patient in hospital. A sick man, Inspector. Oh, I've no doubt he ordered the killing, ordered the brutal way it should be done. We know enough about him to be sure of that. But the fact remains that for the time of the girl's actual death Khan has a cast-iron alibi. Senior doctors. Men at the top of their profession. Men whose word cannot be questioned.'

'Sir, is there nothing that can be done?'

'No, there's nothing. Oh, I know Khan has pulled this trick before. He has been in one hospital or another on two or three occasions when someone who's crossed his path has been dealt with. But when he goes in he makes sure there is no question of anyone being able to prove he was anywhere but in his ward. Private room. Paid for to the last rupee. He leaves the goondas who do his dirty work to fend for themselves. They will be well outside Bombay by now. Out of India even, in some dhow making for the Gulf. Khan's money. No, Inspector, I'm afraid this is one we must just grin and bear.'

Grin and bear? Grin and bear?

There were memos in his in-tray when he went down to his own cabin which he knew he ought to do something about. But he did nothing. As he had glanced at them, picking each one out of the tray, he had hardly been able to take in their contents. All he could do was to boil and ferment inwardly with undissipated rage. Grin and bear?

How could a man like Abdul Khan be allowed to get away with murder? Murder of the most atrocious kind? How could he, when someone who had done no more than take the life of a vicious blackmailer like Chandra Chagoo was almost certain to be nabbed for the crime? Was almost certain to be taken one Thursday to Thana Gaol and there be hanged by the neck until she was dead? While Khan sat there . . . or, no, lay there, lay on his hospital bed, a faker, kicking up his legs and laughing.

And, damn it, while firing his forbidden questions at the Assistant Commissioner, he had not even managed to ask which hospital it was that Khan was in. Not that it mattered. At any of Bombay's big hospitals Khan could buy a private room, produce some symptoms to satisfy the doctors he paid huge fees to, and stay there with a hundred per cent alibi. And in the meanwhile his goondas would be exacting terrible retribution on wretched Nicky D'Costa for doing no more than having tried to discover his next move. Nor would any amount of inquiries, even if he was allowed to make them, break that expensively bought alibi.

He sat with his head in his hands.

The words the Commissioner himself had spoken to him that first time he had sat in the big car and had been given orders to go to the Mira Behn Institute came back again and again into his head. *No, frankly, Inspector, it'll take a better man than you to put paid to Abdul Khan.* He almost heard a chorus of Bombay's squawking crows contributing a harshly derisive comment.

No, Abdul Khan was not for him. The Commissioner was right. A man as powerful as that was not going to be caught by a simple inspector. It would need, if ever that evil career was to be ended, the creation of a special cell of top-class dedicated officers given unlimited resources. Or – he uttered a choked laugh into his shrouding hands – some damn hero of a hundred films punching his way through a dozen goondas at a time, defying death till at last the super-best villain was burnt to a cinder in his own huge house overlooking the damn sea.

The wild thought cheered him a little.

He sat up and began to think what he had to do in the case that he had been given. His duty, however little he liked it.

Yes, there should have been time enough now for the fingerprintwallas to have seen if there were prints on the legs of that stool he had wrapped up so carefully and carried away. Then, if there were, and if they were clear enough to be matched, it would be a question of getting hold of samples from all three of them there in the Mira Behn that night. From all three.

After all, it might be – surely it might be – that the matching prints would not be the set he now had come almost beyond doubt to expect. And dread.

He pushed himself to his feet, went out, and made his way slowly across the dusty compound. He could not bring himself to hurry. What if Chagoo's tall stool was the final stone in the edifice of proof that he had, against all his inclinations, been building up?

Once more he saw it in his mind's eye. Seized by one leg, swung high, brought down first on to the unsuspecting Chagoo's head to keep him quiet. Then with equal force crashed into the Russell's viper's cage. But had it really been Gauri Subbiah who had seized it? Had used it?

'Helloji, Inspector,' Sergeant Nensi, fingerprint expert, greeted him.

'Hello, Sergeant. You are sounding damn cheerful. Were you finding . . .?'

He came to a halt. Unable to complete his question.

'I will tell what I was finding, Inspector. Clear as clear.'

'Yes?' It was a croak, but at least it was a request.

'Damn all, Inspector. Not too much of troubles to find that.'

Loud laughter.

'You are sure? There was nothing? Nothing at all to

show that stool had been picked up by a leg? Or by two legs together?'

'Nothing, Inspector. Less than nothing even. There was one damn good thin layer of dust over all.'

'But— But what about the top? There was a scratch there. I saw same with just only my naked eye. Some blood also.'

'Oh, yes. I have had time to look for those itself. Not my duty strictly, you are knowing. But for you, Ghote bhai, I will do it.'

'And . . .?'

'And that scratch was never made by glass. By something metal. I would say a key, unless I was giving witness-box evidence. And it was made some time ago also. One month, two.'

'But that small bloodstain? What about that?'

'Oil. No need for test even.'

'You are certain? And certain about no prints on the legs?'

'Yes, Inspector. You were wanting to prove this stool was used to break a glass pane somewhere, yes? Well, you cannot do it. I cannot do it. No one can do it. That is that.'

Chapter Seventeen

Ghote knew there was still time to go back to the Mira Behn Institute and question Gauri Subbiah. He was almost bound to find her still at work. But he simply did not have the heart to set out.

He decided abruptly then not to go and sit at his desk but to call it a day. Gauri Subbiah, whether or not she had Chandra Chagoo's death on her conscience, was not going to abscond. She was waiting for the verdict of those referees in France, however sure she was it would be in her favour. Whatever happened she would stay to hear that. So he might as well go home. Go home and try to beat down the fear washing through him that she was not what he had believed her to be. The pure scientist. Go home and try to suppress the black thoughts of the futility of things lurking in the depths of his mind. What if there was in the world nothing certain to hope in?

So it was earlier than usual when he settled himself in his chair as Protima once again began to press his feet. He ought, he knew, to start in his customary way telling her about his day before asking about hers. But he could not bring himself to relate what had happened.

To sit up straighter and tell her that Nicky D'Costa had been mutilated and murdered.

When at last Protima asked, in a not very demanding way 'What you were doing today?' he could do no better than respond with a show of abstracted silence. Eventually she began telling him about her day, and he contrived at least to show enough interest to encourage her to go on talking.

But, he kept thinking, sooner or later I must bring it all out. Nicky D'Costa. Abdul Khan. Inspector Adik. The Assistant Commissioner.

At last Protima ran out of the mild gossip of the neighbourhood.

'And you?' she enquired, a little more pointedly.

Was this the moment?

No, he could not do it. Not yet.

'But Ved?' he asked, with last second inspiration. 'What did he say he would do today?'

'Oh, he will tell me nothing. I was asking and asking, but he would say nothing.'

'Yes, yes,' he said, feeling at last able to produce more than monosyllables. 'But you must remember. Each time you are asking it is making a boy like Ved, a boy like any of his age, determined not to be telling. You should try to—'

He was going to add, almost viciously, *hold your tongue*. But then he remembered with a dart of shame how, the evening before, Protima had totally checked in herself the questions it was against her nature not to ask.

So, to make up for what he had almost said, he began

to leak out at last a brief, censored version of what had happened. Then, little by little, he found himself telling her more and more. Till at last he repeated to her almost word for word his outburst to Inspector Adik.

Finally he brought out what he had dared to say to the Assistant Commissioner. His repeated and repeated question *Why?* And the full stop answer he had had.

Protima had jumped up from her kneeling position in front of him as soon as he had produced his guarded version of what had happened to Nicky D'Costa, leaving his left foot much less relieved of tension than his right.

'But why did you not go on asking?' she snapped out now. 'Why were you falling so pin-drop silent? Why were you not saying, despite all Assistant Commissioner sahib was telling, Abdul Khan must be arrested today even? Why were you not insisting and insisting?'

'But the Assistant Commissioner . . .'

'Assistant Commissioner-missioner. Evil is evil. Justice is justice. Why were you not saying and stating this?'

'But—'

'No, you were not asking enough. You should have asked and asked until he had told whatsoever he knew about Abdul Khan. What hospital he is in? Were you asking even that? Where was he just before he was saying he was sick? Which doctor was admitting him in? What were the symptoms he was saying he was having?'

Now this battering, as unexpected as it was, sent a spurt of fury shooting up in him. What had happened

230

to his wife in twenty thousand? The wife who marvellously knew when not to ask questions?

Why had he told one single thing to this woman? Bound to unloose all this hammer-jammering of asking-this, asking-that. What business of hers was it what he had done or not done? And what business of his or hers was Abdul Khan? He had been taken off the Nicky D'Costa case, yes? Then why was she daring to question about same?

'Listen to me,' he shouted out. 'Listen only. What is Abdul Khan to me, now I have been ordered not to spend any of time about that man? If you are wanting to make complaint, why are you not going to Inspector Adik? Why are you not going yourself to ACP and asking him these Abdul Khan questions? What he is doing? Whether Khan is in JJ Hospital? Or Breach Candy? Or somehow in Cama and Allbless? Or in St George's Hospital itself, British businessmen to left and right? No, I am telling you, it is the murder of one Chandra Chagoo, snake-handler, that is my duty to ask and ask about. That, and that only.'

But he ought to have known no amount of shouting and question flourishing would silence his wife.

'Yes,' she came whirling back, eyes flashing, nostrils taut. 'Yes, and what it is you are doing in that case itself? Days are passing and you are finding out nothing only. Why you are here now, shoes off and socks also, when case is not brought to end? Why it is you have just now altogether forgotten what is your duty?'

'But— But—'

'Why? Why, I am asking.'

'Oh, it is easy to say *Why are you not questioning and pestering?* But I tell you I have asked each and every question there is to be asked at that place. I have asked and asked and asked.'

But, even as he reached that last voice-raised *asked*, he was icily conscious that there was a whole series of questions he had not asked. The questions he ought to have put to Gauri Subbiah. But how to explain to Protima, especially when she was in this flags-flying, shooting-hooting mood, the hopes he had invested in the girl? How to tell her that somehow Gauri Subbiah had come to stand for all he had ever believed about the power of science to overcome the difficulties of the world? How to say that, to him, scientists had been like gods, far above human littlenesses? That in a world he knew to be blackly full of murderers, cheats, liars, thieves – none knew that better than a CIDwalla – he had seen Dr Gauri Subbiah, serious and successful researcher, as being almost a single pure white exception? His symbol of hope?

But something of the faltering he had felt as he had come to the end of his *asked and asked and asked* and had fallen silent must have told Protima she still had the advantage.

In her present mood it was not something she was going to abandon.

'Oh, so you have asked, is it?' she came storming back. 'What it is you have asked? How can it be you have come home so early? There must be questions and questions and questions you have not put.'

'But I have. I have. Damn Commissioner himself

was saying to me I must ask questions. As if that is not what a good detective is always doing. And now you are saying also. But I tell you I have asked. I have asked and asked. I have asked Professor Phaterpaker himself, Director only of the whole damn Mira Behn Institute, I asked him such questions he was at last telling me he has all his life been making false statements in his work, eight–nine hundred science papers and each one lies only. I have asked one Dr Mahipal how it was that, when his father is a brahmin cook, he himself was acting and pretending to be a harijan to gain his seat at medical college. I have asked even the chowkidar at that place at what times he is sleeping, when he is waking, so that I am certain-certain no one could have come into that house when Chandra Chagoo was left to be poisoned by a hundred per cent dangerous snake. I have asked that full-scale lazy idiot Inspector Baitonde, Sewri PS, to check and check no one from Peerbhoy Hospital inside that same compound was coming over to Mira Behn Institute. I have asked—'

But now at last Protima broke into the long, self-justifying tirade.

'What? You were relying and relying on an officer you have called lazy to make be sure no one was coming from Peerbhoy Hospital into your Mira Behn Institute? How could you let that go? What were you asking Baitonde that you were so certain he was not shirking in his duty?'

'I was asking enough. Every bit of enough. I tell you, I am damn sure I am right for once to give Baitonde a clean chit when he is saying no one could have got past Peerbhoy night-securitywalla. How should you know what it is right to be asking a fellow police officer? How do you know what is a detective's work? Do you? Do you? Yes or no? Yes, is it? Or no?'

'It is not needing any detective to know when somebody is not doing their bounden duty. It is needing only a wife to find her husband sitting and sitting taking rest at home when he should be out asking and asking.'

'Oh, yes? And you are so clever then? Well, tell me one question I should have asked and have not. One only.'

But Protima had an answer. And one that gave him a thoroughly unpleasant jolt.

'Yes. What about that researcher-smircher? Name I am forgetting-forgetting. You are not at all telling one thing you have asked her. What bad things she has told you she has committed? Have you asked even?'

'She is Gauri Subbiah. Dr Gauri Subbiah. Doctor. Biochemist. And, yes, I have questioned also. I am knowing my duty. And she has not told me of any *bad things* she was doing. Because, I am willing to swear, she has not done one bad thing in her life. Only she has worked and worked, probed and probed like the best scientist in the world. And she has discovered a hundred per cent fine cure for the hypertensions that are the downfall and bugbear of the West. It will bring into India lakhs and crores of dollars and deutschmarks, French francs, even English sterling pounds. She has used so much of Russell's viper venom for her researches she has drained almost dry every snake the Mira Behn Institute is having. Only with one excep—'

Then coming in from a far distance – he thought afterwards like one of Abhimanyu's deadly arrows in the Mahabharata tale he had heard so often as a child – a doubt penetrated his mind. How was it that, in the register of venom requisitions he had idly glanced at just before they had found Chandra Chagoo dead, there had been a tremendous number of requests under the name of *Dr Subb* in August? In August, after Independence Day, the date Professor Phaterpaker had sent off her famous paper to Paris?

Why had she needed Russell's viper venom then, and in those large quantities, after her paper had been faxed to France?

Yes, there was one question at least he had not asked Gauri Subbiah. So those faint niggles of doubt he had felt about her were, after all, there with reason. And, more, in what she had told him up to now there had been tiny flaws – he recognized it now – little things skipped over. And there should not have been.

He took a deep, deep breath.

'Yes,' he said to Protima, 'you are right. I did not ask enough of questions when before I was talking with Dr Gauri Subbiah.'

Chapter Eighteen

Next morning Ghote, waking after the dream-plagued night that had followed the turmoil of his confrontation with his wife, found one extra task he could persuade himself had to be done before he put his questions to Gauri Subbiah. There had been more than one sore point Protima had put her finger on in the course of her outburst, a finger that had found exactly the places in his flesh causing him most to wince. She had not only picked on his failure to question Gauri Subbiah to as much effect as he had questioned his two other suspects. She had sharply queried his accepting as fact what Inspector Baitonde had found out from the night-security man at the Peerbhoy Hospital.

All right, he still thought it most likely that Baitonde was too cunning in his laziness not to have carried out inquiries easily checked on. But – he had decided at some wakeful moment of the night – before at last coming face to face with Gauri Subbiah he ought to make doubly sure it was truly impossible that some jackal acquaintance of Chagoo's had not crept in the dark from the Peerbhoy over to the Mira Behn.

So he set off from home when it was still hardly

daylight with the object of examining the Peerbhoy compound before getting hold of the night-securitywalla,
Damodar Singh, while he was still on duty.

'No, no, I am not able to have time for eating,' he
had barked at Protima. 'Give those pooris you are mixing
to Ved only. He will eat double all you cook and not be
noticing. I have urgent work.'

She had not uttered then so much as a word of
concerned protest. To his fury. His wife in twenty
thousand.

So at an even earlier hour than he had first rung at
the Mira Behn bell, back when he had thought his task
was to do no more than trace stolen samples of ACE-i,
he rang at it again. He had only to wait a minute in the
misty dawn air – the sparrows were hopping about in
the dust of the road but the crows had not yet begun
their day-long arguments – before the door of the house
opened and Laloo emerged, shaking sleep from his
head.

'Oh, Inspectorji, it is you, good morning, good morning,' he called out, beginning to produce his customary
wide grin. 'You are very much early bird.'

But, all too aware of what must face him at the
Institute later, it was altogether beyond Ghote to match
such cheerfulness.

'Yes,' he said snappily. 'A police officer has work
always. Open gate.'

Laloo, preserving the remains of his smile, hurried
to obey.

'But who it is you are wanting to see, Inspectorji?'

he said, inquisitiveness glinting in his eyes. 'No one is here so early. Even Directorji is sleeping-sleeping now.'

'I am not wanting to enter house,' Ghote answered brusquely. 'All I am wanting is to go into garden.'

He saw the beginnings of yet busier curiosity in every feature of Laloo's face. And stamped on them.

'You may go back inside.'

Laloo, actually looking chastened, made his way back in. As soon as the big door had completely closed Ghote set off on his mission.

What I must do, he thought, is go slowly towards the hospital keeping my eyes damn well peeled. A clue may be anywhere there. Under a bush. On whatsoever path there is. Anywhere. Some footprints. Some fibres. One clue that some badmash on hospital staff escaped the vigilance of that Damodar Singh fellow.

It was perhaps a quarter of a mile to the hospital at the far end of the compound. Once past the well-kept lawns and beds of the Institute's garden, the ground was dotted with low-growing, untended bushes and thick with tall matted clumps of grass.

One damn good place to keep under cover, he said to himself. If anyone in the hospital was succeeding to get past Damodar Singh, despite what Baitonde was believing, then they would not have too much of difficulty in creeping to Institute. And getting in also by that window the mali is using when he is wanting water for his plants.

There may be some clue still to show some person was recently passing this way. After all, nobody has any right to go from the hospital to the Institute, even in full daylight. So, if such an intruder was wearing a lunghi or any other trailing garment, he might have caught same on some thorn bush. Have left a fresh coloured thread hanging.

He went slowly on, eyes down.

The mist among the bushes and tall grass was thicker than it had been out in the road. He felt he had to give his task maximum alertness.

But when at last his slow progress brought him to within reach of the towering hospital building, he had still spotted nothing. With a sigh of frustration he took in the row of wide windows in the private patients' wing, the even longer rows going up and up of smaller, almost prison-narrow, windows in the main block.

Unless Damodar Singh turned out not to be the vigilant fellow Baitonde has painted him as, then there was nothing now between him and the moment he had to begin questioning Gauri Subbiah.

A stinging crack split across his shoulders.

He tumbled forward, footing completely lost. His face plunged into a tangle of wet grass, nose squashed into the earth. His left knee jarred fiercely with the force of his fall. The sudden pain across his shoulders began to throb with rapidly growing intensity.

What— What has happened? he thought.

Then he felt the knuckles of a hand scraping down the back of his neck, as his shirt collar was grabbed, and he was hauled, a limp rag, to his feet again.

'So what are you creeping and crawling here?'

The voice was loud, and ringing with crude contempt.

He contrived to turn round a little way despite the grip on his collar, and saw an enormous Sikh bursting out of a khaki uniform, blue turban on his head, black beard bristling with ferocity, a thick lathi grasped in his free hand.

Shock beginning to fade, he realized who this must be.

'You are Peerbhoy night-security man? Damodar Singh, yes?' he choked out against the tight-pulled collar of his shirt.

'You are damn gatecrashwalla,' the Sikh proclaimed by way of reply.

'No. No. I am Inspector Ghote, Crime Branch. Here on duty.'

'And I am Asha Rani herself.'

A great guffaw of a laugh. Spit showered down the side of Ghote's face.

'No, listen, you fool. I am here—'

But to call this enormous hulk a fool to his face was a bad mistake.

Ghote found himself lifted into the air by his shirt and shaken like a rat.

'No, no,' he gasped at last. 'I truly am Inspector of Police. Coming to talk with you itself.'

'No. Not at all. No.'

'But, yes. Yes. I am just only what I say I am, Inspector Ghote, Crime Branch.'

'No. Police inspector has uniform. Everybody knowing.'

'But, you idi— No, listen. Have you never heard of a CID plain clothes officer?'

'Plain clothes creeping crawling? Why you not coming to hospital entrance, TJ Road? Four times liar.'

God, would he never get this stupid giant to understand?

'Listen, I am investigating murder of the snake-handler at Mira Behn Institute. I was coming this way to check only if killer came by night from hospital.'

'Talking nonsense. No one leaving hospital by night. All doors locked. Damodar Singh on patrol.'

'But— But that is what I was coming here to prove. If any person could have gone over by night to the Institute itself.'

'No. I am saying. Doors locked. Myself patrol-patrolling.'

'Good. Good. I am glad to hear. Now, let me go, and I will show you my identification.'

'No. Damn gatecrashwalla.'

For God's sake, back to where we started.

He tried again.

'Listen, did one Inspector Baitonde, full uniform, come the day before yesterday to ask you if anyone could have left the hospital in the night? Yes or no?'

'No one can leave. Damodar Singh on patrol.'

Having a numbskull fellow like this as night-securitywalla, Ghote thought, must be as good as having damn mines sown round whole place. And just as lacking in brains. Give him some orders, or plant mines in the ground, and they would be there till someone in authority came and lifted them.

241

He took a deep breath, still feeling Damodar Singh's horny knuckles digging into his neck.

'Inspector Baitonde?' he asked again, wearily. 'Did he come to see you? The day before yesterday? In the morning?'

'Ah, that inspector. Pukka uniform. Good friend, liking damn good drink.'

'Right. Well, if we went now into the hospital, you could telephone Inspector Baitonde at Sewri Police Station and he will tell you I am who I say I am.'

Damodar Singh's grasp on his collar had become loose enough now for his bushy-bearded face to be clearly seen. Ghote watched, with what patience he could summon up, as what he had said gradually sank in.

'I will take inside,' the giant responded at last.

'Good, good. In five–ten minutes all this will be cleared up. So, now you can let go of me.'

'Damn gatecrashwalla.'

And the grip on his shirt collar tightened fiercely as ever.

It was very much more than five or ten minutes before the whole absurd misunderstanding was cleared up. First Ghote was manhandled right the way round the big hospital building, past various blankly closed doors, to its front entrance. Then, when he had been unceremoniously pushed up the steps and inside, it became apparent that using a telephone was not one of Damodar Singh's skills. In the end it was Ghote himself, feeling much too bedraggled for his claim to be a police inspector to seem likely, who, after some explaining, persuaded the night-duty clerk at the reception desk to put a call through to Sewri Police Station and ask for Inspector Baitonde.

Who was not, of course, there at this still early hour.

A long wait then.

Sitting on the bench where Damodar Singh had all but flung him, Ghote eventually began to think about things beyond his present ridiculous and miserable situation.

Well, at least, he said to himself, the way I was caught by this idiot Sikh well and truly confirms what Baitonde told me about impossibility of anyone on hospital staff getting over to the Mira Behn. And, from what that fellow at the desk was just now saying also, it is clear at night each and every door in the hospital is properly locked.

He rubbed at his neck, still smarting from Damodar Singh's digging knuckles.

Nothing to be done about the weal on his back where the Sikh's lathi had descended. A bruise there that would last for days, even if wifely hands could be persuaded to paste it with turmeric.

Then the full implications of what had been passing through his mind struck him. It was back now, without the least, last possibility of escape, to the situation as it had been before. Three people only, besides laughing Laloo, had been inside the Mira Behn Institute when the Russell's viper had been freed to send the poison from its channelled fang into Chagoo's helpless body.

Professor Phaterpaker. Dr Mahipal. Gauri Subbiah. And, of those, Professor Phaterpaker had shown convincingly that he had dealt with Chagoo's attempt at blackmail by blackmailing the man himself. Dr Mahipal had argued, as convincingly, that even if Chagoo had known about his father, the brahmin cook, he himself lacked the will to end anyone's life and would have simply paid whatever Chagoo had demanded of him.

Which left Gauri Subbiah.

And, he thought with a slowly descending sense of mud-black despondency, although he had found nothing that Chagoo might have been blackmailing her over, there were things about her and her work that had to be explained. Signs she had something to hide, some of them only tiny. But not to be wished away.

When, making conversation under the tamarind tree in Sewri Cemetery he had happened to ask her whether she had come there in order to think, his question had plainly disconcerted her. He could see now the little whitish scar across the tip of her nose as it had grown suddenly darker. And she had contradicted and contradicted herself before she had found some meaningless answer.

So what had she really come to the quiet of the cemetery to think about?

Was it about what she had done to Chandra Chagoo?

It might have been. It might have been.

So, when he came to see her next, in a few minutes from now, there was more than one unexplained mystery, such as that discrepancy in the dates of her requisitions of Russell's viper venom, that he would have to explore. With whatever cunning questions he could find.

But time must be passing.

He looked at his watch. Eight o'clock. Baitonde should be in his seat.

Craning round the massive form of Damodar Singh, standing directly in front of him like an unthinking, somehow threatening wall he called out to the clerk at the desk opposite.

'Try Sewri PS once more. Ask if Inspector Baitonde has come.'

The fellow dialled, spoke, listened.

'Too early still, they are saying.'

Damn man. Any decent officer should be on duty by this time.

He looked up at Damodar Singh. But the very sight of that huge bristling beard told him there would be no point in trying to persuade him to do anything till he had spoken with Baitonde.

He let himself relapse into a head-sunken reverie.

The thing was he would have somehow to find out from Gauri Subbiah exactly what Chagoo had known about her which she could not afford to be told to . . .

Well, say to Professor Phaterpaker.

Or to anyone. To Asha Rani, for instance, who had to all intents and purposes given her a huge sum of money in the form of that new equipment from France.

But what could it be that Chagoo might have learnt? And how, even if he could get some idea of that from Gauri Subbiah, could he force the full facts out of her? What could he ask that would produce at last the right answer? Nothing. As soon as he began to get near she would sense it, and, if she really had killed Chagoo, she would avoid saying anything that would give him any idea what the fellow had learnt about her.

He sat on in gloom, trying now not even to think of what he had to do.

And then he saw why he was preventing himself thinking more about the young scientist. It was because he knew, in fact, what was the most likely thing about her that Chagoo must somehow have discovered.

He forced himself to reason it out.

Gauri Subbiah was dedicated to her work, yes. She had, it had been plain, almost no other interests. She had avoided marriage. She stayed in some bare hostel somewhere. She got to work early. She left late.

So, if there was anything she could be blackmailed about, it almost certainly must be to do with that work. With her great discovery.

Now other things that had scratched at the surface of his mind as he had talked with her came back into his consciousness. With sickening force. His innocent question in the cemetery about how long it had taken her to perform the hundred-odd experiments she had needed to make in order to confirm her theory about neutralizing Russell's viper venom. At first she had tried not to answer that at all. Then, realizing perhaps this would draw his attention all the more to whatever it was she wanted to hide, she had produced the vaguest of answers. Very different from that directness she had shown in all his other dealings with her. So, for some reason, she had needed to conceal how long those experiments had taken. And then much the same thing had happened when he had, as innocently, asked her how long it took to put together a scientific paper. Once more she had tried to avoid answering, and when she had done so had been as little clear as could be. Unlike herself in every way.

Then something Professor Phaterpaker had said came back to him. He had mentioned, casually, that when he had been at a conference in America he had heard that a research team there had been ordering Russell's viper venom from a snake-worshipping village in Bengal. Later he had gone to extraordinary lengths to get Gauri Subbiah's rapidly completed paper off to France, not even risking twenty-four hours' delay because of the Independence Day holiday.

There could be one conclusion only. Warned that an American team might get in first with an ACE-i similar to the one Gauri Subbiah had nearly finished experimenting on, she had, in Professor Phaterpaker's words, *cut corners* and submitted her paper before every confirming experiment had been completed.

And, yes, that must be the explanation of why she was still now working as hard as ever. She was making sure that the experiments she had failed to perform before the paper went off did actually show what she had claimed they would. That was why she had made frequent requisitions for venom in that book on its shelf outside the Reptile Room after the paper had been sent to France. Altogether illogically.

The knowledge that had surfaced so suddenly in the middle of his quarrel with Protima, he now admitted to himself, had been there in the depths of his mind since at least the time Gauri Subbiah had spoken to him in Sewri Cemetery. In some half-realized form it had perhaps been there from the moment it had been clear there were only three people who could have brought about Chagoo's death and that Gauri Subbiah was one of them.

But he had refused to let the thought come to the fore. He had not been able to abandon his belief, even after he had exposed Professor Phaterpaker, in the power of the scientist to do good. In the benefits of the ever increasing knowledge scientists' questioning brought.

And, yes, another thing. Admitting a doubt about the one scientist he had seen as absolutely fulfilling this idea would have been to admit, equally, that in police work – the work Gauri Subbiah herself had compared to her own – there could not be any hundred per cent pure detectives. That there were times when questions that should be asked would not be put, would go unanswered for ever.

He jumped up from the bench, careless of what reaction it might bring from Damodar Singh.

'Ring Sewri PS once more,' he called across to the clerk, already beginning to put together his empty nighttime tiffin carrier before going off duty. 'Tell them Damodar Singh must speak urgently to Inspector Baitonde.'

And this time Baitonde, apparently, was there. The clerk beckoned to Damodar Singh and gave him the handset.

ASKING QUESTIONS

There was an absurdly frustrating moment while the huge Sikh tried to speak into the phone's earpiece. Ghote longed to shout out, *Has twelve o'clock struck in your head?*, the old jibe that all Sikhs were simpletons who went mad under the noon sun. But he succeeded in holding himself in.

And, at last, Damodar Singh equally succeeded in reversing the handset and made contact, evidently, with Baitonde.

'You are knowing a fellow by the name of Ghote? Inspector he is lying to say?' he bellowed down the instrument. 'I am finding just now in compound, creep-creeping. I am hold-holding just only here now. He is saying you would say who he is.'

Baitonde's reply was inaudible. But, a long moment after it had come to an end, Damodar Singh ceased clamping the handset to his ear and gave it back to the clerk.

'Baitonde bhai will come,' he announced eventually.

'He is coming? Coming here?' Ghote broke out. 'But did he not tell at once I am who I say I am?'

'He is coming itself.'

And not a word more could the giant Sikh be persuaded to utter.

Chapter Nineteen

Inspector Baitonde took his time in coming. And when he did arrive poured out so many mocking questions – his drooping moustache seeming to ride high in jubilation – that Ghote almost wished he had never come at all.

'Hah, is it after all you itself, Ghote bhai? So, what it is you have been doing? Little bit B and E, is it? Breaking and entering Peerbhoy Hospital, yes?'

'I was just only—'

Ghote stopped himself.

Not the most tactful thing to tell Baitonde he had been checking up on him. Yet what else could he say?

'I was just only making double sure that no one from the staff here could have gone to meet Chandra Chagoo over at the Mira Behn in hours of darkness itself.'

'Oh, no need for all that check-checking, my friend. When Baitonde asks questions he gets right answer each and every time. Or whoever he was asking finds one damn boot up his arse.'

'Well, you certainly got the right answer here,' Ghote felt he had to admit. 'Even if I was finding out same in one hard way only.'

Baitonde gave him a broad, smirking grin.

'So my Sikh friend here was not too gentle, yes?'

'No, Inspector. He was not. So, now will you get it into his head he was altogether wrong to drag me in here? And then I can get on with investigating Chagoo's murder.'

'Oh, Inspector, why are you worrying and purrying about that straw-brain? I tell you, all we are needing is to pull in someone like the chowkidar there, Laloo-baloo whatever is his name, and beat out one damn good confession. Case over.'

'Your view, Inspector. However, I think I have come to know at last who was truly responsible. And I would very much like to go ek dum and question.'

He had expected Baitonde to ask who this was. But he had reckoned without the fellow's lack of interest in every aspect of his work – except perhaps beating up witnesses and extracting bribes.

'So, Ghote bhai, you are wanting release from Damodar Singh here, yes?'

'Yes, Inspector.'

'Well, ask only and I will do it.'

For a moment Ghote considered refusing to bow down to such an absurd and humiliating demand.

But the thought of Gauri Subbiah made him bite the bullet. The sooner the appallingly unpleasant business he had with her was over the better.

'Inspector,' he made himself say, trying to keep the least bitterness out of his voice, 'would you be so good as to explain to Damodar Singh that I am who I told him I was, and that I need to continue my inquiries at once?'

'Sardarji,' Baitonde said to the giant Sikh with elaborate courtesy, 'this is one Inspector Ghote, ace sleuth from Crime Branch itself. I think you should be letting poor fellow go.'

Ghote, unable to contemplate crossing the compound again, scene of the fiasco of his final attempt to produce an alternative to Gauri Subbiah as Chagoo's killer, went back to the Mira Behn Institute by road. It increased the distance he had to walk by a good deal, and the sun was beating down from a now cloudless sky. But at least the longer route added some minutes to the time before he had to confront the young scientist.

He had expected to have to go to her laboratory. But, just as he came in sight of the Institute's ever-locked gate he saw her. She was standing on the opposite side of the road, apparently engaged in a vigorous dispute with the old bonesetter there.

His immediate instinct was to hurry over and intervene. How could that disreputable old man have ensnared her, he asked himself. Was he demanding money? Was he harassing her in some other way?

But, even as he dodged the cars, autorickshaws and goods-crammed little tempos zooming along the clear road, he realized Gauri Subbiah's situation was not what he had thought. Above the noise of the traffic he had just caught the sound of her laughter – had he ever before heard that serious scientist laugh aloud? – and then there was something in the way she was standing, looking down easily at the old man beneath his ancient star-holed umbrella that also made him see he had got things wrong.

Whatever it was, by the time he reached the safety of the far pavement he knew the dispute between two such unlikely contestants was, for all its evident vigour, entirely peaceful.

It was being conducted, he heard as he came nearer, in that mixture of Hindi and Marathi – execrably pronounced by the young Pondicherry incomer – with a liberal sprinkling of words in English that was the all-purpose language of Bombay. But, for all the crudity of the medium of communication, the debate itself was on a surprisingly high level.

'But Bonesetter sahib,' Gauri Subbiah was saying, 'you cannot call what it is you do as science. Must I tell you again? Science is the process of finding out, by asking and asking the right questions, until we have discovered what is causing something to happen. Until we are knowing the why, it is no use trying to put right whatever may be wrong.'

'Madam, not at all,' the aged bonesetter answered, his eyes gleaming with delight at the combat. 'You are making great mistake. Not at all necessary to know what-what is happening inside body. It is enough – it has always been enough for our greatest sages of India – just only to know what will make the wrong once again right.'

'But that is what has been the matter all down the ages in India,' Gauri Subbiah came back. 'Lack of proper scientific method. All this guess-and-see work. All right, sometimes people like you or any Ayurvedic practitioner may succeed in curing a patient. But not always, and until—'

'Madam. No, no. Tell me, is it that the Western doctors, such as yourself and those Mira Behn-Shira Pain fellows just opposite, are effecting cures to one hundred per cent in each and every case?'

Gauri Subbiah blushed. But in a moment she went back into battle.

'Oh, Bonesetter sahib, you really must not rest your arguments on single cases only. Yes, of course, doctors practising Western medicine sometimes lose a patient, even sometimes also because they do not know enough. But all the same it is by proper scientific enquiry' – *scientific enquiry*, the English words stood up like two pointed rocks in the ebb and flow of the restless sea – 'and by scientific enquiry only that we are making our progress.'

'And so much of time you are wasting-wasting with your enquiries this and your enquiries that,' the bonesetter cheerfully replied. 'Miss sahiba, would it not be better if you were to stop asking and asking and just only do what it has been found and found will cure whatever illness you are treating?'

Ghote, despite his sympathy for the medical detective Dr Mahipal had once compared Gauri Subbiah to,. felt just a little convinced by the argument the surprisingly resourceful old bonesetter had produced. To quash that doubt at least temporarily he stepped forward and intervened.

'Dr Subbiah,' he said loudly, 'I was just only coming to see yourself.'

And then he realized that, however little he wanted it, he had at last taken the first step in his interrogation. Now there could be no going back.

'Bonesetter sahib,' Gauri Subbiah said, her face still alive with the joy of the combat, 'another day, another time. Yes?'

'Whenever you are daring to come, Miss sahiba.'

The old man seemed as filled with combative delight as Gauri Subbiah. But Ghote, as he turned away with her, suddenly realized why it must be she was so obviously full of the joy of existence. There could be one reason only. She had finished the experiments she had failed to make before Professor Phaterpaker had faxed her paper to France, and they had fully confirmed the facts and figures she had sent away unproven.

And it was now that he was going to have to accuse her of the murder she had committed in order to preserve the secret of her failure to make those experiments when she should have done.

'Madam, you have left your work,' he said. 'Where it was that you were going when you began talking with that fellow?'

'Why, why, Inspector, I don't really know.' She looked up at the sky. 'I was— I was just only going out. I have finished— That is, I do not have anything in particular to do this morning, and I thought I would just go out. I think I might go for a walk in the cemetery. Yes, why not? I'll visit the famous tamarind tree again where you were wanting a plaque to be put up to me.'

And she gave him a beaming, roguish smile.

'Madam,' he said, his heart spiralling downwards, 'may I please accompany?'

It would be terrible, he thought, to bring her hopes, her life even, to an end at that very spot. But he could not let her go now.

Perhaps he would get an opportunity to start a full interrogation before she reached that shoes-off spot. Or he might, straight away, simply say something to her that would make it plain the search for Chagoo's killer was near its end. Then he could march her along to Sewri Police Station and ask his questions there. True, that might risk Inspector Baitonde muscling in, either to spoil the pattern he had seen his questioning taking or, worse, to try to get a quick result by brutal means. But, however things happened, the tamarind tree in the cemetery was not the place for this final confrontation.

He would just have to see how it went.

They walked along side by side, Gauri Subbiah chattering non-stop about anything that came into her head.

Or about, he thought, anything that comes into her head bar one subject. The subject she almost certainly wants and wants to talk about, the successful end to her research.

'You are very silent today, Inspector,' she said suddenly. 'What is it you are thinking?'

Was this the moment? He could say *Madam, I am thinking about the death by snake bite of one Chandra Chagoo*. And then he could begin with the series of questions he had in his mind. The questions that would lead him he hoped – or was it feared? – step by step to a final accusation.

But they had not yet reached the cemetery gates, and the public road was an impossible place to conduct any interrogation.

'Oh, madam, I am not thinking of anything really. Just some thoughts passing through my head. My wife. What I was saying to her when I was leaving early this morning.'

Gauri Subbiah smiled.

'And what was that, Inspector?'

What had it been? Oh, God, yes. Telling Protima he would not be eating the poories she was preparing, and his hidden fury that she had not begged him to stay till they were cooked.

He could hardly tell Gauri Subbiah that. Especially not when, in a few moments now, he would need to appear to her as a figure of hard authority.

'Oh, madam, I am altogether forgetting. Not very important.'

And now they were at the gates.

The guards in their flapping khaki were standing at attention, he saw.

Why?

Then, looking back along the road, he realized what the answer must be. A funeral procession was approaching, a coffin carried by four men, a shuffling crowd of mourners following it.

Must be one of those Christian burials, he thought, stepping aside to let the procession pass.

Together with Gauri Subbiah, who had managed to

subdue the bouncing excitement she had been showing, he stood in silence as the coffin went by, the four podgy, very Goan-looking men carrying it, sweating copiously in the heat of the sun.

Not far inside the cemetery, he saw now through the railings, a priest was waiting, white robe blowing about as occasional puffs of wind sent dust whirling between the pink, green and white marble tombstones. With him were two small boys also in white robes, one swinging an incense-pot on a long gold chain. Wafts of deep-blue smoke rose up from it.

'I think we can go on inside now,' he said to Gauri Subbiah.

'Yes. Yes. I suppose I do still want to. You know, I hate to think of anyone having died when I myself am feeling so on top of the world.'

'Well, perhaps it is some aged man only. After a long life.'

But it was not.

As they went discreetly past, the priest who was standing receiving the coffin and mourners, began to speak in a loudly resounding voice.

'Brothers and sisters in Christ, we are gathered here today on the saddest of all occasions. To bury a young woman who in the fullness of her youth has been foully done to death.'

And at once Ghote realized who this young woman must be. Nicky D'Costa.

He had wondered to himself the last time he had come to the cemetery if there would one day be another D'Costa grave here. And perhaps at the very time the thought was passing through his head Abdul Khan's goondas had begun to track down the woman the smuggler had believed was betraying him.

He came to a halt. Unable to move a step onwards.

'Inspector? What is it? Are you ill?'

'No,' he answered mechanically. 'No, I am not at all ill. It is— It is just that I think I was knowing the woman they are burying just now. She must be one Nicky D'Costa. I had by chance caught her smuggling in some drug. She is— She was an air stewardess. And I had forced her to spy on the man, her lover, who had made her bring in the drug, one Abdul Khan.'

'Abdul Khan, the ganglord? I was hearing his name somewhere just two or three days past.'

'Yes, the ganglord. And he—'

He could not go on.

'Oh, yes,' he dimly heard Gauri Subbiah saying, 'I know when it was. One of the technicians at the Institute was telling me. That man, the ganglord, was in a private ward in the Peerbhoy itself. But, Inspector, what happened? Why is this woman you caught now dead? Was it . . .?'

'Yes,' he answered. 'It was because I forced her to spy on Abdul Khan, and he guessed why she was asking him so many questions and ordered some of his men to kill her. And to torture her first. Yes.'

Gauri Subbiah's face was suddenly drained by dismay.

'But— But that's terrible,' she said. 'Terrible. I can understand how you must feel, Inspector, though I'm sure you cannot be altogether to blame.'

'Well,' he replied after a moment for reflection, 'I suppose I am not one hundred per cent to blame. You see, when I was first sent to the Institute, to inquire about the missing samples of your ACE-i, I was taken off the Nicky D'Costa case and it was given to one Inspector Adik, who, I regret to say, was too much pushing that girl for answers.'

'But that's appalling. Truly appalling. Listen, wouldn't you like to go somewhere else? You don't want to stay here and see her being put into her grave.'

He would have liked to have accepted her suggestion. To have turned and walked off with her as rapidly as he could. But he felt uneasily that, if he did, he also would be running away from what he had to do. Somehow to accept Gauri Subbiah's suggestion, to go with her somewhere far from the burial taking place a few yards away would be to make her his accomplice. And to make him, in an indistinct reversal, her accomplice.

No, he must stay where he was. Stay and interrogate here and now this woman who, in all probability, had committed a murder of her own. A murder as callous, in its different way, as the one Abdul Khan had committed. Each of them, when you thought about it, had left it to some other agency to commit the deed. Khan to his goondas, so that he could establish his unbreakable, guaranteed alibi. This woman beside him, Dr Gauri Subbiah, to that long, curling, coiling, poisonous Russell's viper.

'Madam,' he answered her at last. 'No. No, it is best that we stay here. Madam, I have some questions I must put to you. Now itself.'

Chapter Twenty

'Look,' Ghote said, 'there is an ancient tomb just there, under that neem tree. We could sit.'

Gauri Subbiah was looking at him with an air of slightly bemused surprise.

Could it be she had not realized what the questions he said he had to ask her would be about? Could she have somehow succeeded in thrusting away every thought of what she had done that night in the Reptile Room? Knocking Chandra Chagoo unconscious or half-unconscious? Smashing open the Russell's viper cage? Watching the deadly snake begin to emerge, angry and seeking an enemy? Taking Chagoo's key and quickly leaving, slamming and locking that steel-plated door behind her?

Had she really blotted out all that? Did she think at this moment that all he wanted was to sit somewhere in the shade and recover from the shock of finding himself present at Nicky D'Costa's funeral? That the questions he had spoken of were going to be no more than a few more enquiries about the way scientists worked? Simply taking up again the passing-the-time chat they had had further on in the cemetery under, not a neem tree, but a tamarind?

It seemed so. Tranquilly, she went over to the low, mouldering stone tomb he had pointed to, swept off it a few freshly fallen long, narrow, dark green leaves.

Could she, even, be thinking of the custom of eating a few bitter neem leaves at the start of the year to ward off sickness? Contrasting it with her discovery of a very different, more effective preventative? She really seemed unconcerned enough for just such thoughts to be running idly through her head.

Satisfied that the top of the tomb was clean, she swished her sari round herself and sat down.

Ghote, despite having suggested they both sat, chose instead to stand looking down at her.

'Madam,' he began, 'I was saying I have questions to ask. I must beg you to answer with the truth itself.'

Now she looked thoroughly surprised.

'What— What questions are these, Inspector?'

'Madam, they are questions that must be asked. And answered also. For instance, the very first time I was seeing you I found you in your laboratory and already at a very early hour so busy at work you hardly took any notice who had tapped on your door. Now, why it was you were so much occupied?'

She did not answer for a moment. And when she did it was with clear signs of uneasiness.

'Why shouldn't I be occupied, Inspector? You must know by now I am dedicated to my work. Too much so, my friend Dr Mahipal sometimes tells me.'

'And it was pure dedication also that was keeping

you just as busy later, when I was coming again to question you about Chandra Chagoo? You were saying then you had a *mountain of work*. Why was that?'

But now she was more in command of herself.

'Why was that? Quite simply, because it was the truth of the matter. What is this, Inspector? Why are you asking me such questions?'

He ignored these demands, suspecting them to be no more than an ever-thickening smokescreen.

'Madam, I am asking why you seemed to have so much to be doing when the paper you were working on had long before been sent to France? How does that come about, madam? And why, just only some minutes past, after you were talking and discussing with that bonesetter fellow, did you begin to say *I have finished*, and then were stopping yourself and were saying just only you did not have anything particular to do? Again I am asking, madam, why was that?'

But she was not ready to yield yet.

'Oh, come, Inspector, you are making, as they say, one mountain out of a molehill. What difference is there between saying I had finished what I happened to be doing and saying I had nothing in particular to do? A researcher does not stop work altogether when a major project is completed. There are always lesser projects you may carry on with.'

'And that is your whole explanation, madam?'

'Well, yes. Yes, it is. If what I happen to be doing in my laboratory needs any explaining to the police.'

'Perhaps what you were doing first thing this

263

morning does not, madam. But here is something that does require explanation.'

'Yes?'

Was there a flicker of fear in her eyes now? If there had been, it had gone quickly enough.

'Madam, on the day we were discovering Chagoo lying dead in the Reptile Room, while I was waiting for you to find the key, I chanced to look at the requisitions register lying open on the shelf there. It was out of idle curiosity only. But what I was seeing was that long after Professor Phaterpaker had sent your paper to Paris, that evening before Independence Day, you yourself were making many requisitions for Russell's viper venom. Madam, why this was?'

A silence.

In the distance the voice of the priest consigning Nicky D'Costa's mutilated body to the earth boomed away in waves of sound too indistinct to be made out. In front of him Gauri Subbiah had begun unconsciously to tug at the rough bark of the neem immediately behind her.

He pressed into the gap in her defences that he seemed to have created.

'Please to answer. Why were you needing venom after your paper had been sent? Why also, when we were just only chit-chatting here in this cemetery, were you finding difficulty to answer when I was asking how long your one hundred experiments had taken? Or, when I was again, just only from curiosity, asking how long it took to write a scientific paper why did you at first not at all answer? And then, when up to that time you had been altogether detailed in what you were telling, did you give a reply so weak that, if it had been a good-for-nothing from the slums I had before me, I would have slapped his face?'

'Inspector,' she almost shouted out in reply, 'why are you badgering and pressuring like this? What right have you to be asking me such questions? What business is it of yours what I have done or not done?'

He knew now that this stage of it all was near its end.

'Madam,' he shot back, 'the reason is simple. It is because I have come to conclusion your paper was sent to Paris before the full work on it had been completed. That you were cheating itself.'

Although he had not put a direct question to her, he thought that now his best chance of forcing a reply to all he had asked was to let a silence grow between them.

So he stood, looking down at her as she sat on the blackened old tomb, keeping as far as he could his eyes without a flicker in them or any change of expression from his face.

Gauri Subbiah was not looking back at him. She was, if anything, minutely regarding the scatter of dried or freshly fallen dark green, spiky neem leaves on the ground at her feet.

The seconds passed. A minute. Perhaps another half-minute. Then there came the flooding-out words.

'Oh, why hide it any more? Why not tell the world? Yes, I faked my results. I agreed to let Professor Phater-paker send the paper when he must have known I hadn't had time to replicate my experiments. There.

There you have it, Inspector. I lied about that. I invented figures for those last experiments. I lied about scientific fact. That is the sort of researcher I am. A liar. A faker.'

The tears were spurting from her eyes now. As if two little pumps were in there behind them, working full out.

'But why? Why could you allow yourself to do it?'

That was not the question he knew he should be asking. He should be pressing onwards, moving from this confession to whatever chance it had been that had laid her open to Chandra Chagoo's blackmailing. And on to what she had done to silence that blackmailer for ever. But the outright confirmation of all that he had feared about this admired figure had brought that irrelevant question shooting out of him every bit as involuntarily as the tears that were squirting from Gauri Subbiah's eyes.

But, in answer, she did look him fully in the face again. With something of the directness that had first planted in him his admiration for her and all she stood for.

'Why did I let myself cheat?' she asked. 'Oh, half a dozen things entered into it. But— But, I suppose, underneath it was that I was weak. Weak. Weak.'

'But, madam, what half a dozen things?'

He wanted to know. He wanted to be able to store away some excuses for what she had done. He needed to counter the feeling of hopes betrayed permeating his whole mind.

'Oh, Inspector . . . What? What were they? Ambition, if you like. That was one. I wanted passionately to achieve something no other scientist had succeeded in. I wanted, yes, to see my name in heavy print at the top of that paper published by the Académie des Sciences. And – why not claim what I can? – that ambition was at least not wholly for myself. It was for the poor and ignorant of India, such as I once was. Daughter of a maidservant and a mali, destined to become a maidservant myself. It was for all those in as downtrodden a state as myself who happened to be gifted with some powers that could make a difference in the world. It was for them. And, yes, it was for women, too. Women still get a poor place in the world of science, at least in our country, Inspector. It is men like—'

She checked herself. Then a look of fierce determination came through her on her tears-blotched face.

'Yes,' she said. 'It is men like Professor Phaterpaker who run everything in science. And who run it as a sort of club. Women not admitted. Or not full members. Oh, yes, there are women scientists in India who have great achievements to their credit, who occupy prestigious posts even. But most of us are, all the same, side-lined. By the Phaterpakers, the lookers-after their own reputations. And, yes, that was another reason for what I did. Ashamed to say it as I am, I was bullied and cajoled by that man to get my paper published before the American team he had heard about had completed their work, just for the greater glory of the Mira Behn Institute.'

He saw that, after all, his questions about why she had done what she had were not as useless as he had thought. Answering them had enabled her to emerge from her welter of misery and tears. She was in a fit state now to hear the other questions he had.

The questions that – it looked yet more certain now – would lead inevitably to a confession to worse than scientific fraud. To a confession to murder.

He swallowed hard.

From behind him, where the mourners were clustered round the priest burying Nicky D'Costa there came distantly the heavy droning of some prayer being offered up. '. . . Holy Mary, Mother of God . . . hour of our death. Amen.'

'Madam,' he said, 'there is more I must ask.'

'More? More? What more can you want to know, now you have heard the full extent of what I have done?'

So she was going to make a fight of it.

He half-admired that. The spirit of it. It was, he reflected wretchedly, the same spirit that had taken her from those lowest-of-the-low beginnings to become a researcher at one of India's prime scientific establishments, and on to being about to have a paper of world significance published in a journal in distant France.

Except that, once she was an under-trial on a charge under Section 302, Indian Penal Code, it was more than likely that Professor Phaterpaker would see to it that the paper never appeared as her work. Worse, it was quite likely to appear with the name Phaterpaker in that heavy type at its head.

But, if Gauri Subbiah was going to fight, he must fight too. His duty. However hard.

'Let me go back,' he said, 'to that morning when we were first meeting, when I was coming to see you just

only to find out some more about how your stored specimens of ACE-i might have been smuggled out to be
sold by a drugs-dealer to the film community. I was
announcing myself as Inspector Ghote, Crime Branch.
And then, for just only some few seconds, you were
saying nothing. Nothing, madam. Do you remember
that meeting? Can you remember what thoughts passed
through your head when you found an inspector from
Crime Branch was there to talk?'

But this was a question too easy to deflect. Too easy
for a guilty woman to deflect.

'Inspector, I do remember you coming up to my
laboratory. But I can hardly be expected to remember
what I thought when you gave me your name. Why are
you asking this?'

'Very well. If you are saying you cannot remember,
then I cannot be making you. But let me come down to
something else. To what you were doing in the time
before you were opening that door with those steel
plates and we were seeing Chagoo's body.'

She was succeeding, he realized, in holding fast to
an expression of simple puzzlement.

But what thoughts, what fears, must be churning
behind that? The knowledge that, yes, when she had
first heard his name and rank the thought must have
been there that somehow already her crime had come
to light? Waiting with him outside that steel-plated door
she must have been full of apprehension. Of coldly
rising dismay. Of fear that, once the door was open,
there would be something there to betray her.

'Yes?'

'First, I am thinking, madam, you were doing utmost to delay that moment of the door opening. You were telling and telling about how snake venom is extracted. You were telling and telling about Village Sitala and the mela that is held there at the Naag Panchami festival. Then, when you were finding that door locked— Was it you were pretending to be surprised only that the door was locked?'

'Pretending, Inspector. I do not understand.'

Fight, fight, fight.

And perhaps in the core of my heart I am hoping still you would win.

'No, madam? And what about your talk-talk about premonitions? The premonition that you would find something bad in that room? You were saying even a scientist is allowed sometimes some premonitions. But, madam, I do not think a scientist will truly have such. I am believing what you were saying was just only one more attempt to give yourself time to put on a good face. For what you were about to see. What you knew you were about to see. Yes? Yes?'

'Inspector, no. Are you suggesting that I somehow knew Chagoo had been killed in there? But how could I? He was killed at some time in the night, yes. And, true, I may have been there in the house when it happened. But I was up in my laboratory. I was – you forced me to admit it – working as hard as I could to catch up on experiments I ought to have done before my paper went away. I knew nothing of what might have been going on elsewhere in the house. Nothing. How could I know?'

'No, you could not know. If you were all the time in your laboratory. But, let me remind, you were one of the three people only in the house that night, leaving aside poor Laloo.'

'Well, yes, Inspector, you told me that before. And I told you that, whether what you said was right or wrong and whatever suspicions it cast on Professor Phaterpaker and even on Ram Mahipal, I did not leave my laboratory once I was in the building, right until the time I asked Laloo to let me out to go back to the hostel.'

Still fighting, still asserting.

But what else was there she could do? Except admit what had happened. What he still had to believe had happened.

'So you are saying, madam, so you are saying,' he went on, forcing his way forward. 'But nevertheless when I was asking you questions concerning your relations with Chagoo, after we had dealt with the matter of his possible sexual advances, I was just only asking what other contacts you had had with the fellow. But, to my surprise, you were very much of dismayed by that small question. Now, madam, why was that? There should have been nothing there to stop you giving one simple answer. And yet you were replying with anger almost. Madam, why?'

'Was I? To tell the truth, I do not at all remember. But if I was, it was because I disliked Chagoo, as I told you, Inspector. The mere mention of his name must have made me angry. I cannot say more than that.'

He felt a sense of dull obstinacy building up inside him. Yes, he would have liked the situation to be such

271

that she might have an absolute explanation for all these hints and half-explained hesitances he had noticed. He would have liked nothing better than for there to exist a different *duniya*, a world in which there was no shadow of suspicion against her. But the way she had brushed aside his every probing question had begun to set up in him a desire to have at least one of them fully and completely answered.

'No, madam,' he said, his voice now sharp rather than sombre, 'not remembering and not remembering is not at all good enough. Let me tell you fully what is your situation. You were inside the Mira Behn Institute when Chagoo was killed. You have admitted you at least disliked the man. I believe now this was something more. I believe Chagoo had worked out from his requisitions register what I also came to work out. That you had sent away your ACE-i paper before your experiments had been fully done. I believe Chagoo, a confirmed blackmailer, was in the end blackmailing you also. To yield to his advances, yes? And I believe you made up your mind then to get rid of the fellow. I believe you were creeping down to the Reptile Room when you had reason to think he would be there on his rat-feeding duties. I believe you had some chat with him on this and that only, and then when he was turned away for one moment you struck him on the head. And, while he was not able to prevent, you smashed open the cage with in it that Russell's viper. And at last you were snatching Chagoo's key and locking him in leaving that viper to do its deadly work.'

'But— But— Inspector—'

She looked now totally bemused.

'Inspector, let me get this right. Are you saying Chandra Chagoo died from snake-bite?'

'Madam, what else? He was killed by that snake. That snake you had deliberately released, and angered even, so that it would do for you the work you could not bring yourself to do with your own hands.'

'Inspector, that is nonsense.'

She was unexpectedly calm. Ridiculously calm even. Something like a smile seemed to be hovering at the corners of her lips.

'Nonsense? It is not at all nonsense.'

'But, Inspector, can it be you don't know? Didn't you see Chagoo lying there? Was his body never sent for post-mortem examination? What is this? Chagoo was strangled. I saw it as soon as they turned him on to his face. Anyone could have seen it. His protruding tongue. The bruises at his throat. Do you mean to tell me you didn't notice those?'

He felt as if every substantial thing around him was whirling madly about: Gauri Subbiah, who in her amazement had jumped up from her tombstone seat, the spreading, shady neem tree above her, the forest of carved marble gravestones, the band of Nicky D'Costa's mourners as they filed away out of the cemetery.

'No,' he said. 'No. Madam, I never saw Chagoo except lying flat on his front side. You remember, I was saying almost at once a simple death was not at all a Crime Branch matter? You were protesting at me, but I was going and summoning an officer from nearest police

273

station. In accordance with procedures laid down. It was from Sewri PS. It was Inspector Baitonde who—'

He broke off.

'Baitonde,' he burst out. 'Baitonde. That damn man was never giving me Examiner's report from JJ Hospital. Never. It may be on his desk itself now only. I was not knowing there were the marks of strangulation. I was not knowing there was no sign of any bite of a snake. I was knowing nothing.'

He felt tears springing up behind his eyes. Tears of sheer frustrated rage.

'Inspector,' Gauri Subbiah was saying, 'didn't you realize this also when you were coming fully to investigate? What, I admit, in the first moment of seeing Chagoo dead there I did not think of, was that I had been requisitioning so much Russell's viper venom the chances were almost certain the snake crawling over him had been milked dry. That it was as harmless as a kitten. Is all you've been telling me true? Can there really have been a misunderstanding like that?'

'Oh, yes, madam,' he answered bitterly. 'It is only too true. You see, in police work we cannot all the time have same standards as you scientists. We cannot—'

He stopped himself.

Scientists, he had just learnt, even the best of them, were, too, at the mercy of human weaknesses.

'Well, madam,' he said, gulping back the feelings turbulent within him and beginning to think, 'this is putting whole different complexion on case. If it is a matter of strangling . . .'

'Yes, vicious and brutal strangling, Inspector. I saw

those marks on Chagoo's throat. And I think I know, too, what you are beginning to work out.'

'Madam, you do. It is plain. This cannot be the crime of a woman, such as yourself. You would not have had the strength to strangle a tough fellow like Chagoo. And there is more. Dr Mahipal has a withered right arm. He could not possibly have been Chagoo's murderer. And Professor Phaterpaker? Well, can you see that old man succeeding to kill Chagoo in that way, even if he had needed?'

'No, Inspector. That's hardly the Professor Phater-paker I know.' There was definitely a smile on her face now. 'No, I can see our Director committing various crimes against scientific truth. But, with all the will in the world, I cannot see him strangling Chandra Chagoo.'

She sobered up then.

'But in that case,' she asked, 'who did strangle him? Who on earth could have done it?'

'Madam,' Ghote answered. 'I know. Now, at last, I have been told the truth about the body of Chandra Chagoo, and I am knowing who must be his murderer.'

Chapter Twenty-One

A different *duniya*. Ghote had wished often enough as his inquiries seemed to lead step by inexorable step to Gauri Subbiah, that there could somehow be a different world running just parallel to the facts of his existence but in which there would be one small significant difference. A difference that would mean the young scientist he so admired could not be the person who had killed Chandra Chagoo.

Now, thanks to the brutish inefficiency of Inspector Baitonde, he had to all intents and purposes stepped into that world. A world where Chagoo had been killed, not by a bite from the venomous Russell's viper, but at the hands of a vicious strangler.

And he had realized, almost simultaneously with learning how Chagoo had actually died, that the very man possessed of the savagery to have killed him in that fashion had had an excellent opportunity. And, very likely, reason enough.

Abdul Khan.

Just before the had begun his interrogation of Gauri Subbiah, when he had been overwhelmed at finding Nicky D'Costa's burial taking place, the young scientist had casually said she had heard Abdul Khan was a patient in the Peerbhoy Hospital. He had hardly paid attention at the time, just barely noting at the back of his mind that the Peerbhoy was the answer to the half-idle question he had put to himself from time to time ever since the Assistant Commissioner had told him Khan had fabricated a hospital alibi.

But now everything came clicking into place. Khan had on this occasion chosen for his customary alibi, probably by sheer chance, the Peerbhoy rather than any other Bombay hospital. Once there, he must have realized the Mira Behn Institute stood in the selfsame compound. The very place from which Chandra Chagoo was supplying him with illicit ACE-i specimens.

First-class opportunity to get new supplies. In the depths of the night, at a time he knew from past experience Chandra Chagoo would be feeding his rats, all he would have to do was slide open the big window of his private wing room and drop down to the ground. Then slink past, if necessary, the enormous, noisily patrolling Damodar Singh, something ridiculously easy to do if you were watching out for him instead of going along intent on finding clues. Next enter the Institute through the window the old mali kept unfastened so as to fetch water for his beloved plants. Finally, slip down to the basement to conduct his transaction, making sure he was safely locked in with the snake-handler against any chance of intrusion.

But something must have gone wrong. Blackmailer Chagoo asking for a higher price on the threat of giving the gang leader away?

Not something you did to a man like Abdul Khan.

He saw the scene, vividly almost as if he had been there watching. The sudden fixed rage behind the big Pathan's invariable glare glasses. Hands reaching for a throat in one single instant. Perhaps a ground-out accusation. And then the pitiless squeezing. At last, when Chagoo's body was limp in death, the final vicious hurling of it away. Only for the dead man's head to crash against the thin glass of one of the snake cages. The one housing the Russell's viper.

The beast, maddened already by the banging and movement just outside its man-made lair, gliding out at once. Khan, however little frightened he might be of any man walking Bombay's streets, horrified now at what he was seeing. Racing over to the door. Unlocking the door. Hurrying back to the safety of his hospital bed. Undetected.

But no.

The whole scene sharp in his mind, Ghote recalled the Reptile Room door as he looked at it, with some intangible foreboding, when Gauri Subbiah had first opened it for him. Just a second away from the instant he had seen Chagoo's body and the long black snake sliding over it.

That door did not unlock at a twist of its key.

You had, Gauri Subbiah had eventually remembered, to pull it from outside hard towards you before the tongue of the lock would slide back. So, correspondingly, on the inner side Abdul Khan would have needed to discover that the key would not turn unless the heavy door was pushed, by just a fraction, away from himself.

While all the time the Russell's viper would be slithering towards him.

He saw the man in his desperation. What would he have done? Answer: he would at last have hit on the fact that you had to push hard at the door. At the steel plates on the inside of it, like those on the outside.

So on those plates, at about chest level, there would – surely there would – be palm prints. Fingerprints.

Perhaps in the course of the days since Chagoo's murder fingerprints might have been blotted out. Perhaps other hands had pushed at that door to unlock it. But why should they have? Who was likely to have planted their hands on those steel plates? No one would have locked that door from the inside now Chagoo was no more. No one.

'Madam,' he said to Gauri Subbiah, standing blinking with surprise in the shade of the rough-barked neem tree where she had just heard herself accused of Chagoo's murder. 'Madam, kindly excuse me. If I am right in what I have thought, I have to secure some evidence. At once.'

'Oh, but go, Inspector. Go. Find out what it is. As you will, I know. I can see you're a good experimentalist.'

But as he turned away, she put a hand for a moment on to his sleeve.

'No, wait. Just tell me just one thing. Inspector, why did you not ever ask how Chagoo had been killed? Why didn't you ask that obvious question?'

For just an instant he asked himself why that had been. Then he answered.

'Madam, it was because I never thought to do it. Just

that. The question I ought to have asked. I thought I already knew the answer and I did not ask it.'

Less than an hour later he welcomed into the Mira Behn Reptile Room Sergeant Nensi, fingerprint expert.

In the tormented time he had been there, guarding the place, he had asked himself over and over again, was he guarding nothing? Had Abdul Khan actually pushed at the steel plates on the door with his sweaty palms? And, even if he had, a dozen other people for a dozen different reasons might have pushed at the door as well. Covered it with their damn hand marks? Obliterated everything on it? Wiped it? Washed it even?

'You have brought Abdul Khan's record sheet with you?' he asked Nensi, snapping out the question in an agitated snarl of distrust.

'Inspector, I am very well knowing my job.'

He brought himself to a check.

'Yes. Yes, of course. But, tell me . . . I mean, I am just only making sure of everything. If you are finding some good marks on this door, will you be able to say there is proof Khan was in this room?'

'Inspector, did they teach you nothing when you were under training? You must be knowing for proof by fingerprints there must be at least sixteen points agreeing. So, if I am finding seventeen, or sixteen only, there will be proof. If fifteen, no proof. Fingerprinting is a science, you understand, an exact science.'

For one terrible moment the thought of all he had learnt about science and its exactness under the strain of ambition, carelessness and timidity came back into his head.

He thrust the thought aside.

'No, sixteen points I am well knowing,' he said to Nensi. 'And, please God, when you come to make a hundred per cent thorough examination, you will find them, or seventeen points or twenty-four. The we would be able to start shaving Abdul Khan's head. But for now, Nensi bhai, just only tell me if what I am suspecting is at all right. Was Khan here itself? Is there at all any evidence?'

'Inspector, if you would be letting me begin work, you will all the sooner be getting your answer.'

He stepped aside then. Pointed mutely to the steel plates at the top half of the door.

Would this be the moment, soon, very soon, when he would have the proof that could send the mighty Abdul Khan, head shaved, to gaol?

He watched, every muscle tense, while Nensi set down his big, black plastic case on one of the glass-topped rat runs, glanced back to the surface he would have to deal with, took out his insufflator and set it on the glass beside the bag, selected from its depths a little glass jar of powder, then, with a quick look of thoughtfulness, replaced it and brought out another. Of slightly darker powder.

But at last he went over to the door and blew a cloud of powder on to the dulled silvery surface on which Khan's hands might have pressed.

Ghote, even from this distance he was forcing himself to keep, could see that marks in plenty had shown up under the powdering.

Were they? Or . . .?

Nensi went trotting back to his case, took out a large magnifying glass, returned to the door, examined its surface with maddening care.

'Yes?'

He had been unable to keep the question in.

Nensi turned away from his peering at the door.

'Inspector, if I am not having Khan's record in front of my eyes only, how can I be answering such a question?'

'Sorry. Sorry. Carry on. Carry on.'

Nensi went back once more to the big black case and rummaged inside it. At last he brought out the buff-coloured card on to which Khan's prints had, long ago when he was no more than a small-time goonda, been firmly implanted. Solemnly he took it across to the door. Solemnly he held up his oversize magnifying glass once again.

Ghote, strained to sweating point with impatience, watched Nensi's head go from the card to a particular patch on the door. From the patch to the card. From the card to the patch.

Then at last . . .

'Yes, Inspector. It is Abdul Khan. I cannot under present conditions make detailed count. But definitely sixteen points. Twenty even.'

Then Inspector Ghote allowed to float into his mind certain words spoken to him by the Commissioner of Police, Bombay. *No, frankly, Inspector, it'll take a better man than you to put paid to Abdul Khan.*